THE LUCKY PREPPER

Emma Zeth

First published in Great Britain in 2019
Copyright © 2019 Emma Zeth
The moral right of the author has been asserted.

All rights reserved.
No part of this publication may be reproduced, stored in a retrieval system, or transmitted, in any form or by any means, without the prior permission of the author.

This is a work of fiction. All names, characters, businesses, events and incidents are products of the author's imagination or are used in a fictitious manner. Any resemblance to actual events, or to real persons, living or dead (or imaginary), is purely coincidental.

Acknowledgements

Many thanks to my family, who provided encouragement and sustenance, whenever it was needed.

Also thanks to Elizabeth and her wonderful charity: the Community Learning Partnership.

Thank you for all your excellent work, for allowing me to sit and write during crafting sessions, and for all the fabulous suggestions.

And finally,
thanks to the Tai Chi Friday Lunch Club,
for all your unstinting support.

Contents

Chapter 1: Home 1
Chapter 2: Outbreak 13
Chapter 3: Security 25
Chapter 4: Travel 44
Chapter 5: Harvest 66

Chapter 6: Missing 87
Chapter 7: Meeting 97
Chapter 8: Hiding 107
Chapter 9: Waiting 116

Chapter 10: Decisions 130
Chapter 11: Attacks 144
Chapter 12: Benefits 153
Chapter 13: Questions 162

Chapter 14: Help 176
Chapter 15: Escape 194
Chapter 16: Disaster 213
Chapter 17: Regroup 220

Chapter 18: Researching 235
Chapter 19: Finding 247
Chapter 20: Planning 255
Chapter 21: Freeing 270
Chapter 22: Conflict 290
Chapter 23: Community 300

1

Home

Thursday I was supposed to go to school. I didn't. I called in at seven and left a message, adding a few extra coughs and sneezes for effect. The school hated anyone taking the day off, but I felt pretty awful; tired and aching, with a scratchy throat that was threatening to turn into a full blown, jelly-and-ice-cream-only affair. I staggered into the kitchen and switched on my computer. Then I put on the kettle. I grated some ginger into a mug, added a spoonful of honey, and poured in the boiling water. Stirring the steaming liquid, I sat at my desk and cobbled together some lesson plans for my head of department.

Thursday was a good day to get ill, only four lessons and two of them were A-level Biology, with students who could cope with a bit of independent study. If it had been Friday, I would have stumbled in, just to avoid giving anyone my year 11 class. Twenty-eight stroppy teenagers; they were okay with me, but would do nothing for a cover teacher, and their exams were coming up fast. I made some activity sheets for my year 9 group, squinting at the screen and catching, at the last minute, a spelling mistake that turned a perfectly innocent word into something highly inappropriate. Then I switched off the computer, went to the bathroom, and staggered back to bed.

I could have gone to work really, but taking a single day off, right at the start, was much better than waiting until I was dying on the job, and then having to take a week off to recover. Whenever I caught an infection, I would go straight to bed and give my immune system a chance to fight, let my white blood cells do their work, raise my body temperature, and destroy the pathogen before it had multiplied. No paracetamol or ibuprofen, just lots of fluids and sleep.

A couple of hours later, when I woke up again, I had three text messages, the first sent at around break time at school. They were all from Katy, who taught chemistry in the classroom opposite. 'Where r u?' she had texted, '16 staff off today, also 300 kids, mostly year 8, r u ok?' and then, a bit later, 'P4 class cancelled!' The message ended with a load of party emojis.

I ran my hands through my tangled hair. I felt a little groggy, maybe I'd read it wrong, but nope, 300 students were off ill. One of the teaching assistants, Gabby, had been sneezing and coughing during the year 8 assembly on Tuesday... surely she couldn't have given her bug to that many people? But it had been so hot that we had the fan going at the back of the hall... and she had been standing right beside it. I taught science, I knew that a single sneeze could contain over 100,000 germs. Even so...infection rates for the flu were only about 5%. For 300 kids to be ill, the bug had to be incredibly contagious. I meant to text her back, but I fell asleep again on that thought.

I snuggled up in bed all day, periodically getting up for salt gargles and raw ginger tea. Towards the evening, I could feel the sore throat starting to give up against the bombardment of astringent salt and fiery ginger. The next morning I blearily opened my eyes as the alarm went off and dragged myself out of bed. I made myself a large flask of honey and lemon, and went back to school. It was Friday and I wanted to give my year 11 class one last revision session before their exam. I knew it was clutching at straws for some of them, but I couldn't help myself. My poor students…they would be lucky to be able to answer even a quarter of the exam paper; they tried so hard in class, but very little stuck from week to week.

I walked in, smiling at the kids and sniffling into a tissue whenever I saw management. I was feeling better, but that evaporated when I looked at my first email of the day; it was from the cover supervisor, taking my only free period. Morning briefing was a car crash; there were only twenty-three teachers present of about eighty. At thirty-four, I was one of the more experienced members of staff, and I knew I would be roped in to do extra duty. I sighed in resignation as I ditched my plan of eating a healthy snack from the canteen; it would be a bar from the chocolate box again. There was some talk of closing the school, but it was too late, half the parents would have been on their way to work already; they'd have slaughtered us if we rang them up to send the kids back home.

Sure enough, on my way out of the meeting, my head of year grabbed me to double up my form class and cover break duty in the playground. As I walked up to the science department, I passed by the staffroom. Usually it was empty in the morning, as teachers scrambled to get themselves organised for the chaos ahead, but today there was a distinct murmur of voices that made me pause. I did an about-turn and stuck my head around the door. There was a gang of teachers crowded round one of the work computers, staring at something on screen, I wandered closer; what had caught their attention so thoroughly? I was surprised to see the familiar colours of BBC news.

'What's going on?' I asked.

'Hey Zoe,' replied one of the English teachers, 'Do you know anything about this new virus?'

I peered over her shoulder and scanned the page; an article on a possible new virus with flu-like symptoms. It was short and had remarkably few real facts, but there were lots of colourful pictures of viruses. 'Nope.' I replied, 'But at least it's not the vomiting bug that was going round last year'

Up in the science department we were so short staffed that I ended up teaching multiple classes all crammed together in the same room. My year eleven students were glad to see me at least, and we went over as much as we could of the GCSE biology syllabus; cells, enzymes, the heart... I could see the lack of knowledge in their desperate faces when I asked quick-fire questions at the end. No matter how hard I tried to motivate them, they always left the revision until the last minute. They should have started back in January if they really wanted to do well. It was impossible to learn it all in just the few short weeks they gave themselves. I handed out some last minute cram sheets and wished them good luck for their exam on Tuesday. Just before period four, management sent out an email closing the school and we all went home.

After changing into a comfortable cotton skirt, which suited my slightly chubby figure better than my work suits, I went out into the garden. I walked down the concrete path and into my new cedar greenhouse, to water the seedlings. It was the start of May and we were in the middle of a heatwave. I was so tempted to plant all my seedlings out into the ground; let them spread their roots and enjoy the sun, but a cold night could stop growth for weeks, and a deadly frost was not impossible. So even though it was twenty-three degrees, and felt like summer, I left everything crammed inside.

I plucked a couple of weeds from the raised beds on either side of the path and checked the fruit trees that lined the brick wall on the left side of the garden. I had hand-pollinated the flowers in March, using an artist's paintbrush to dab pollen from flower to flower, and hundreds of tiny little apples and pears now covered the miniature trees. I never saw the point of growing normal sized fruit trees; I was only five foot two; normal trees were just too tall for me to harvest and impossible to prune without a ladder. I grew fourteen different varieties on dwarfing rootstock, and had an abundance of fresh fruit in autumn that I could pluck straight from the tree and eat whenever I wanted.

I checked for the fluffy white spots of woolly-aphid, and sprayed a couple of tiny infestations, then I lay in my hammock and called home.

Home is a peculiar word, it means so much more than you might think, 'home' for me, has always meant where I grew up, my parents' house. But home was also my little bungalow where I felt so comfortable and at peace. When I thought of home, I thought of my bungalow, but when I called home, I was calling my mum.

My brother picked up almost immediately. 'Hey Zoe.'

'Hey Vik, I got a half day off!' I said happily.

'Nice,' he said, 'are you coming over?' His tone was upbeat; it looked like today was a good day.

'I'm not sure, what are you up to? Do you know anything about this new virus?' I asked.

'Not much, I've only just had breakfast,' he replied. The household generally rose about midday as my brother was a computer geek who worked from home, staying up half the night talking to America, whilst mum loved to sleep in. 'How did you get the day off?' he asked.

'Half the school was off ill with a new virus, so we closed early,' I responded, 'I was off yesterday but seem okay today. Have you had it?'

'No, but we've not been out much.' he said, 'the car still needs to go to the garage'

We discussed scrapping the old Toyota, the advantages of having Friday afternoon off work, and the symptoms of the virus. I said I'd look it up and let him know, and then asked for mum. After a couple of seconds I heard her voice and then a long yawn, 'Hey mum, did I wake you?' I asked.

'No, no, I've got to get up anyway,' she said, 'I'm just enjoying the sunshine.' Mum's bed caught the morning sun and she loved lying there in the mornings soaking it up. 'How come you're not at work?'

I explained the school closure again and we chatted a bit about nothing. I ended the call and lay in the sun thinking about the virus. Then I decided to go to the shops...just in case.

There is a section of society called preppers, you never hear much about them, as (just like fight club,) the first rule of prepping is that you don't talk about prepping. I once saw an eye-opening film in which there is a week-long power cut in the UK. In the film, several scenes focus on a prepper who lives in central London. He cooks on a barbeque in his tiny garden, whilst smugly gloating to his wife about his foresight at stocking up, but his neighbours see the food and come over, so he has to share what he has. In the evening, he turns on his generator so they can have light, and during the night has it stolen. Violently. He did the opposite of what a prepper generally does. In reality, preppers mostly believe that resources should be hidden; otherwise desperate stronger people will take them. I was all in favour of helping others in need, but if it came to the crunch, survival of the fittest seemed only natural. Stock up on resources and hide…it was a good plan for someone like me.

I had an emergency kit in the loft; it seemed silly not to. Just some sugar and salt, a bag of rice and some lentils, a load of vitamin pills and some painkillers. One birthday Vik had bought me a lifesaver bottle that purified water. I'd never used it, but it was reassuring to know I'd always have access to clean water. I looked through my cupboards, checking my supplies. Urgh…nothing, just some sweetcorn, and a solitary tin of mushroom soup. How had my stock got so low? Ok, so I was busy with the exams, but really? When was the last time I had cooked? Fillet steak…was that last week? Or the week before…anyhow, I'd obviously used up everything. Off to Tesco, to stock up before the crazies started panic buying.

It's funny how you think you are being clever until you realise that almost everyone else is doing the same thing. It wasn't panic buying, not yet, but I could see other people had had the same idea as me. Tesco's car park was almost full. On a Friday afternoon I kind of expected it to be busy, but this was different. Lots of crying kids, parents looking stressed.

I grabbed a trolley and headed for the tinned food. This aisle was mostly empty, only a few other random professionals like me, given the afternoon off work, winding their way down the aisle. Were they also teachers? I smiled at a couple as we manoeuvred around each other. I filled my trolley with tins of sweetcorn, baked beans and pulses, and packets of dried soup mix and barley, not enormous amounts, stuff I would eat anyway.

I lingered beside the couscous; this would be great for meals; tasty and quick. I began loading up my trolley with one of every type and brand; coriander and lemon... roasted vegetable... tomato and chilli. Soon there were over twenty packets, was it too much? I rifled through my choices, it was more like taste testing the different brands, not panic buying. I grabbed some more sugar, and was happy to see that Cadbury's hot chocolate was on special again. I took down a jar, and then another, and then one more, why not? It would be used eventually. The confectionery aisle was next. I wheeled my trolley down the aisle, piling in one of everything that was on offer. A pack of four Whispers for a pound. Nine Twix fingers for one twenty five. If the shops ran out of food, I would need a decent chocolate supply.

I paused and looked down at my trolley. I was going to get so fat if I ate all that...and my resistance to chocolate was almost zero, if we were back at school on Monday how long would it all last? About a week probably. I almost put it all back, but left it in the trolley and added a couple of bags of toffees and some Malteasers. If the worst happened and there was serious panic buying then I wanted to be prepared.

I wandered around the shop, picking up items that had a long shelf-life; foods that I could just added water to, like dried pasta and porridge, and things I liked snacking on; crackers, Baby Bel cheeses and cartons of pineapple juice. When I'd filled my trolley, I stood in the shortest queue I could find; it still stretched up into the aisle and I was jostled several times by impatient shoppers, pushing to get past. A baby near the front was crying; piercing shrieks that were making everyone restless. Eventually I reached the checkout, paid, and wheeled the trolley out to the car park. The atmosphere was even more chaotic than earlier, with horns sounding long hoots of the truly frustrated, as cars queued to get in.

I looked to see the cause of the blockage; up by the entrance there were two police cars and an ambulance. Something had obviously happened, although I couldn't see exactly what. Shoppers were pausing to watch, some looked concerned, but others seemed animated by the drama; chattering into their phones, and snapping pictures. I quickly turned the other way and pushed my trolley over to my little black Corsa, which I had parked near the exit. The urge to avoid trouble was deeply ingrained; I just wanted to get home, where it was calm and safe.

Home was in Carpenders Park; a quiet suburb of Watford that was technically outside of London, but inside the M25. I lived by myself in a two-bedroom bungalow. Unlike most people, I was naturally happy alone. As long as I had mum and Vik, my tai chi group and my friends on Facebook and Whatsapp, I was content. My mum was going crazy over my single state. She was convinced I must be lonely, but I wasn't. For ages I didn't really know what loneliness was, until someone explained it in a way that I finally understood. I had a friend; a lovely older lady from my tai chi class. She lived alone; her husband had passed away, her children grown up and moved out.

She explained to me that she enjoyed going out with friends, or to church events and concerts, but when she walked through the door, and sat on the sofa in her empty flat, a lump would grow in her throat and she would feel like crying. She missed having people to come home to, and felt lonely. I was the opposite, when I came home, I would flop into a chair and sigh with relief, I loved being home on my own.

I parked in the drive and unlocked the front door, picking up the four heavy bags and shuffling sideways into the narrow hallway. I walked past the spare room and living room; cosy rooms with large bay windows overlooking the front drive. At the end of the corridor were three doors; my bedroom overlooking the garden at the back, a tiny bathroom, tiled all in white, and a large kitchen/diner, full of warm pine cupboards. I levered down the door handle with my elbow and gently shouldered the glass paned door open, then dumped all the shopping bags on the kitchen counter.

The back door led straight out of the kitchen into the garden and I unlocked it and looked out. The garden was the best thing about the house…it was my pride and joy. Secluded and tranquil, it was a haven after the never-ending demands of work. The garden behind was overgrown with evergreens, brambles, and a large ash tree. The house was owned by an elderly couple who I had seen perhaps three times in the five years I had lived there. Their neglect had turned their garden into a jungle, but the huge tree in the northern corner shielded my garden from the surrounding houses, without casting shade over the plants.

My house was on a corner so the left side of the garden was bounded by the road. I would occasionally hear pedestrians walking by, but felt secure, as the wooden fence had been replaced by a tall brick wall by a previous owner. It was two meters high with thick piers every two meters along to strengthen it. That wall blocked out the noise from the road and soaked up the sun.

I did a quick circuit of the garden, checking the roses that grew up the piers and then ran across the top of the brickwork. Every autumn they were severely pruned to keep them from taking over but the new growth was already reaching up on wavy stems. I had grown the fan trained and espalier miniature fruit trees between the piers to take advantage of the warmth retained by the bricks but the heat wave was drying out the soil rapidly. I turned on the hose and lay it at the foot of the trees then went over to check the grape vine. It was a white seedless grape called Lakemont and grew on a post and wire trellis against the wooden fence that bordered my lovely elderly neighbour on my right. That vine was the bane of my gardening life as it grew at an astonishing rate and required pruning every couple of weeks in the summer. The new leaves were already growing larger and I made a note to sharpen the secateurs.

Back inside, I resisted eating any of the chocolate, and made boring pasta with a jar of sauce for dinner. I surfed the internet, passing time and before I knew it, hours had gone by. It was dark outside when I dragged my eyes from the screen, disturbed by the sound of rising voices. There were flashing blue lights on the walls of the kitchen. I hadn't noticed before, but they were obvious once I looked up. I could hear crying, and a voice, raised in denial. The cries intensified until the person was almost screaming. I stood hastily and moved to the window to see several police cars and an ambulance parked askew in the side road.

I stood at my kitchen window with the lights off, watching the bits of road I could see and trying to work out what was going on. Ambulances were not an unusual sight, in a road full of bungalows. When I moved in, the estate agent called the place 'the waiting room to heaven', full of older, retired people. It suited me just fine. It was normally peaceful and quiet, with a friendly horticultural society and a community book sale every month. This screaming was something new and very disturbing. I watched for a long while but eventually turned away, shut down my computer, and went to bed, drifting off into a restless sleep as the cries diminished to an intermittent sobbing.

The next morning was Saturday. No work, but I woke up at seven anyway. The emergency vehicles had disappeared and all was quiet. Online the BBC was running a 'breaking news' and a 'live update' page on the virus. Still not many facts, but accounts of people collapsing, accidents, and even a cancelled football match. There were the usual stories of the NHS struggling, unable to cope, along with advice on staying in, taking paracetamol, and drinking lots of fluid if you were ill. It all looked very bad and I didn't know what to do, so I decided to go to the garden centre.

2

Outbreak

At first glance it might have seemed an odd decision, but the garden centre was a two-minute drive away, had a wide range of products, and I wanted a sweet potato plant. It was early, and therefore almost empty. I meandered through; looking at the expensive exotic plants and tables of pretty alpines and ferns. Then I moved on to the vegetable plants. Tomatoes… more tomatoes… peppers… pumpkins… sweet potato! I picked up the plant, and then looked back along the row. I could get more, just in case. Perhaps some courgettes? I had only grown them once before, because as it turned out, I didn't particularly like courgettes. The plants had produced non-stop all summer. I harvested so much, I had difficulty finding people to give them away to. And if I didn't pick the courgettes, they turned into giant marrows which were even more difficult to get rid of. I looked at the pots; they might not be my favourite vegetable, but they were filling and healthy. I made a face and picked up a strip of three plants.

I looked over at the potatoes. I had some 'first early' potatoes in small pots at home, every year I harvested them as new potatoes in June. Watering the plants in summer was a time consuming job, so I never bothered with main crop potatoes. However it wouldn't hurt to do a little extra prepping…have some growing in the ground as insurance in case the virus turned out to be more than an especially virulent strain of the flu. Scientist had been warning about a new pandemic for years, they kept talking about Spanish flu and bird flu and the inevitability of an outbreak.

I looked around at the many different varieties; I wanted something that was blight resistant but tasted good. The seed potatoes were in baskets, with labels and a short description above. I read them all, geek that I was. I vacillated…Carolus or Maris Peer. I had grown both before; Maris Peer grew big and tasty, but I picked the Carolus. Blight resistance was the winning characteristic.

I browsed the barbeque area; would this be the year I finally got a barbeque? I scanned the products displayed and my eye was caught by a cute little camping stove, I added it to my basket, along with a couple of tins of gas. I would use them on the camping trips I ran at school, for the Duke of Edinburgh Award. I hated camping; the cold, the rain, the hours pacing around the campsite telling the kids to go to sleep…but it was worth it to see the kids have fun for once. I took a group out every year and the next trip would be after the exams. This year's group were a bit accident-prone but I was looking forward to it anyway.

The area for seeds was undergoing reorganisation and as I wandered past a sign caught my eye; 'Seeds Packets: 50p'. Wow! That was good value. Of course, there were plenty of unopened packets at home, piled up in the shed, waiting to be sown. I pictured the seedlings growing in the greenhouse, but then shrugged. 50p! I could always give some to mum, or the horticultural group. I searched through the trays; flower seeds, wild flowers, lots of sweet peas, ah here were the veg. I scooped them up and sorted them out; broad beans, runner beans, French beans, haricot beans and dwarf beans. I picked a couple of each. Multipacks of sweetcorn seeds and herb seeds. Those went into my basket too. Then I saw that they had packets of peas and carrot seeds. I went crazy; I got at least twenty pounds worth.

I carried on through the pretty solar lighting area, but I had plenty of solar lights and couldn't justify the cost. Then as I approached the tills, I saw a wonderful sight; boxes and boxes of Cornish fudge. No one would seriously expect me to resist, and they would make lovely presents for the teaching assistants when the current situation was over, and we went back to school.

At home, I planted the sweet potato in an old cracked water butt that I had filled with compost and then potted up the courgettes. I filled the watering can from the new water butts which were connected to the greenhouse guttering and gave everything a good drink. I kept meaning to attach the irrigation system to one of them, and install an automatic valve, but I hadn't had time. Maybe now I would. I checked the news again; there was an abundance of stories highlighting the chaos in the hospitals, and everywhere I clicked there were alarmist reports of food shortages with pictures of supermarkets with empty shelves. It wasn't helpful news, just clickbait.

It was too early to phone home, so I walked down to the local shops, to see what was happening. My bungalow was on a corner plot near the southern end of the estate. There were four distinct areas in Carpenders Park, the bungalows in the middle and running south, the blocks of flats at the northern end, and the houses to the east. To the west was the railway, which divided it from the ex-council estate of South Oxhey. To the north were woods, with overgrown paths that eventually led to Watford. The other sides were bounded by two wide roads, beyond which lay open fields.

I sauntered past bungalows and neat front gardens, and in less than eight minutes, I was walking past the pub, towards the couple of shops that made up the hub of the estate. There were cars everywhere…not just in the normal spaces, but also on the double yellow lines, the bus stop, and up on the grass verge.

The main shop was a co-op, and I could see, inside the store, that people were obviously panic buying; packets of meat and fresh vegetables were scattered over the floor. I walked towards the entrance but paused as I looked in. What was this? A middle-aged woman, on her knees amongst the scattered packets, looking up at another, similar aged woman who was standing over her, clutching a packet of sausages. I could hear fragments of the conversation, 'sorry, but you shouldn't have pushed me… I had it first….' There was a crowd surrounding them, shocked faces, looking on in fascination, their purpose forgotten for a second. A few people edged past them, deeper into the store, grabbing stuff off the shelves as they went. The tableau broke and the woman surged to her feet, shoving the other away.

I backed up and walked round to the chemist where there was another altercation going on, this time between the pharmacy assistant and a large man holding a crying child, with two kids crowded beside him, eyes wide, looking from their dad to the petite lady in front of them.

'I'm really sorry sir, but there is none left in the stock room either,' said the assistant, giving a patient, but impersonal smile. As I watched, several agitated-looking parents, clutching kids, entered the tiny shop, and made a beeline for the counter, I quietly backed out; the situation was starting to look tense, and if it was tense here, in calm, peaceful, Carpenders Park, what on earth would it be like in London or Watford? I googled 'London riots' on my phone and was reassured when the top results were all about 2011.

More cars were pulling up, double-parking. It was getting crowded. I looked around at the anxious faces, the crying children and shouting adults. My gaze fell on a group of three; an older man waiting patiently at the bus stop, along with two elderly women who were looking nervous. As I watched, I saw them confer and shake their heads, then they stepped away from the bus stop, walking away from the chaos. They had it right; I would be better off at home. I walked slowly back up the hill towards my bungalow. For some reason the situation felt much worse than 2011; immediate and real, rather than a news item. Just as I arrived, I saw my neighbour getting into her shiny electric-blue mini. She waved as she pulled out of the driveway. 'I'm off to stay with my son and the grandkids for the week.' she called out of the window, 'Take care of yourself.' I waved weakly as she drove away.

Back in my kitchen, I called mum. She was awake, which was good but getting ready to go to the library, where she volunteered a couple of times a week. 'But mum,' I said, 'have you not looked at the news? This virus looks really bad … there's panic buying in the shops…it's not safe to go out.' I should have saved my breath; my mum totally believed she was invulnerable.

'Really Z!' she huffed, 'don't be silly, I'll just walk down to the library, I told Rose I'd do the 2 to 5pm slot.'

'Mum, I'm serious, it's dangerous out there; people are desperate. I think someone died here last night… there was an ambulance and police and everything. A lady was screaming and yelling for at least an hour. You shouldn't go out.'

'I said I'll go, so I'll go, it will be fine, I'll get Vik to walk down with me.' she responded. I'd made it worse. Now it wasn't just mum at risk; my little brother Vik, who disliked confrontation and hated going out, would be at risk too.

I was kicking myself even as I said the words: 'I was thinking of coming round, how about I give you a lift down instead, then I can have a look at the new library, see what they've done with it.' I hadn't been thinking of 'coming round' at all, but that was the way things went in our family.

'We're having a Caribbean show-and-tell this afternoon,' said mum, 'you can stay and help if you want.' Her voice was light and enthusiastic - she was happy I was coming over.

I doubted very much that there would be any sort of show-and-tell but kept quiet, I felt enough of a killjoy as it was. 'See you in twenty minutes then mum. Bye.'

I picked up my bag and grabbed the keys. Yet again I had volunteered to do something I didn't really want to do. But family was important, and if they weren't going to properly take care of themselves, then it was up to me to do so. I stomped outside and got in the car, turning the radio on loud.

The twenty-minute drive to mum's house was busy and slow, there seemed to be more cars on the road than normal, and I counted five ambulances. There were a lot of young people on the streets, gathered in small groups. The mood was quiet and slightly sombre, none of the usual laughing and clowning around. I turned the radio off; it didn't seem appropriate somehow.

I took mum to the library, which was insanely, still open. She hadn't believed me about the virus, but when I went to pick her up, a couple of hours later, she reported that Gillian, another member of staff, knew someone whose child had died, 'It was so sad, only four years old, this flu is really serious!' she said. I sighed; she believed her friends absolutely but never me. When would I learn that she would never change? I took myself off for a chat with Vik, while she made dinner.

'Vik,' I said, 'we need a plan.' His computer screen looked like gibberish as usual; some forum post in the top half, with a load of code beneath. 'I know,' he replied but didn't say any more. This was typical, Vik was smart, incredibly smart, but he wouldn't volunteer ideas or suggest a plan himself, he was very good at analysing and evaluating, but he was passive. I had to be the assertive one, organising, and even a little bit bossy perhaps. Even if sometimes I didn't feel like it.

'Perhaps you guys should come and stay with me?' I said tentatively. My place was much smaller, but somehow I felt it would be safer.

'Mum won't leave; come and stay with us if you're worried.' he responded.

'What do you think is happening? Do you think we should be worried?' I asked. 'This area has way more people than Carpenders Park and if we get riots and stuff…' I tailed off; I didn't really know how to explain the unease I felt, or how to talk about an epidemic without sounding stupid. He shrugged in response. I went down to do the crossword with mum, ate dinner when it was ready, then left, mum waving bye from the door like she always did.

That evening, as I watered the forty or so pots of potato plants, I listened to the sirens wail nonstop. The pots were tucked all around the house against the walls to stay warm during the night. They were all first-early varieties, I had a lot of Epicure, which was cold tolerant, and had been planted at the beginning of March. But I also had Kestrel, which were nice potatoes with smooth skins, and Yukon Gold, which tasted delicious. Most of the plants were a foot high, at least, and growing spectacularly well in the heatwave. It wasn't forecast to rain for a while, so I topped up the water butts, and then went online again to see what I could find out.

People were dying, in their hundreds if not thousands; I couldn't stop reading, the stories were horrific. Hospitals were overwhelmed; corridors filled with patients and emergency departments crowded with terrified and angry relatives, struggling to get help. The BBC had a map of the outbreak. They were encouraging people to tweet their symptoms, with the hashtag #Ihaveflu, so they could track the epidemic. There was a list of closed A&E departments, and where to go instead. The advice from Public Health England and the NHS, was to stay at home, and if a member of the family became unresponsive, to call NHS Direct.

I remained glued to the computer until the early hours of the morning, trying to understand what was happening and how to best stay safe. When I woke up late on Sunday, I checked the BBC again. There was an in depth analysis, comparing it to Spanish flu and other pandemics. It was more widespread than I had realised, with cases being reported in Europe and America.

The UK map of the outbreak was covered in red circles; London had the largest circles, indicating many cases, but Manchester and Birmingham were similarly covered. Some rural areas seemed to have almost none. I looked around my kitchen, would it be safer further away from London? I would have to stay in a B&B or hotel if I left, and persuade mum and

Vik to come with me...was it really worth it? I did a bit of research on booking.com and even rang a couple of places, but everywhere was either fully booked, or closed. After a couple of hours of research, I left the computer. The best strategy would be to stay in, hide, and wait until things went back to normal.

I tidied up a bit, then looked up at the loft hatch in the hallway. A flick of a long metal pole had it falling open. I pulled down the ladder and climbed up. The sun shone through the Velux windows in the roof, dust motes danced through the rays of light, which also highlighted the fine strands of cobweb, hanging from the rafters. At least there weren't any wasps' nests. The loft was light and bare, a large open area, great for a loft conversion if I ever needed the space. I stepped onto the boarded floor, juggling some of the extra items I had bought at the garden centre. I ducked under one of the supporting beams and opened the largest of several crates that were stacked on one side. The crate contained my emergency kit. It was much as I remembered, but there was also a six-pack of bottled water, five tins of sardines, and some custard and dried milk powder. I checked their expiry dates, and then added the camping stove, gas, and the hot chocolate and climbed carefully back down the ladder. I closed it all back up and then went back online, but this time to the prepper websites.

The prepper sites were interesting but scary, I scrolled through; did people have guns in this country? And what was with all the knives? I decided to take the advice about leaving the lights off, and closed the doors to the front bedroom and living room. Okay, anyone looking at the front would see an empty house. I dug out the old net curtains and put them up for more privacy. Then I started to flag, was this really what I wanted to do on my day off? I'd be knackered by Monday at this rate, and I still had marking to do.

Sunday passed and around 6pm the school sent an email saying it was closed for the forthcoming week, and to provide homework. I checked the school website and sure enough, there was a notice:

'Due to the recent outbreak the school is currently closed. Please click on the links below to find the homework for your child. Please check this website regularly for updates.'

I spent the rest of the evening writing homework booklets and creating resources to use with my favourite science website, before emailing it all off to the website administrator just before 10pm. Then I sat back, stretching, this wasn't just a one-day closure, like a snow day in winter. The school was closed, and it didn't look like it would be opening again any time soon. My year eleven GCSE students would be ecstatic, but what had started out as a fun exercise in prepping, seemed to be turning deadly serious.

The rubbish collection trucks came round Monday morning as normal, waking me from a lovely dream about gingerbread. The news confirmed widespread school closures. The infection rates in schools were so high; I could see it made sense. But as the morning progressed, the news reported disruption to many other services, as parents stayed home looking after children or ill relatives. The scale of the outbreak was reaching wider and wider, and my Facebook feed was filled with posts of condolences as people lost family and friends. A couple of cousins who did go to work, found no-one there, and turned around and came home again, so we spent the day Whatsapping each other and reading the news.

It all felt remote to me; no one close to me had died, and although I had a lot of work colleagues and acquaintances, my circle of close friends was tiny. But I could feel the danger of getting caught up in the mass grief, so I closed Facebook and concentrated on the factual stories from the BBC and updates from the CDC. There were some worrying stories of panic buying and food shortages. I had seen the panic buying first hand, but it seemed rather soon to have food shortages. But I was a single person, living alone, maybe large families would run out of food much faster.

There were some lovely stories of restaurants staying open to feed friends and neighbours, but fresh produce seemed to be running out quickly, especially things like bread and milk. There were also stories of people knocking on doors, demanding food. People weren't used to doing without and there was a lot of unrest building; it made me uneasy.

I spent the day moving between the computer and the garden. I planted the courgettes and then began to clear weeds with fresh zeal. This year they would not get on top of me… I needed the space. I looked around as I worked. What would be the best layout for maximum food production?

The front half of the garden was a small lawn, divided down the middle by a concrete path. There were flowerbeds in the middle of the garden, with trellis dividing the front from the vegetable garden at the back. I had removed the lawn from the back, and built L-shaped raised beds using decking boards. The greenhouse was in the centre of the raised beds, and the paths were just wood chippings, laid over weedstop fabric. The beds were easy to maintain, as the raised sides kept out some of the weed seeds, and made it easier to cover them with fleece or netting.

The L-beds usually contained the onions, carrots, tomatoes, beans, sweetcorn, and other veg. But maybe I should try the Three Sisters method and grow the sweetcorn beans and pumpkins together? I grabbed some paper and began to plan.

I decided to turn some more of the lawn into beds for the main-crop potatoes. Throughout the day, I alternated between energetic bursts; lifting the grass and piling it onto the compost heap, feverishly drawing and redrawing my plans, and then staring at the computer; researching subsistence farming.

Later in the evening, I walked down to the shops to see if there was anything left. The place was very different to Saturday afternoon; just a single car, parked askew and very few people, all scurrying by, scarfs wrapped over their mouths and keeping their distance from anyone else. The fear was palpable. The shops were all closed up, I squinted through the gaps in the co-op shutters; the shelves inside were entirely bare. The staff must have locked up early, taken the remaining food, and gone. Would they be open tomorrow? Next week? It was a good thing I had powdered milk in the cupboard. Walking round to the chemist, I was shocked to see the front window had been shattered, with pebbles of glass scattered on the ground below. A large hole had been ripped out of the toughened glass pane and the store inside was a chaotic mess of products. The previously neat shelves and displays were just a memory. I stood, disturbed by the violence implicit in the fractured glass, it must have been hit hard, over and over again, to make that hole. I looked around me and shivered in the sunshine, then turned and walked away.

3

Security

Tuesday I stayed in. There were fewer sirens on the estate but more people on the streets. Online, the big story was the actions of parliament. The previous day COBR had invoked the emergency powers in the Civil Contingencies Act 2004 and were creating new regulations left right and centre, to keep the electricity, gas, and water running and protect fuel deliveries. The BBC had a picture of just a handful of politicians, gathered around a table, looking earnest. I was reassured in one way but also alarmed; I didn't know much about politics but weren't those emergency powers usually reserved for wars or natural disasters? It seemed the government also thought that the outbreak was deadly serious.

Wednesday the riots began. I had been expecting them, and was only surprised they hadn't started earlier. One of the central London hospitals had closed and the locals had organised a peaceful demonstration outside parliament to get them to reopen it. I watched the BBC livestream on and off during the day, as the small group of demonstrators swelled with grieving relatives, demanding answers. It quickly turned ugly. There was a lot of activity on social media, which brought out opportunists who started the looting. The disorder spread to other areas, and although the police around parliament quickly restored order, in other regions, they were so short staffed that they abandoned entire districts. As usual the BBC had a pretty graphic, this time to show the areas that people should avoid.

It was Thursday afternoon and I was reading an article on 'home hardening' when I heard the knock. I froze, listening intently, and the knock came again. I didn't get up; the article had been about home security and had made me nervous. Who would come knocking on my door without texting me first? I waited and then slowly got up out of my chair and moved to the window. There were two youngish women walking down the road, dressed in summer dresses, bags slung over their arms. Had they knocked on my door? I didn't recognise them. What did they want?

One of the women crossed the road and stepped onto the driveway of the bungalow three doors down. I frowned, were they knocking on particular doors? I had a clear view across the road as an elderly man answered her knock. They spoke for a bit. Was she asking for help or offering it? It seemed odd that she had left her friend behind. The man shuffled away and then, after about thirty seconds or so, came back with something that she put in her bag. She walked back to her friend, took the package back out, opened the top, and handed her something small. Was that a biscuit? Well, that was one way to get food. It seemed risky to me, and also rather shameless; they hadn't worked for that biscuit, paid or traded anything for it, just asked and been given.

The women didn't seem dangerous or desperate but I didn't want strangers, who were potentially infected, knocking on my door asking for help. My car was out front, tomorrow I should probably move it to the side road, then the driveway would be empty… like next door. I would pretend to be out if anyone knocked. It was selfish but also felt like the sensible course of action.

After that, the knocks came fairly often, several times a day. I never answered the door, but sometimes I watched them from behind the net curtains at the kitchen window, as they made their way down the street. Some of the knockers offered money to people, but others were quite intimidating. I saw an elderly lady answer her door and shake her head to a young couple. She began to close the door as they shouted and swore but they shoved it open and barged past her into the house. Luckily a dog began barking from inside, and they backed out pretty quickly. I was tempted to go over and check she was ok; I waited for the road to clear of knockers, but when I looked an hour later, her car was gone. People were leaving, the streets were unsafe, and with the shops closed, and the bus service unreliable, I saw very few of my neighbours anymore.

Not having to go to work, I got into a routine; early mornings were spent in the garden. The knockers wouldn't arrive before mid-morning, so I would get up early, have a quick shower, get dressed, and set the hose to a quiet trickle whilst I weeded around the plants. It was peaceful. Like a holiday. Later on, when there was more activity on the streets, I would stay indoors and read, or do some of the house upkeep that I had fallen behind on. I still phoned home every day.

On Monday, after I had been at home a week, Vik phoned me late in the evening. 'Hi Z,' he said. I was surprised, as I had phoned earlier in the day for my usual chat.

'Hey Vik, what's up?' I asked, swivelling on my chair in front of the computer.

'I don't want to worry you,' he began, 'but some of the older kids have taken to hanging around the top of the road and accosting people as they go past.' he continued. 'They're not asking for money; they're asking for food.'

I stopped spinning and sat upright. 'We have people knocking on the door asking for food.' I replied. I hadn't told them about the knockers as I knew they would worry. 'They canvas whole streets and carry shopping bags. Some can be quite intimidating.'

'Yeah, these kids are pretty intimidating also,' he said, grimly, 'this afternoon Jenny, from across the road, was tripped as she walked past, and fell quite hard. They helped her up and accompanied her home, but then ransacked her kitchen, filling bags with food and valuables. She's ok but has decided to leave London to stay with family in the country.'

As he spoke, I could faintly hear shouting in the background. I was alarmed. Individually young people were generally nice, but as a teacher, I knew how quickly a large group could get out of control. I hadn't always worked in good schools and I could distinctly remember how kids could gang up, when they were together in the playground.

'Are you keeping the lights off?' I asked, 'And maybe you should talk to mum about staying inside for now.' Mum had been regularly visiting with the neighbours, as she had a lot of friends on the street. Because their place was in an affluent neighbourhood, I knew that mum and Vik felt they were safe. Although they were happy about all the precautions I was taking, they didn't see the need to do the same at their house. If Vik was phoning me though, he had to be more worried than he was letting on.

'Yeah, maybe.' Vik replied. 'Anyway I just wanted to let you know. Mum's making dinner so I better go.' We said our goodbyes and rang off. I was worried, although their house had enough food to last for at least a month, mum didn't grow many vegetables. She grew chilli plants, herbs and spinach, but you couldn't really live off those. I wondered how I could get her to come and stay with me, but deep down I knew that was impossible. She would never leave her house. It was her home.

In the garden, the roses had put out a lot of new growth, and I put some thought into weaving the long stems so they would fall over the wall and deter any of the knockers trying to climb up. The brick wall made the garden fairly secure, and in the corner I had planted a large pyracantha bush, also known as a firethorn, to deter thieves from climbing over using the neighbour's trees. The only weak point was by the house; the flimsy side gate leading to the driveway.

I stood at my front door, looking up at the sky. The air had that early morning crispness, and the atmosphere was one of undisturbed tranquillity, but I was out front for a reason. I had been home a week; the school wasn't re-opening and the food shortages were getting worse. My research on home hardening had made some things quite clear; I lived in a bungalow in the suburbs, not a cabin in the middle of the woods or a castle with a moat. My bungalow had few features to protect it. The only way to stay safe was to be invisible. Not actually invisible of course, but to blend in, not showing anything of value, and to make it as unappealing as possible.

I looked around. The front garden was completely unsecurable. The driveway was large and open, without gates of any kind. The side of the driveway was bounded by a copper beech hedge, which at this time of year, was a lovely rich green colour with new leaves. It wasn't particularly tall, but it was thick and impenetrable. The front drive was separated from the back garden by an extension to the brick wall, which ran sideways until it met the house. Inset into the wall was a wooden side gate, which allowed access to the garden from the drive, so I could carry plants and compost through from the car.

The side-gate was the only way into the garden from outside; it had a single bolt that could be padlocked. The hinges were flimsy, and I imagined the whole thing could be kicked in very easily. My research had suggested three options; camouflage, strengthening and diversion. I could disguise the door so people didn't see it, I could reinforce the door so it couldn't be kicked in, or I could rig it so it looked broken, and the garden looked wild and overgrown so people wouldn't bother going in. Of course, I chose all three. First, I needed plants big enough to hide it, which meant a trip back to the garden centre.

I planned quite carefully; I didn't want the roaming knockers to see me come out of my house, so I needed to go early. I also needed my car, as a plant large enough to hide my doorway would be too large to carry. I didn't know if the garden centre was open. If the gates were shut it would be very difficult to get in without breaking in through the chain-link fence that surrounded the garden centre. I couldn't imagine doing anything like that, it would be vandalism, I was happy nicking some plants, but criminal damage was a step to far. It was only two weeks into the epidemic and I still mostly believed that things would go back to normal fairly soon. I didn't want to wake up one morning to the police knocking on my door to arrest me.

I decided it would be best to check the gates first; walk over at night, when there would be less chance I would be seen. I set a very quiet muffled alarm to wake me up at 2:30am and slept restlessly for a bit. I dressed in black jeans, a dark green jumper, and black sketchers. Then I paused; watching the knockers every day had made me nervous. I looked round for a weapon. I ruled out a kitchen knife as being too extreme, and instead, opened my toolbox. I rooted around until my fingers closed on something cold and heavy; a pair of large snub nosed pliers. I pulled them out, then swung them in the air. Not bad, a hammer might have been better as an actual weapon, but this felt right; weighty and solid. Not that I could imagine using it, but it was better to be safe than sorry.

At 3am, when the streets were entirely empty, I opened the front door. The night sky was clear, and after the heat of the day, it felt much cooler, almost chilly in fact. Most of the streetlights were off, as it was after midnight, but there was one up at the top of the road spilling white light over the junction. There was a bit of a moon, and because my night vision is fairly good, I could see quite well. I stood by the side of the hedge trying to be as still as possible as I slowly scanned up and down the street.

It was empty, so I stepped out onto the pavement. Carpenders Park at night didn't scare me in the slightest; I had spent too many winter evenings walking around in the dark trying to burn off some of the frustrations of school. The dark felt familiar and safe. I was in two minds about what to do next, I wanted to walk down to the shops and explore the estate…sheer curiosity, but I also knew that I should focus on the garden centre. I turned and walked up the road towards the T-junction, moving slowly and steadily, swinging the pliers slightly so anyone watching could see them.

At the top of the road, I stopped in the mouth of someone's driveway, in the shadow of a large overgrown hedge. The streetlamp cast a wide blanket of cold pale light, and there wasn't really anywhere else to hide. I listened intently. The road in front of me was the southern boundary of Carpenders Park. It was lined with houses on my side, but opposite was just a hedge, with a dark field beyond. To the right, the road led to a single-lane bridge, which took traffic over the railway line. To the left, the road led up to the traffic lights and the main road running north into Watford and south into Harrow. I turned left and walked along the pavement, past the houses, until I reached the side entrance to the cemetery.

The cemetery was a familiar place to me as my dad's ashes were buried there. It was a large lawn cemetery so there were no headstones. Lots of people planted flowers over the graves, and had signs and other memorabilia, but as time went on the grass would spread over, and all would be left was a small plaque in the ground. It was a quiet and peaceful place, even at night, with large trees showing inky black against the sky. The cemetery occupied the whole corner of Carpenders Park, wrapping around the garden centre, which was right at the end of the road, on the junction.

As I passed the cemetery I glanced in and was surprised to see bobbing lights in the distance; there were people here. I briefly wondered what they were doing but moved quickly on. The trees from the cemetery overhung the pavement and created a dark shadowy space. I could barely see, and was uneasy now that I knew there were people around. I knew the garden centre must be on my left, but I couldn't see it. Then the trees thinned, and I saw the gates; they were open!

I stood at the gates, the moonlight highlighting the silver metal against the dark background. My task was done, but it felt exciting to be out at night, after being stuck inside for so long. Perhaps I could check how easy it was to get to the tall plants at the back of the garden centre.

I slipped into the empty car park and walked round the windowless building, down toward the entrance, hugging the wall for cover. I was aiming for the entrance porch, which opened straight into the plant yard. The security lighting was on; bright lights on the rails surrounding the car park, but the porches were in darkness. The large outer doors were pushed back, but I couldn't see past the darkness to the inner automatic glass doors.

As I passed the exit, by the tills in the building I noticed that its outer wooden doors were also open. I paused listening; there was silence. I slipped into the opening and crunched loudly down on something. I froze, crouched, and reached down with a hand. My fingers brushed something smooth with a sharp edge: glass... my eyes swept the darkness in front of me as I reached forward. The inner glass doors were completely smashed.

I waited a long time, crouched down, listening, but couldn't hear anything. The pitch-black darkness inside was frightening and my nerve failed...there was no need to go inside...I could just check the main entrance was open and then leave. I rose, and as I pivoted to step away, the glass crunched again. A torch light flashed on in the store, and a voice murmured. I darted out of the porch, and, dashed back towards the gates. As I reached them, flashlights circled light round the carpark and up toward me, I heard an exclamation, but I didn't wait to see what they would do; I ran.

I was not a runner; I could do a ten-mile hike easily but never ran anywhere. It was much harder than you'd think. My breath ripped in and out, and my limbs felt heavier than lead, I could hear my shoes pounding against the ground and after a couple of hundred yards I had to stop, just to breathe. I staggered back to the T-junction and fell behind the shadowy hedge, gasping for breath. I waited, trying to quiet my breathing, but no one followed. My right hand clenched tight around the pliers. That hadn't gone quite as planned. I brushed the sweat from my forehead. The garden centre was too risky to go in at the front, but these pliers…they were the perfect tool to get in from behind.

Back home I was too wired to go to bed, so I turned on my computer. I opened google maps, and as the sky slowly lightened, started planning another outing, this time to the cemetery.

The next day I slept in; I hadn't gone to bed till after sunrise at 5am, so it wasn't surprising that I slept to mid-afternoon. I was awakened by a knock at the door, and, being half-asleep, had risen and taken several steps before I caught myself. I waited, as they rattled the door handle, calling out for 'just a little something… whatever you can spare', hoping they would go away and leave me alone. When they had finally left, I turned on the computer and returned to my research.

The back of the garden centre had a boundary with the cemetery. I checked the ordinance survey maps online, and saw that there was a bit of scrubland between the garden centre boundary and the cemetery proper. I could drive in, walk into the scrub, cut through the fence into the garden centre, and …well I would take it from there.

The next morning I watched out of the window as the cars went by… where were they going? The empty shops? To the closed hospitals? Or were they trying to get to family and friends? I waited until I couldn't see anyone from my windows, and then left, pushing my wheelbarrow in front of me. I walked casually on the pavement, turning down the side road to get to my car. There was still no-one about, so I opened the boot, folded down the back seats to make more room, and wedged in the wheelbarrow. Sometimes the ignition gave trouble, but as my eyes swivelled left and right, searching, the car roared to life.

I drove round to the cemetery, and turned in. The car park was full, and as I looked around, I saw at least three hearses parked along the roads that crisscrossed the green lawns. This must be where some of the cars had been going. There were small groups of people standing around fresh graves, and there was a large digger working up at the top of the cemetery. I was surprised; with the chaos going on everywhere else it seemed astonishing that the funeral business was carrying on as normal, but I supposed that they were used to dealing with difficult situations, and the dead still needed to be buried. Funeral directors were probably just as important as the police and firemen during an outbreak, and the bodies wouldn't be infectious, so there were fewer risks than being a doctor or nurse. I drove past one of the hearses and turned my car to the far side of the cemetery. The area I was aiming for was empty. I drove down the paths towards the garden centre and reversed up onto the grass until the boot was at the base of a slight bank.

Out of the car, I was glad I had dressed in thick jeans and walking boots, as the bank was covered in waist high vegetation. I looked around, but there was no one near. I grabbed the pliers and pulled my wheelbarrow out of the boot. Forcing a path up the bank wasn't hard; luckily it was mostly weeds like rosebay willowherb, rather than nettles or brambles. Beyond the bank was a slight depression in the ground and then the back fence of the garden centre.

So far so good, but this was the point where I moved from law abiding citizen, to trespasser and thief. The fence looked much older on this side. It was green, plastic coated, chain link fencing, held up by posts every six feet. On the other side were the bamboo plants, perfect, if I could get to them. I looked carefully at the wire. I didn't need to cut a line down through the links; all I needed was to open the link at the top and un-weave one single strand of wire. Then I could roll back the fence and would have a large six-foot gap to go in and out.

I paused, Now that I was standing outside the fence, I was unsure. I had been good all my life; apart from dodging the occasional train fare when I was younger, and a couple of recent speeding tickets, I obeyed the law. What I was going to do was criminal, and I didn't even know if it was necessary… The government might have organised things by next week, I told myself… There might be food supplies and maybe even a vaccine… And school might even be back open; I might be back at work. I half turned, then straightened and reached up to the first link. I told myself I could stop at any point if it didn't feel right, but I kept going. It was fiddly work, but after half an hour, the two sides of the fence sprang back from each other and sagged backwards, leaving a two-foot gap.

I pulled three bamboo plants through. They had small pots but were at least eight feet tall. I put them in the wheelbarrow and turned to make my way back. The long stems blocked my view, making it almost impossible to steer over the humps in the ground, but eventually I made it and stowed them in the car.

I paused resting; this area of the cemetery still had no-one in sight. It had been so easy to get the bamboo...maybe I would push my luck, and go back for some bushier plants. I returned to the fence and rolled the opening a bit wider, so I could slip the wheelbarrow in through the gap. Pushing it in front of me, I looked carefully beyond the bamboos to see if anyone was about. It seemed clear, so I moved further into the yard, past the Japanese maples and ferns. I suppose I was distracted by all the plants, but just as I came upon the perfect Red Robin shrub, the noise in the background resolved itself... I could hear kid's voices. I turned, looking for somewhere to hide. The noises suddenly sharply increased in volume and I heard shrieking and running, and then a girl, primary school age, maybe nine or so, burst into view. She skidded to a stop and stared at me, frozen. Uh-oh.

'Hi.' I said, smiling nervously, letting the wheelbarrow fall.

Two smaller boys joined her. They didn't say anything, just stared. I needed them to not call out, and I was usually good with children; I quickly decided to try a bit of distraction. 'Which do you think I should get?' I said, gesturing to the two plants in front of me. 'I like the red leaves on this one, but the shape of these is lovely.' The second plant was a castor oil plant with large, bright green, lobed leaves. I touched one of the leaves. 'What do you think?' I said again. If I could just get them in conversation, they wouldn't run off and call for help.

The smallest boy pointed to the red robin shrub. 'I like this one.' he said. The other boy immediately pointed to the other plant, 'No this one is nicer.' I relaxed ever so slightly. The boys were on-side, but the girl still looked tense. I smiled.

'You have the deciding vote,' I said. 'I like the red robin, but...' I tailed off, desperately hoping she would say something.

'Yeah' she said, 'it's nice.' 'What are you doing here?' She asked.

'I need some plants for the garden.' I said, as if it was the most natural thing in the world, 'It looked a bit scary at the front, so I came in the back way.'

'There isn't a back way.' she replied firmly.

'There is a gap in the fence by the bamboo plants.' I pointed back the way I had come. Luckily, the gap was small, and they might think they had missed it. 'Could you guys help me lift this?' I asked, tilting the red robin onto its side. If I could keep them occupied, they wouldn't run off and tell their parents I was here.

I grasped the pot, and after a second the boy who had chosen the red robin grabbed hold of some leaves as if to help. 'Thanks,' I said, after we had manhandled it into the wheelbarrow.

'My name's Zoe.' I brushed my hands on my jeans and held one out towards the other boy who was standing back a little way. Younger kids were always a little perplexed when I shook hands with them. It would help keep them off balance.

'Um, I'm Lucas,' said the boy, who looked at my hand, and then suddenly reached out and shook it, looking shy. I turned to my helper, holding out my hand again.

'I'm Toby' he said, shaking it and smiling.

Then the girl, I held my breath as I held out my hand. 'I'm Daisy' she said, reaching out her hand and solemnly shaking mine.

'Great, can you guys help me, so I don't crash into anything?' I asked, as I picked up the wheelbarrow and turned it around. 'See if you can find the bamboo plants, they're really tall with thin leaves'

'It's what pandas eat,' volunteered the girl.

I smiled at her, and with Toby still holding some of the leaves at the front, set off for the way out. We reached the fence without mishap, and more importantly without any adults turning up.

At the fence line, Lucas stopped and stepped back. 'We're not allowed to leave.' he said.

'Uncle Ben says this place is forty…fortif…fortible,' said Toby.

'Fortifiable,' I corrected, 'that's true, it's a great place with lots of resources.' It sounded like his uncle definitely wouldn't be happy with my trespass and burglary. I turned to Daisy, 'you should tell him about this hole in the fence,' I said. 'So he can fix it.'

They stood and waved goodbye, as I wobbled across the scrubland, and after a quick check that the coast was clear; down the bank to the car. I looked back one last time before they disappeared out of sight. I hoped they would be ok.

The red robin was awkwardly large; wide and leafy with a pot that was much bigger and heavier than the bamboo pots. It was almost impossible to lift out of the wheelbarrow, but eventually I closed the boot on the squashed branches and sat back in the driving seat to take stock.

It was still only mid-morning. There would be knockers about and people watching from their houses. I drove back, parked in the side road, but left the plants in the car to remove later that evening when the roads were empty.

The side road was a short access road to the street behind mine. I walked along the length of the brick wall beside my garden, and then along the fence of the house behind mine. The fence was old and neglected with several feather boards missing. Could I get inside somehow? I felt along carefully; there were several loose boards either side of a narrow gap. If

I swung two boards aside, I could get into my neighbour's garden. I looked around, but there were no houses overlooking this strip of road, so I quickly pushed the boards apart and ducked inside.

As expected, the garden was a wilderness. I could barely see the bungalow at the end, and what I could see looked abandoned. My elderly neighbours must have left years ago and the place had remained unsold, slowly decaying away. The original shrubs had gown straggly and tall, and the ground was covered in weeds. But what really impressed me was a massive conifer at the centre of the garden. It was some sort of cypress, with a large pyramid shape. It must have been planted ages ago, and it probably looked fine for a couple of years, but now, well, it dwarfed the bungalow behind it and covered almost two thirds of the garden. The foliage was dense and dark green, and the branches drooped so that they were touching the ground, with no trunk showing at all.

I moved right, towards my garden, but the way was blocked by an impenetrable undergrowth of viciously-thorned brambles and damson saplings, that covered the back all the way to the fence. There looked to be a path on the other side of the cypress, but I just couldn't reach it. I would have to wait where I was.

I brushed away some of the leaf litter from the tiny oval of patio paving that I was standing on, and sat cross-legged on the stone. I looked around. Well it wasn't a terrible place to wait. I shifted my legs, and decided to do a bit of meditation to pass the time.

About thirty seconds later I opened my eyes, reached forward, and lifted the nearest trailing branch of the cypress to check. Sure enough, the inside of the conifer was mostly dead wood, and much less dense than the outer foliage suggested.

Maybe my meditation technique was rubbish, but my chattering mind had come up with a fairly decent idea. With a bit of judicious pruning, I could clear a space at the base, to crawl through to the other side. Only one problem; I didn't have anything to prune it with; all my tools were in my house.

I stood up and walked towards the back of the bungalow, At the side, half hidden, under a tangle of ivy, was a derelict greenhouse. The glass was cracked and opaque with years of dirt and neglect. I found the door, removed some of the blocking vegetation, and managed to shove it open wide enough to slip inside. Spotting a brush that was propped up against the staging; I waved it in the air to clear most of the spider's webs and looked around. The greenhouse was a veritable treasure trove of broken things, but beneath a pile of pots, I found a pair of old secateurs; jackpot.

I spent ages beneath that cypress, trimming away at the dead wood. I couldn't just cut away the branches because I would lose all the concealing greenery at the end of the branch. I had to painstakingly work along each branch, snipping away all the dead wood, and then repeat for the branches above and below. The inside of the tree slowly opened up as I gradually worked further inwards. The large bits of wood I pushed to the edge of the tree, and the ground became carpeted with dead needles as they broke off and rained to the ground. When I reached the trunk, I snipped out some of the dead branches and turned around. The tunnel was fairly spacious, but I would have to cut at least a couple of branches to move round to the other side of the tree. I backed out and went looking for the ancient garden saw, I had seen earlier.

Back under the tree I carefully cut a couple of branches at the base of the trunk, then I had to work my way out again, snipping along the branches to the other side. When I finally reached the edge of the cypress, I saw that there was indeed a path to my garden, and with the trees up against the fence, climbing over would be, if not easy, at least possible. I scrambled over, avoiding the sprouting dahlias as I dropped the six feet on the other side. Once inside my garden I relaxed; I couldn't get into the house as the back door was locked, but I could lie in the hammock and rest, and most importantly, feel safe.

After dusk had fallen, I opened the side gate, went around the front, and let myself in. I was starving. I made a note to stash some crackers in the boot of the car, and then cooked some pasta with tomatoes, olives, and sweetcorn. Later that evening, when the streets were clear, I went out to the car and brought my loot round to the front of the house.

The bamboo plants were taller than the brick wall and leafy. The sturdy Red Robin in front would keep them from falling over, but although the door was disguised from a distance, up close anyone would be able to see it, and worse, see that someone was trying to hide it. I dragged round a couple of pots of potatoes from the front, but what it really needed was a load of trailing ivy and some weeds. It looked entirely too neat and tidy. I was a little discouraged, but perked up when I tallied up the successes of the day; not only had the main objective been fulfilled, but as a bonus, I had found a way of getting in and out of my bungalow undetected.

Phase two was to reinforce the door to make it harder to break open. Now that I had found a back way into the garden, I could seal off the front semi-permanently. I might conceivably need to use the side-gate to get large loads into the garden, but most of the time I would probably use the cypress route. I decided to kill two birds with one stone; I would dig up some of the brambles from the garden behind mine and plant them by the gate. If some of the roots were intact, it would probably survive, and would soon send out new shoots. I would use the long whippy branches of bramble to weave across and over the gate. It would help with the disguise, and would make it very difficult to open, but if I needed to, I could just cut all the stems with a pair of loppers in order to open the door.

The plan worked like a dream. The bramble stems were extraordinarily long: four meters at least. They had obviously been growing a while. They were incredibly difficult to dig up, and eventually I took the garden saw to the thick taproot. I just hoped there were enough smaller roots to keep it alive. I planted them at the base of the wall, tied to a stake, and trailed them up over one side of the door frame, and then wound them round the slats of the door before tying them to the other side. With the plants in front, the overall effect was one of natural chaos. It looked like the brambles were escaping the garden, but it also meant that anyone trying to break in the door, would also have to break all the bramble stems.

I stood back from the door and looked at it. Was it a bit over the top? Did I really need to be so paranoid? The knockers were a little worrying, but, apart from work, life was carrying on as normal. Nevertheless, it didn't hurt to be prepared. Who knew what might happen over the next couple of weeks.

4

Travel

During the early hours of Saturday morning, the weather finally broke and I woke up to a drenched garden and the news that, starting that afternoon, there would be rolling power outages.

The article on the BBC listed when the power would be out for each area. Mine was due to go off mid-afternoon. I put my phone on charge and then looked at the fridge. Both my fridge and freezer were tiny. The fridge was mostly empty; no milk or yogurt left, although there was some butter and Flora margarine. There were also opened jars of jam and marmalade, a load of sauce bottles, and the Baby Bel cheeses I had bought at Tesco.

I took some plastic take-away containers, filled them with water, and put them in the freezer. I gave the fridge a thorough clean and stacked the remaining items neatly near the bottom. When the ice packs were ready, I would put them on the top shelf. They would cool the air, which would hopefully drop down and form a cold layer over the food.

The freezer was also mostly empty. Just some packets of frozen veg that I hadn't got around to using up. I took out some cauliflower for lunch and crossed my fingers for the rest. Cleaning up the fridge and freezer set me off on a cleaning binge that lasted the whole morning. I sorted through all my food stocks, moving some up to the loft and bringing the sardines down. The crisis seemed to be ongoing, and my strategy of 'stay in, hide, and wait' was not a long-term solution. I had been expecting the government to provide emergency food supplies, but that didn't seem to be happening. The electricity supply was now intermittent; maybe things weren't going to go back to normal. I had think seriously about the food I was growing. I went to open a spreadsheet on my computer, and realised that 2pm had passed; the electricity was now off. I picked up a pen and went to find a notebook.

It was nearing the end of May, so in a couple of weeks I would start getting the first of the new potatoes, I also had some small carrots, and the onions I had planted in autumn were now a decent size. The peas were looking well, and the beans in the greenhouse could be planted out fairly soon and would crop from mid-summer. The tomatoes would be ripe by the end of august, and the sweetcorn would be ready in September. If I planted the bag of maincrop potatoes now, I should be able to harvest them in early autumn and store them in the shed over winter. As long as they didn't get damaged by frost, they would be fine. The courgettes of course would start cropping in about ten weeks, and would produce until the frost killed them, which might not be until November. I might not like them, but they were a good bulking vegetable. The apples and pears would be harvestable in autumn and some of the varieties were good for storing until January, as long as I boxed them up carefully.

I looked at the notes I had made, it seemed like I would be ok. If I stayed in my bungalow and kept my garden safe, I should have food to spare through the summer and autumn and if I was careful and stored the produce carefully, I might be ok for winter as well.

Sunday was still too wet to be in the garden, so I began sorting out my clothes; moving my work outfits to the spare bedroom closet, and bringing my summer wardrobe over into my bedroom. With the rain and the net curtains, it was dim and gloomy, and I had turned on a light, thinking that no knockers would be out in the wet. I was happily working away in the front room; when I was interrupted by the doorbell ringing. I paused, was there someone actually at the door?... or was the wireless doorbell playing up again. A series of heavy knocks rattled the door in its frame. I didn't move, looking at the window and the light; should I switch it off or leave it be? The door banged again and the doorbell rang. I stepped towards the hallway and peered down towards the front door. The letterbox opened and I quickly drew my head back into the room as I heard a voice shouting 'Oi...I know you're in there...open the door...please...my kids are starving' It was a man's voice, deep and harsh.

What to do? I had food, but I was loath to open my door to a stranger. But the thought of kids going hungry had me hesitantly stepping forwards. Then I heard a second voice; 'Fucking open the door, bitch.' The door rattled hard against the frame. 'We know you're in there, we're going to fuck you up if you don't open this door right now' I froze in place, heart racing. The door shook violently and then loud banging started on the windows. As I stood paralysed, the noise moved round to the side of the house. I slipped into the hallway and looked into the kitchen; the curtains were closed and I couldn't see anything behind them, but I could still hear noises. It sounded like they were trying to get through the side gate. I heard swearing again but this time in pain; ...the brambles...doing their work. There was the sound of wood splintering and then more swearing. Then the voices grew louder, moved past the kitchen window, and back up of the drive, gradually fading away as I sank into my chair and shook uncontrollable.

I sat for ages, cold inside, listening as hard as I could, but eventually, when I was absolutely certain they were gone, I persuaded myself to get up. It was time for some chocolate. I desperately wanted to phone home, but I knew they would worry, instead I found the superglue and sealed the letterbox shut. Doing something proactive helped immeasurably with the shakiness I was feeling. I took the spare duvet and stuffed it round the front door to reduce the chance of people hearing me from outside. It was a trick from the prepper website that I had discarded as being over the top, but now I began to prep my house in earnest. I taped the net curtains to the edges of the windowsill and put tape over the light switches so I wouldn't forget and accidentally switch them on out of habit. I then went online and looked into the security of my UPVC doors.

I was appalled; it looked like the panels could just be kicked in. The internet had helpful suggestions of door bars and grills, but where exactly was I going to get those? I scratched my head for a bit, and then in the interests of security, I sacrificed my shower rail and some solid wood shelves to create a bar across the weakest part of the door. I cut the shelves into two 8 inch squares. Then I cut U shapes into the wood the width of the bar. I drilled holes in the brick walls either side of the front door and screwed the pieces of wood flat against the walls with the opening to the U at the top. The thunderstorm that started on Sunday afternoon helped disguise the drilling and after it was all securely attached I cut the shower rail to size and dropped it into the slots of the wood. I then glued the rest of the shelf to the UPVC panel, building up the layers until the wood was pressed against the bar. If someone tried to kick the panel in, they would be kicking against a metal bar, attached to a brick wall. It took all afternoon but I felt an enormous sense of satisfaction when I finished.

On Sunday evening, I put out my bins in my neighbours driveway, but Monday, the rubbish van didn't show. I checked the local Facebook community group and sure enough, there was a post from the council, apologising, and giving notice that a special collection had been organised in coordination with the army. I went back to the BBC and read the breaking news that the Home Office was utilising the armed forces to assist as emergency personnel, helping at hospitals and crematoriums, and driving the refuse lorries to collect the rubbish. I was impressed and waited to see if they would also be supplying food.

The news had a lot of discussion on the food shortages. The warehouses were making fewer and fewer deliveries; staff shortages at all levels meant that the food just wasn't getting to where it needed to go. There were fewer staff at the warehouses, fewer drivers, even the people that could have coordinated the remaining drivers were at home looking after their kids, or ill themselves. And more people were getting sick all the time.

The bug I had caught had disappeared completely after a couple of days of home remedies and sleep. I wasn't sure whether I had just had a cold, or if it had been a mild version of the virus. Online there was some speculation about its mechanism. It seemed that it was fairly harmless, until it had been in the body long enough to multiply. At sufficient concentrations, scientists thought that the virus could possibly cross the blood-brain barrier. Once there, they speculated that it destroyed the parts of the brain stem responsible for the important things like breathing, heart rate, and consciousness. The initial symptoms were much as I had experienced, but the virus usually progressed past the flu symptoms, to confusion, sleepiness, and then the sick would suddenly go unconscious and their hearts or breathing would just stop. If my illness had been caused by the virus, then my day off had probably saved my life; the virus had been destroyed before it had crossed into my brain.

After such gruesome reading, I had to phone home to check on my family. Vik answered on the second ring. 'Hi Z,' he said, sounding unusually alert for this time of the morning.

'Hi Vik, what are you doing up so early?' I asked.

'My friends in America have stopped coming online.' he replied, 'The virus is there too, but things are much worse; lots of gun violence, and a lot of people have left the cities to be with family in the country. Also, we're keeping the lights off, so it's just easier to go to bed early.'

'Have you checked when your power goes out?' I asked, 'mine went off at 2pm, but I think yours is later, starting at 2am.'

'The power's going out? Why? What's the problem? He asked.

'Some of the power stations still work…hydroelectric wind…solar, and the grid is still connected, but there just isn't enough electricity to go around' I replied.

'But why? asked Vik.

'I've been reading online a lot, and there was an in depth article on the BBC.' I said, 'It's partly due to not enough fuel; the gas and oil supplies are unreliable, and partly because the power plants are short staffed.'

'Really?' said Vik, 'That seems a bit crazy.'

'Yeah,' I replied, 'but I'm just happy that there's still power.'

Neither of us said anything for a moment, I almost mentioned the knockers, but then Vik said hesitantly, 'Mum went out yesterday. She wanted to see how Maria was doing.'

'What!' I exclaimed.

'I tried to talk her out of it, but you know what mum's like,' said Vik, 'I was going to go with her, but she was already gone before I could get ready.'

I looked unseeingly at the computer in front of me. Why would mum do that? It was so stupidly risky. 'Is she ok?' I eventually asked.

'Yeah, she didn't stay long, I think Maria was ill,' replied Vik.

'Is she there?' I asked.

'Hold on, I'll see if she's awake.' He responded. There were some muffled noises then mums voice, 'Hi Z, what's up?'

'Mum,' I said, 'I thought we agreed we would stay in and hide, till things got back to normal'

'Well, it's been two weeks and Maria is just down the road,' she said defensively, 'I just wanted to check on her. It's a good thing I did, because she's almost out of food and was a bit under the weather. I invited her to come and stay with us, but she said no. She's hoping her son will be coming and wants to wait for him.'

This was crazy, mum was wandering around as if we weren't in the middle of a crisis, and now she was talking about taking people in. Her food was going to run out in no time. 'I'm coming over' I said. 'We need to talk about a long term strategy'

I looked back through the notes I had made in my notebook. I could grow enough food to feed me, but probably not all of us. However, mum still had lots of food at her house. She usually bought extra-large bags of rice and lentils as it was cheaper, and tended to stock up on stuff when it was on offer in the shops, storing it haphazardly in the kitchen cupboards and larder. They also had Costco multipacks of instant mash and noodles that Vik bought, and there was an enormous cupboard in the garage, filled with tins of tuna and chickpeas bought in bulk, and bottles of coke and sprite.

It felt like a lot to me, but we really needed to take everything out and work out how many people they could feed, and for how long. If you continuously harvest runner beans from a beanstalk, they will keep flowering and producing more, for as long as the plant is still alive, but a larder wouldn't magically fill up again once it had been emptied. Mum wasn't thinking about finite food supplies, she just knew that she had plenty and wanted to share what she had. I needed her to see that this wasn't necessarily the prudent thing to do.

I used the new back route out of the bungalow. I had dad's sturdy old stepladder; heavy metal frame and wooden treads, which I placed against the back corner of the fence. I pressed the feet into the hard ground. The weather had changed again and it was windy and much cooler in the garden, with scudding clouds above. I had extracted an old tarp from the shed, along with a bag of spring clamps, and I chucked them over, before climbing up into the garden beyond.

I spread out the tarp, and using the clamps to pin it to the branches, lined the tunnel under the cypress tree: it would keep some of the bugs and dirt off me as I crawled through, and stop me getting so scratched by the needles. I peered out of the gap in the fence and when I was sure there was no one watching, I pushed the loose boards aside and stepped through.

I was carrying my smallest backpack with some crackers and a bottle of water, which I hid under the junk in the boot of the car. There was already a first aid kit, picnic blanket, boot liner, spare waterproof coat, woolly hat, and old walking boots in there, along with jump leads and an air pump. It's surprising what a single person, whose main hobbies are gardening and walking, ends up with in the boot of their car. I got in, started the engine, and drove out of Carpenders Park.

It was mid-morning, but there were almost no cars on the road. I turned south at the main junction and headed towards Harrow. I wanted to avoid the town centre in case there was looting still going on, so headed left along the A410 Uxbridge road, and then round a roundabout to go into a smaller side road. I immediately hit a snag. Two cars had been parked at an angle across the entrance to the road, completely blocking it. I slowed, looking across. Behind the cars, I glimpsed a group of garden chairs, on which lounged several people; they were barricading the street! I saw the people look up and start to rise, as I continued round the roundabout and then sped back the way I had come.

Now on alert, I noticed that many of the streets had been blocked off; the local residents seemed to have got together and organised themselves. I wondered what the barricades were there to block; I hadn't seen any other cars or pedestrians so far; were they to stop people entering the area or to stop people leaving? I drove back, but I didn't want to give up yet. I would try the route south via the town centre. The area was residential and seemed peaceful, but as I drove, I began to smell smoke. I crested a slight rise and could see, straight ahead, that the shopping centre was on fire. Black smoke billowed from the large green dome of the roof. I slowed to a crawl and stared into the distance, I was still about a mile away, but I could see the orange flicker of flame. I watched dismayed, as the flames leapt higher. I had shopped there for as long as I could remember, bought all my stationery in WHSmith, tried on numerous outfits in TK Maxx, and sat in the cinema with my family and friends. My eyes filled and I blinked rapidly to clear them, swallowing the sudden lump in my throat. I turned around yet again and reluctantly drove back to my bungalow.

Back in my kitchen, I called home again and explained what was going on. I would still go home, but I would do it at night and I would walk there. I worked out a route using google maps, which said it would take at least two hours, and then printed it out just before the electricity turned off.

I slept from 5pm to 2am, and when I woke, the power was back on so I checked the weather forecast. There was a forty percent chance of light rain. I didn't know if that was a good thing or not; rain would keep people off the streets, but it would be horrible to walk in. If the power in Harrow was off, it would be very dark without streetlights and the clouds and rain would make visibility even worse…but if I couldn't see much, then people wouldn't be able to see me either.

I dressed in my waterproof trousers and a gortex coat, and put my hiking boots on. The trousers looked like normal heavy walking trousers but were breathable, waterproof, and windproof, and this outfit would keep me completely dry. The coat and trousers were both a dark navy blue. I gave my brown leather boots a quick coat of black shoe polish to darken them further and then looked at my backpacks. Both of my smaller packs were bright, light colours. One of them even had reflective markings, which was not great for staying out of sight. I would have to do without. I stuffed a small torch in the large thigh pocket on my trousers, put the map in the inner map pocket of my coat, and was ready to go.

I left via the front door, went out to the car, and took my Leki walking stick from under the passenger seat. Bought several years back, when I had sprained my ankle on a walking holiday in Ireland, it lived in the car. Its most recent use had been at my tai chi class, when we had learnt part of the walking stick form. I did tai chi as a meditation and as a social activity; I had learnt the applications of the form, but I very much doubted that I knew it well enough to use it, if I got into trouble.

When I was at university, living in central London, I had joined a martial art class. It seemed only sensible at the time; to learn to defend myself, but I had never needed to use what I had learnt; the confidence it gave me seemed to deter any would-be assailants. Fifteen years later, I hoped I still wouldn't need it. I had no idea how much I remembered or even if I could hit a person hard enough to hurt them. I was pretty sure that sparring in class was nothing like reality.

I swung the cane thoughtfully, and then put it back under the seat; I felt better with both hands free, and it would probably just get in the way. I paused after closing the car door, and mentally ran through my checklist. I was as prepared as I could be. It was time to go.

The walk to mum's house was fairly simple. Once I was on the main road it was a straight line south towards the shopping centre, and then I would veer east into Kenton. I started walking, the same route I had taken to the garden centre, but continued past, up to the traffic lights and turning south.

I set a steady pace downhill along the main road and reached a large roundabout after about thirty minutes. The roundabout was in darkness; the power was off; I was now out of Hertfordshire and in the suburbs of London. I paused for a good listen but at 3am there wasn't anyone about. I made my way slowly round the roundabout, and onto the road heading south.

The wind had died down a bit and gaps in the clouds allowed the moonlight to come and go. When the moon was behind the cloud it was pitch-black and because the pavement jinked in and out around patches of grass verge, I kept losing the path. I walked into a tree trunk, and then, thirty seconds later, a parked car in a driveway. I paused as I rubbed my knee and moved into the middle of the road. It wasn't like there was any traffic anyway.

I made good time and the rain held off. After about forty minutes I started to smell the acrid scent of smoke…I must have reached the shopping mall but I couldn't see anything. I waited for the moon to come back out, and then backtracked a little and turned east. I had planned to use some of the side streets, but I missed the first turning so I walked along the deserted main roads until I was almost home. The sky was just beginning to lighten as I turned into mum's road, and when I knocked on the door, Vik opened it immediately; he had been waiting up for me.

Later in the morning, after mum had cooked breakfast and I had recounted my uneventful trip, I took a deep breath and brought up the subject of food. 'Mum', I said, 'how much food do you actually have?'

'Oh, don't you worry; we have plenty,' she responded, 'how about you?' I explained about the veg seedlings in the greenhouse and the extra potatoes I had planted.

'Mum,' I said, 'what happens if you run out of food?'

'Zoe,' she replied, 'you worry too much, we have rice and flour, we can bake, and I have some tomato seedlings and apples in the garden…and anyway, the government will do something, they can't just do nothing.' she said with conviction.

'But mum, what can they do?'

'They can use the soldiers, there has got to be food somewhere, farmers will have sown crops in the fields, they just need to get it to people'

Maybe mum was right; it seemed only logical. I had been sticking to the main news outlets and the government was still saying that help was coming. However, I was naturally sceptical of the government's competency and couldn't let it go. 'But what if they don't?' I said, 'Everything I've ever read or seen on TV says that the best thing to do is get out of the city. To get to somewhere secure and rural, where you can grow food and protect yourself.'

Mum wasn't impressed, 'where would we go Z? How would we get there?' she paused and when I was silent, continued, 'We'll be fine here, I've got a big garden, I can grow whatever I need'

'Ok' I sighed, 'but what about people like Maria, people who run out of food, you shouldn't take in people or you won't have enough food for yourselves'

'Maria's my friend,' she said, 'If she needs help I'll give it, we have plenty of room here.'

I gave up. I knew I wouldn't persuade her any differently and we would only end up arguing. After the power cuts yesterday I was beginning to think things weren't going to go back to normal any time soon, and if mum was determined to stay, I was better off talking to Vik about fortifying the place and keeping her safe.

Vik and I went round mum's house making a list of all the improvements he could make. I knew he disliked DIY but was perfectly capable of screwing in extra boards to strengthen doors and barricade windows, if he had to. Then I thought about how I would get home.

It was at this point I hit a snag. Mum didn't want me to go. 'I have more food,' she said,' a bigger garden…'

'And our garden is surrounded by other gardens so it's less vulnerable.' chipped in Vik.

'But I have all my stuff at my house,' I said.

'We have more than enough here you could use' said mum. I could see she had thought it all out carefully, before raising it with me.

'Or you could go home, pack up a bag and walk back.' said Vik, 'You said yourself that the journey was easy.'

'But I like living at my place,' I said, I was floundering, how to explain? 'Carpenders Park is outside London… it's cut off from the suburbs and surrounded by fields,' I said, 'whereas all around here…'

Mum interrupted me, 'round here is very nice, and our house is bigger' She was starting to sound irritated.

Of course, I knew what was really being said…I should be with my family. We should stick together. But I really wanted to stay in my bungalow, and it wasn't that far. I could pop over any time if I walked at night. 'No guys, I'm not staying' I said firmly, going over to mum and giving her a big hug, 'if things get worse then I'll come back.'

I could tell that Vik thought I was being stubborn, and perhaps I was, but really, if we were talking sensible, it would be much better for them to move to my place…I had so much more food growing, and I could always use my neighbour's garden to grow more. If they wanted us to be together, they should really come and stay at mine. I didn't say anything though, there was no point, for them, leaving was unthinkable.

After that I really wanted to get home. It seemed silly to wait till night, and Mum also thought that it would be safer during the day. I was tired, the walk had been long, and I really wasn't looking forward to another two hours walking back, especially not up that final hill, but I desperately wanted to get home. I sat for a while, flicking through an old newspaper while Vik washed the dishes. My gaze snagged on a picture of a cyclist and I had a brainwave; I would take my old bike; it had been a long time since I had ridden it, but it would be so much quicker. I could go down the hill outside mum's house, cut through the park, and take the side roads back to mine. I pulled it out of the garage, brushed off the dust and pumped up the tyres.

Vik tried again to persuade me to stay the night, but I was adamant. Home was calling and I responded. I borrowed some leggings and a T-shirt – cycling during the day was going to be a whole lot warmer than walking at night. Mum loaded me up with some containers of home cooked food and I strapped them and my waterproofs to the back of the bike. I wheeled it through the side gate to the front of the house. Outside the road was clear, up at the top were two kids, but they melted away as I looked at them. I gingerly got on the bike, pushed on the pedals and was off.

People say you never forget how to ride a bike, and it's true. But when I got on, after a gap of so many years, it was nerve wracking. The bike wobbled and I felt slightly out of control. It seemed quite hard to get to the top of the road. Once there I turned left and freewheeled down the hill. It was scary, I kept pressing the brakes to slow down, but about half-way I finally relaxed and let the speed build up. At the bottom I veered into the park. This was great; a ten-minute walk had taken 30 seconds.

I sped through the park, sticking to the paths and heading towards the middle. The park was split into two sides by a narrow stream. The road I was aiming for was on the far side. There were large trees and a play area, people were walking in groups and sitting on benches, and the atmosphere seemed normal, just like it had been when I rode here with Vik when we were kids.

Where the bridge spanned the fast-moving shallow stream, there were overhanging trees and bushes. I slowed the bike a little as I crossed. Suddenly, from the side, a large figure stepped right into my path. I swerved and fell, hitting the ground hard. I lay there, stunned for a second, then untangled myself from the bike and sat up, looking to see who I had almost hit. The figure was a six foot tall youth, big but still only a youth, probably only around fifteen or sixteen. 'Look where you're going.' he said belligerently.

'Sorry' I said, rubbing my elbow. I suddenly hurt all over. I pulled up my leggings to look at my knee, which felt horrible, I was sure it was bleeding. As I did so, he took a threatening step forward. I looked up… oh no, this was not good; I could feel the vibe in the air. I had been caught up in the exhilaration of riding the bike and had forgotten the situation. I scrambled up onto my feet, and looked at him properly. Apart from the lack of uniform, he looked much like the kids I taught; full of attitude. He was wearing a dark hoody and grey tracksuit bottom. He stared back trying to intimidate. 'What are you doing here?' he asked, shoulders bunched up and hands fisted at his sides.

The next few seconds were crucial; kids had a finely honed sense for the hierarchy of power, but having been a teacher for so long, I was used to grabbing the initiative and projecting authority. 'I've been visiting my mum,' I said, 'I'm just cutting through the park to get home'. I injected confidence into my voice and straightened my posture, it was working…he started to step back, but then another smaller youth stepped out from the bushes and joined him. There were now two of them staring at me, and this changed things considerably.

I picked up my bike and turned to face the edge of the park, I was now between the kids and the bike; they couldn't snatch it and run. I wouldn't catch them if they did and I refused to give it up. However, they were now quite close. Too close. The first one took another step in. 'Lend me your bike' he said, reaching out with his hands. I batted them away.

'No!' I said loudly and aggressively, 'Back off!' I let go of the bike, which fell to the ground again, and turned to face him fully as I said it. He raised his hands, backing up a step. Then I saw him change his mind and lean forward. I reacted on instinct, my hand formed a fist, my feet planted in the ground, my torso twisting as I pulled back my arm and then shot it forward. I hit him with all my strength, powering up from my back leg as it pushed against the ground, striking the middle of his chest and then pulling back. I stood there, fists up, bouncing on my toes, full of adrenaline. 'Back off!' I yelled again, turning to the smaller kid as I said it. He stepped back, and I picked up the bike and ran with it to towards the road. At the edge of the park I turned back; the larger youth was bent over, clutching his middle. The other was beside him, looking helpless. They were no longer a threat, but as I watched, three more youths drifted in towards them, looking up towards me. I quickly took the bike down into the middle of the road, got on, and peddled away.

I was high on adrenaline and the success of that punch, and wasn't paying much attention to my surroundings. I cycled on, mindlessly crossing the main street and coasting down along a flat curving road for a couple of minutes before crossing another junction and slipping between two parked cars half blocking the road. It wasn't until I glimpsed the men rising from the chairs behind the cars that I realised I had drifted into one of the barricaded areas.

I won't pretend I wasn't terrified. I was already going at a decent speed and I pumped my legs round and sped out of there as fast as I could. I veered into the next left I came to and kept going. The area was a maze of streets, and once off the main road, none of them looked familiar. After a minute, I reached another junction, right or straight? I couldn't decide. I turned right. I was trying to get north, up to the big Uxbridge road that bounded this whole area.

The road I was on was fairly wide and it seemed to go on forever, but eventually it came out at a junction I recognised; a large roundabout, with trees and grass, and with people having a barbeque. I slowed to a stop. There was a nursery on my left with brightly coloured play equipment in a small covered outdoor space. Behind it was a small carpark. I got off my bike in the car park and leaned it against the railings surrounding the nursery. I needed space to catch my breath and work out how to get home.

My hands were trembling slightly, and my back was covered in sweat. I needed to stop and breathe. I sat down cross-legged between two cars, so I couldn't be seen, and took two minutes to close my eyes and slow my breathing. The punch replayed itself over and over in my mind; I couldn't believe how well it had worked. My hand hurt, a lot, but so did my elbow and knee. I took a deep breath and let it out slowly. I had to move on, and get out of the guarded enclave. I kept breathing, and after a minute or two, I felt a semblance of calm returning. I opened my eyes and took out my phone.

The roundabout was large, with a parade of shops around the outside, a pub, and a petrol station. Looking round I could see there were families in the middle of the roundabout, on the grass under the trees; parents and kids, playing and having fun. They all seemed to know one another. As I watched, I heard a car approaching and a black BMW drove up from the road on the far side of the roundabout. Four adults got out, three men and a woman. One of the men sauntered over to one of the family groups and dropped the car keys onto the grass. I could see that there was some good natured banter going on, before several adults stood up, walked to the car and drove off. The new arrivals dropped to the grass and lay back. I wondered briefly where they had come from; it almost looked like a change of guards. I was tempted to go over and find out, but it looked as if everyone there knew everyone else. Although they looked relaxed, I didn't know how they would react to an unfamiliar face in the middle of their territory. I couldn't believe that they would become violent in front of the children, but I did think they might take me away for a chat and that might get very unpleasant. I disliked confrontation, and after the scuffle with the youths, I decided I would be better off avoiding them. I was curious where they were getting their food though. There weren't any large supermarkets locally as far as I was aware.

I had phone signal and data, so I opened google maps and turned on the satellite overlay. It looked like there was an alley at the end of the carpark, that ran behind the shops up to the road I needed. I looked further and realised I was stuck. All the exits onto the Uxbridge road were the ones I had seen yesterday, blocked off. To get through I would have to go through at speed, and surprise them. And that just wasn't going to work, as I would need to slow down to make the sharp left turn onto the main road.

I rubbed my face with the bottom of my t-shirt, wiping away the sweat. Okay, maybe there was another way. I pushed my bike through the crowed alley and peddled along the road until I wasn't far from the junction. I couldn't see the barricade, but google maps indicated that I was close. I searched for a good spot to hide the bike, and eventually stashed it under a parked van, hoping no one was watching. I walked quietly up the road and slipped into the front garden of a house, a couple of hundred meters from the watching guards. I could easily see them but was sheltered from sight by an overgrown garden.

There were four people, it looked like two men and two women; husband and wife teams maybe. Whilst I was watching, one of the doors to a nearby house opened and a child came out and walked up to the barricade. It was a girl, pre-teen, carrying a plastic box. She handed it to one of the women, her mother perhaps, as they had the same dark hair and thin faces. The mother took out a couple of sandwiches, or perhaps they were wraps; I couldn't see but it was something edible anyhow. They all tucked in to the food whilst the girl chatted a bit, then walked back to the house with the empty container.

I felt reassured. These people were family people, and were well fed. I could try plan B. I went back for the bike, and wheeled it quietly into the nearest side street behind me. I waited until the watchers had settled down again after their afternoon snack, then got on the bike, and not even attempting to hide, rode slowly straight up to the barricade.

They were sitting facing outwards towards the barricade, but one of the women saw me and stood up. She was tall and athletic looking, wearing jeans and a navy down jacket. The others were in similar clothes and as she stood, they turned and rose also. I waited until I was almost upon them and then got off the bike. 'Hi' I said, smiling at them all and then directing my gaze at the woman who had stood first.

'Hi,' she replied, 'who are you?

'My name is Zoe and I'm trying to get home' I said straightforwardly, 'I need to get onto the Uxbridge road, I'm heading towards Watford. Can I pass?' I looked round at them all, meeting their eyes and smiling. Then I looked down and fiddled with my bike, giving them time to decide, wondering what would happen if they decided not to let me through.

I felt them look at each other and one of the men asked, 'Where did you just come from?'

'Kenton,' I said, 'I accidentally zoomed past a couple of you guys, not realising this area was off limits, I'm very sorry', I looked around again and tried another smile. I felt fresh sweat break out over my face and my palms were damp with nerves. I looked back at the tall woman. 'Is it very dangerous out there?' I asked, trying to start a dialogue.

The other woman with the dark hair and thin face chipped in before she could say anything, 'Yes it is,' she said, 'you shouldn't be out here by yourself.'

'I'll get home as quickly as I can,' I said, 'can I go through?' I indicated the gap between the cars with my hand. After looking round at the others, the tall woman nodded.

'Of course,' she said, 'try and keep safe'

'Thanks', I replied as I pushed my bike through the gap and out to the small roundabout ahead. I turned the bike side on and waved back at the group. Then I got on and cycled away, sighing in relief. It had only worked because I appeared non-threatening. People responded positively to smiles and I hadn't given them any reason to stop me.

I rode on, my legs were starting to ache now, and I was tired, but this was the last stretch. I worked up some speed on a downhill slope and zoomed past the barricade roads. The hill up to Carpenders Park was empty which was lucky, as I had to dismount and push the bike up most of the way. I was tempted to ditch it but kept going, until finally I found myself back at the traffic lights and the junction to home.

I reached my house close to exhaustion, wheeling my bike up to my driveway I stared down at it; what to do… my brain wasn't working anymore, and in the end, I removed my waterproofs and the food containers and pushed it under a big van parked in the side road hoping for the best. Once inside I took a long delicious shower and tidied up my grazes. I was tired of the tension and conflict, of being scared and worrying. I wasn't good at meeting people at the best of times, now every interaction was a positive minefield. I was going to stay put for a while; I relaxed back into my armchair, there was no reason to go out, mum and Vik were fine, and I had everything I needed. I was happy, here at home.

5

Harvest

At the start of June, I put my faith in the weather, and planted out the seedlings into the garden. Leaning over into the middle of the bed, I stabbed at the soil with my trowel and scooped out a hole. The sweetcorn seedling was about a foot high and already had several sets of leaves. They flopped out at the sides, with the newest leaf forming a spike at the top. I tapped it out of its pot and placed it in the hole, crumbling the soil back in around it and pressing it in firmly. I plunged my trowel in again, about a foot away, making a new hole, and placed a second plant so the leaves were at right angles to the first. It was a space saving trick that seemed only logical.

The next hole I planted a Crown Prince squash. At the moment it was just a short vine, less than eighteen inches long, with small hairy leaves, but I could imagine it; lush and full, curling among the sweetcorn stems and producing football sized, bluish-grey pumpkins with bright orange flesh. Stored correctly they would last until the middle of winter.

Fifty minutes later the sweetcorn were all in. The bed still looked bare, the plants tiny and forlorn in the expanse of soil but I wasn't fooled, if I planted them any closer they would crowd each other out and I wouldn't get as high a yield.

I walked over to the peas, and ran my hand through the plants, searching for pods big enough to pick. They had been planted in February and were flowering continuously, producing long fat pods full of peas. I had been harvesting them before they were fully mature, so that the plants would keep flowering a little longer. Peas were good at sensing when they had produced seeds and would shortly after shrivel and die. I wanted to put that off for as long as possible.

I shelled the pods as I went along, stripping the peas into a bowl and chucking the empty pods onto the compost heap. When I was done, I went into the greenhouse to pick up some more bean seedlings. I had been planting them, a few at a time, in any available space. I glanced at the label; these were climbing beans. I grabbed a couple of bamboo poles and some string, and strolled over to the bed along the back fence. A couple of minutes later I had a tepee of poles and began pushing them deep into the ground. The moist soil allowed them to slide in easily, until I began hitting stones in the clay. Time for some excavation work.

It was a day pretty much like every other this past week; June was the busiest time of year for gardening and I was determined to get it all done. I was working hard in the mornings before the knockers started roaming the streets. Then I would go in and relax for the rest of the day, doing small chores and surfing the internet until they left. It was still early, and I hadn't heard any knockers yet, but I decided to take a quick break. I picked a couple of leaves of peppermint to make tea and went online. Reports showed that the government had survived, but one of the consequences of the government's new emergency powers was the side-lining of the other political parties. No longer did the BBC talk of Conservatives or Labour but only of 'The Government'. It made sense; they needed to get things done quickly and there wasn't time for debate or questions. COBR and its subcommittees were running almost everything. Some of the new laws they produced were very restrictive; even allowing the government to imprison people who threatened the order and stability. There was some chatter that they were shipping journalists and activists out to isolated areas and abandoning them there, far away from food or clean water. I took it all with a pinch of salt and concentrated on my garden.

The last thing on my list was the tomatoes. They were an early cropping variety called Matina, maybe not ideal as they were prone to blight, but they had one very unusual property: their skins peeled off easily. When ripe I could use my teeth to peel the outer skin right off, leaving just the juicy sweet flesh behind. They were my favourite tomato and I had started growing them in March, before the outbreak. It had been a bit too early and they were growing tall and lanky, and really needed to be planted out.

I dug a deep hole, double the depth of the pot, and buried the plant deep. Sometimes tomatoes would grow more roots from the stem, giving it a bigger, stronger root system. I wound the stem up the twisted poles and stood back. That would do. Hopefully, with some decent sun and warm nights, the leaves would bulk out and they might start to look a little healthier.

I pinched off the side branches from the tomatoes, took them back to the greenhouse, and pushed them into pots of soil. They would root and give me more plants. I looked around the still crowded shelves and at the trays on the floor. Maybe I should stop sowing seeds; there was not a scrap of room left, and some of the plants were getting quite big.

I walked over to the last of the L shaped beds, which was covered in fleece. Lifting up a corner, I peeked inside. The carrots were coming on nicely, with thick ferny growth on top. The carrot roots themselves were beginning to bulk out; they were a cold-tolerant variety and had been optimistically planted in February under fleece. They had taken ages to germinate but the head start had let them take full advantage of the heat wave. I made a note to add some mulch to keep the shoulders of the carrots from going green and I hunted around to find the largest. I pulled a couple up for lunch, along with some spring onions, then I extracted the packet of carrot seed from a pocket and sprinkled a couple in the disturbed earth. I pressed it flat and pulled down the fleece, looking around in satisfaction. Progress was good. I went inside, wishing vaguely that there was someone to share it with. Phoning home was ok, but I wanted them to see it in person. Just occasionally, even I needed company; I was beginning to feel lonely.

The news had said that the army would begin distributing emergency rations today, and I was eager to get online and see how it was going. However, when I opened the BBC News Live, I was dismayed. The reporters were using drones to film from overhead, and there was a lot of chaos around the distribution; mobs of people swarming the trucks, grabbing boxes of ration packs. It was madness; if people had stayed calm, they would all have been given food. The drone zoomed in on people fighting, other people running and yet others smashing windows and looting shops. Seen from above, they were just faceless blobs with limbs flailing, but I could imagine the desperation and fear.

There had been a lot of social media pressure calling for the army to be used to restore order, but the government had been adamant that they weren't trained for civil unrest. I could see in the videos that they weren't using their weapons. I watched as one truck was overrun and the soldiers retreated away down the road, leaving it behind. It looked like the city had descended into complete anarchy.

I wondered if it would spread. What would I do if it did? Would I leave? I was probably better off where I was. The electricity, water, and gas were still running, if intermittently, with the rolling blackouts happening at the same time each day. I had food and shelter, which wouldn't be guaranteed anywhere else. I was not one of those survivalists that could shoot rabbits and forage in the woods. If I left, I would have to find a way of taking food with me, and I would have to be aiming to get to a particular place with supplies. But if the chaos moved this way I would need to be prepared.

I called home to Vik. He answered after a couple of rings, 'Hey Z, what's up?'

'Nothing,' I said, 'I'm just watching some videos on the riots and food distribution.'

'Why do you watch that stuff?' he asked, 'you know it only makes you depressed.'

'I just wonder what's happening,' I said, 'how my students are doing, and the people from work…I miss them.'

'Do you have friends you can go and see?' asked Vik, 'people near you who you could visit?'

'No, not nearby; my neighbour has left and I don't know any of the others on my street well enough.' I replied, 'it would be nice to see some of the guys from tai chi or friends I know in South Oxhey, but it just doesn't feel safe outside.'

'Have you tried online?' asked Vik, 'I log on to several forums each day; connecting with people keeps me sane.'

It was a good idea, I had been looking at the news sites and reading Facebook, but I made a note to start looking for community groups and forums that I could connect with. We talked desultorily about things for a bit, I think Vik was trying to cheer me up, but eventually I rang off and went back out to the garden.

I had been impatiently waiting until the first potato plants had started flowering, and now as I walked around, examining the pots, I realised that some did have small flowers, bobbing in the slight breeze. I scraped away some of the soil in the pots, feeling down with my hand to see if there were any tubers. The soil was cool and damp and my fingers brushed something solid and round. A potato! I gradually worked my fingers around it, careful to avoid scraping the skin. My fingers slipped underneath and I gradually eased it up towards the surface. Perfect! It was the size of a golf ball, knobbly but with a very thin skin. I broke it off from the root and gently patted the soil back down. Then I went and tried another pot.

I poked through the roots, but felt nothing. Either it was not ready or they were hiding. I was impatient and curious, so I rolled the pot on its side, grasped the haulms and gently eased the plant out. The roots had spread out round the pot, binding the soil together, and halfway down I saw the smooth white surface of a potato, I eased my fingers behind it and it popped out. Then I carefully placed the rootball back into the pot, straightening the stems gently. They flopped over, looking unhappy in the way that only plants that have been mistreated can. Oops. I left the other plants in the pots, but my less invasive furtling still produced five potatoes. I washed them gently under the tap, the delicate skins sliding off.

I was coddling the plants, watering constantly and feeding with seaweed fertilizer so they would go on photosynthesising, producing glucose, and storing it as starch in the remaining potato tubers. I would harvest some a couple of times a week; to get a handful of potatoes to cook and eat. In the meantime, I made a vegetable stew with the carrots, peas, and potatoes I had just harvested, flavouring it with spring onion and garlic, and adding some lentils and soup mix to thicken it. Pre outbreak I would have posted pictures on Facebook, showing my harvest. Now I felt a complex mixture of pride in my achievements, sadness that people were going hungry, and guilt that I wasn't sharing when I had so much.

I followed Vik's advice and joined a couple of self-sufficiency forums. I read voraciously, drawing comfort from all the others out there, also trying to get by. The main forum I followed had a core group of users from before the outbreak, but just like me, most people had discovered it whilst trying to survive the food shortages. Many of the issues we faced were climate and environment dependent; often advice from someone in Cornwall didn't relate well to someone living in Scotland, so just after I signed up, someone suggested the newbies and more experienced members set up groups together by location. I was reassured to see that there were many others living in the suburbs around London, but I just lurked for a while, reading through old threads.

One sunny afternoon I was sitting in the garden after a failed attempt to cook a late lunch. It had been one of those rare occasions when both the gas and electricity had been off. I was hungry and annoyed with myself; almost all the food I had required boiling water, if the power went off permanently

I would be in trouble. As the sun shone down, I took out my phone and went online to research how to make a solar cooker. The concept seemed simple, foil or mirrors, conductors and insulators, but I needed specific instructions. I found a couple of different versions and eventually I logged onto the forum and started my first thread. I began to get replies almost immediately; the response was overwhelmingly positive with lots of hints and tips to make it work better. I stayed online all afternoon, working on some tentative plans whilst chatting to people. I began to contribute to another discussion, and although they weren't actually here with me, for a couple of hours I didn't feel entirely alone.

Two weeks passed; the number of cars driving around grew fewer and fewer, the ambient noise decreasing until all I could hear were the birds in the garden. But one morning I was disturbed by the sound of a large vehicle. It sounded like a truck but I couldn't see anything. When it eventually rolled into sight, I saw that it was a green army vehicle, open at the sides but with shelves stretching all the way across. It was accompanied by soldiers walking along the road. I watched as people came out to talk to them, I hadn't realised there were so many people left in the area. I wondered what they had been doing. Had they been hiding like me? They all looked anxious and stressed.

The soldiers were going door to door, with ambulance trolleys. As I watched, one group knocked on a door, which was opened almost immediately by an elderly lady. There was a very brief exchange and then they entered the house. I waited but nothing seemed to be happening. I had a grim feeling. As I looked around I saw another team of soldiers on the other side of the street, knocking on another door. They knocked several times, banging hard on the door and the window and then moved around the back. They returned and then they took out a door ram and within a couple of seconds had the front door open. They stopped to put on masks and then entered the house. They came out almost immediately and took one of the trolleys, went back in and returned with a body, which they wheeled towards the truck. I noticed that the soldier up on the bed of the truck was filling in forms and attaching them to the bags, as they were loaded. Meanwhile the elderly lady was walking slowly back towards the truck bedside a trolley with a filled body bag on. She looked upset and very frail and I was tempted to go out and help her, but as I watched, her neighbour ran up, took her arm and led her back to her home.

The body was loaded and the truck moved forwards, slowly inching down the road. I gazed at the soldiers, their faces looked grim and in their camouflage uniforms, it seemed unreal, like a film or documentary; a step removed. I continued to watch through my kitchen window, feeling detached from it all.

When they got to my bungalow, I was ready and waiting by the door. Opening it, I spoke first, 'I'm ok, it's only me here.'

The soldier had tired looking eyes, and hair flecked with grey. He nodded and turned to move away and I quickly asked 'Do you have any news?'

He turned back but shook his head, 'Not much, all I can say is that the government advice is to move out into the country.'

'What about food?' I asked.

'Food distribution is via local authorities through county, district, and parish councils,' he replied, it sounded like a spiel he had said many times before, and my forehead knotted in puzzlement. He sighed and said wearily 'they're not supplying food to anywhere inside the M25, if you've friends or family in the country I suggest you go to them.'

I nodded, 'Thanks' I said, as I closed the door; my worst fears realised.

The next morning people started to leave. There had been occasional departures, but now they packed up their stuff and their kids and drove away en-masse. By the middle of the week, most of the properties were empty.

Thursday was the summer solstice, and the morning light woke me up at a ridiculously early hour. I tried to go back to sleep but after an hour I gave up and got up. The empty streets outside looked inviting, I hadn't been out for over two weeks and it was so early; no-one would be out yet. As I walked past the empty driveways, it was easy to tell who had gone; the lack of car in the driveway and the discarded objects in the front gardens, in their hurry to leave, most people had made quite a mess.

I spied a picnic blanket lying in a driveway, then a couple of doors down, a duvet. It looked like people had difficulty fitting their stuff into their cars. I walked a little further then stopped and backtracked, the extra blankets might come in handy at some point. Later that afternoon, as I grated carrots in an attempt to make carrot cake, I saw more knockers, moving down the road. Two men and a woman; all wearing pink t-shirts with the same slogan. They looked relaxed, and as I watched, they approached one of the houses that the soldiers had broken into. I saw them enter and then quickly back out again, hands over their mouths. They moved down the street, spitting and swearing. I watched disgusted and fascinated at the same time. Then they picked a new house, the one that had the picnic blanket that morning. What were they doing? There was no one there and the door was locked. There was a thudding sound as they kicked at the door. In just a couple of seconds, the jamb broke and the door swung open. The knockers had moved on from knocking. They came out with arms full of tinned food, and walked off down the road, laughing and shoving each other.

In the morning, I moved my car back in my driveway to discourage the knockers, and went back to the house they had broken into. I took a large backpack and searched thoroughly. I was surprised; the knockers had left behind lots of the good stuff; pasta, flour and an unopened packet of porridge oats. I found a tube of tomato paste, a bottle of pepper sauce, and hidden in one of the revolving corner cupboards was a jar of golden syrup. I took almost everything, even some of the seasonings and baking ingredients. I could use the internet to find some recipes. I missed toast, and surely I could make bread at home? That afternoon I tried making flatbread, it wasn't exactly a success, but it was edible.

I combed the estate, going out early to avoid the knockers, and only picking houses they had already broken into. I collected a lot of half opened containers of sugar and coffee, lots of condiments and oil. It was surprising what people left behind. I also picked up firewood and charcoal whenever I found them. Few people had open fires in their houses, but a surprising number had wood burning stoves. Often, if I could get into the garage, I would find a bag or two of chopped wood. I stored the wood in my neighbour's garden and began searching for a barbeque; something to cook on. The first one I found was a tiny portable thing, round and coloured like a football with a domed lid. I soon upgraded when I found a better one, and then upgraded that several times more. I wanted to make sure that if the gas stopped, I would still be able to cook food and keep warm.

Mum called one afternoon a couple of weeks later, 'Z, I've found some dried chickpeas in a cupboard in the kitchen,' she said, 'do you think they would grow?'

'Try germinating them on damp paper towel' I replied, 'Do you have any left? Or tissues?'

I heard her calling Vik, there was a muffled shout back, and then she replied, 'we have some boxes of man-sized tissues'

'Put a couple of tissues in a take away container, add enough water so it is completely damp, then place the chickpeas on top, spaced out, one per square inch,' I said, 'leave them somewhere warm, maybe on a sunny windowsill during the day, and then in the airing closet at night.'

'Ok' she said.

'Check them each day; if they sprout tiny white roots, then they can be planted outside.'

'Great, thanks Z,' she replied, 'but will they grow in the UK?'

'Yes, but mum,' I said, 'chickpeas only give two peas per pod. It's going to be really time-consuming picking off the pods and shelling… it might not be worth it.'

'Well I'll have a go,' she replied, 'there's no harm in trying.'

'I could come over,' I said tentatively, 'Bring some seeds? It would be nice to see you guys.'

Mum replied immediately, 'No, it's too dangerous, we'd love to see you too, but after what happened in the park, you're safer where you are.'

'But there are not as many people around as there were,' I said, 'Lots of people moved out of the city, when they stopped distributing food.'

'No Z,' she paused, then continued more softly, 'what's the matter?'

'Nothing.' I said. How could I explain that I felt lonely, when I had been so adamant that I was fine on my own?

It was still light past 11pm, and one evening, as I wandered, bored, around my bungalow, too hot to sleep, I remembered the joy of speeding down the hill on my bike. Maybe it would feel cooler… I retrieved my bike and slowly peddled around; ending up at the top of a slight hill on the far side of the estate. I looked down the hill and began to peddle, faster and faster. It was exciting and I felt reckless, the speed combined with the danger. I glided round the estate, looking at the houses that had become so familiar. As evening fell, I saw lights switch on in one house, and a TV flickered light through the windows of another, the music blaring in the night. I stopped, listening; it was unmistakably Jurassic Park.

The next morning I found myself staring at bikes as I scavenged. Maybe I could get a better bike, something with paniers so I didn't have to heft the stuff I found in my backpack. Most of the bikes I saw were better than the one I had brought from home, and eventually I found something suitable. I 'borrowed' a large robust bike for carrying stuff; it made life so much easier, and soon after, I also acquired a super-light road bike that I used for speeding around the estate in the evenings.

It was the last Friday in July when I rang home and no one picked up.. The call the previous day had gone as usual, a discussion of what we had harvested and meals we had made. New ideas we were thinking of trying, some speculation on how friends were doing. Mum recounted a weird dream she'd had during the night, Vik reported on the new garden he had explored that day, cheerfully describing the pear tree he had found.

When they didn't pick up the phone immediately, I didn't think anything of it. We had avoided using the landlines, because although they were more likely to work, a ringing phone was very audible, now that there was no traffic or ambient noise. We were using our mobile phones on silent instead, and sometimes, if you were busy, you just didn't notice it was ringing. I rang a couple more times that evening, but when they still didn't answer, I began to worry. What could have happened? I fretted as I prepared and ate dinner and then decide; I would walk over and see.

It had been months since I had left Carpenders Park. The time in the garden had been very relaxing, but I didn't really know what was going on around me. The news sites had been reporting less and less and I was now getting most of my information from the forums. One of the posters had described gangs on mopeds, who were siphoning fuel from parked cars, and another had mentioned packs of dogs roaming around.

I was an animal person before the outbreak, but I had no idea how a dog would behave if it were starving; they were descended from wolves after all. Most of the cats seemed to be doing fine; they had been nocturnal hunters before the outbreak and friends had often described how they would wake up to presents of dead mice from their lovely pets.

I was glad there were cats around, as they probably kept the rat population down. Dogs however, were not used to feeding themselves. I had assumed that they had been put down by the army, now I wasn't so sure. I wouldn't want to be in the open, surrounded by a pack of feral spaniels, poodles, and Labradors, which seemed the most common breeds in my area. I could only be glad that German Shepherds and Rottweilers didn't seem to be so popular any more.

It was July so no deliveries had been made for three months. There were enough empty houses that remaining survivors would have been able to scavenge food but what about large groups of people, like those behind the barricade? They must have moved away like my neighbours; there was no way they had enough food to stay. Anyone left would be desperate; gangs on mopeds sounded about right. So if I walked to mum's I could be facing feral dogs and dangerous gangs, but there wasn't any question really, I needed to know they were ok.

I waited until 3am then left the house. I weighed up the choice between walking, cycling and taking the car. Walking would be slow and exhausting but I had been exercising on the road bike most evenings around Carpenders Park, and was now quite a bit stronger and more confident than I had been on that first trip. I figured that I could go fast enough to escape any dogs, and the bike was light enough to lift over walls or barricades if I needed to. Then I looked at the car; it would be even faster, I would be protected inside, and I would be able to transport mum and Vik back with me if I needed to. However, the car would attract a lot of attention, and if there were still barricades, I would be forced to find alternative routes. I went back and forth between the choices but in the end I picked the car. At the last minute I pulled down the back seats, opened the boot, grabbed the road bike from where it was stashed under a van, and shoved it in as backup.

The car sounded incredibly loud in the darkness, The noise was an assault after the near silence of the previous days and I hunched into my seat. I moved off as quickly as I could. It was lucky my car was an automatic, I was so nervous I would have stalled it for sure, if it had been a manual. As it was, I clipped the curb going round the corner. I swept up the road to the T-junction and then turned left to the traffic lights, which were red. I ignored them and carried on through; it seemed a bit pointless to obey the traffic laws when mine was the only car on the road. The empty downhill slope had my car quickly reaching 60mph. But at the roundabout I slowed. There hadn't been a single soul so far, I sped up again, the engine roaring in the night; if there was anyone around, I didn't want to give them any time to block the road. I powered along the straight, zipping round the mini roundabouts. This was fun, like freewheeling on the bike but better.

At 3am Harrow was on blackout so my headlights were the only light around. The night was still and warm. I wound the windows down but couldn't hear anything over the engine noise. I was still doing about 40mph, even accounting for all the mini roundabouts, and as I approached the first crossroads, I craned to see if it was blocked. It seemed clear so I raced through, flooring the pedal and heading south for the shopping centre. The noise of the car carried through the air and I could see doors opening as I sped past, luckily at the speeds I was going, no-one had a chance to get out onto the road.

I knew I would have to slow at some point to turn east. When I had walked this route, I had gone past the junction, as it had been so dark. This time I had headlights, but it still caught me by surprise. I stamped on the brakes, which squealed as I turned the car sharply left. The car skidded and swung wide, and I pulled the wheel tighter, I had been going too fast and almost didn't make the turn; there was a signpost just ahead, and the front of the car bumped up onto the pavement and down again onto the road, missing it by a hair's breadth. I straightened out too quickly and almost lost control again, before accelerating away down the road. After a second or two, I took the speed down a notch; that had been too close.

The next few turns were much wider, and then I was on the main road to mum's. The turn off had speed bumps and I was forced to slow right down. I still got an awful jolting. I cut though a few side streets and then I was on the road beside the park. Mum's house was on a crescent off this one, and I was approaching quickly…if I didn't want to bring everyone to her door, I would need to park up before I got there.

I saw an empty driveway and made a split-second decision. I pulled in and switched off the engine. Then I jumped out, pulled the bike from the back, locked the car, and quickly cycled away. A couple of lights flashed on in the surrounding houses as I quickly slipped into mum's road. I had made it safely through, now I just needed to find out what had happened to mum and Vik.

I got off the bike and slowly wheeled it down the road to mum's house. Everything seemed relatively quiet. I walked into the drive, holding on to the bike, and paused in the porch. It was pitch black and I couldn't see anything. I reached out with my hand, groping towards the door, but my fingers met only empty air…the door was open. My breath came faster and I strained to see. I didn't want to go in. I couldn't see anything, and I didn't want to alert everyone to my presence by shining a light in the darkness.

I called quietly. 'Mum?' 'Vik?' but there was no response. Where were they? What had happened? I stepped back and round to the side gate. Again it was too dark to see if it was open or closed, but as I groped forward, I felt the solid wood against my fingers. It was firmly closed. I went back to the front door and hovered, undecided. After waiting what seemed like forever, I propped the bike against the wall of the porch and stepped over the threshold and into the house.

I was petrified of what I would find. I couldn't hear or see anything; there was a slight smell I couldn't identify, but I could feel no movement of the air. I needed to see so I pushed back the door behind me until it touched the doorjamb, then pulled out the torch from my pocket and flashed it on and off.

In that quick flash of light I glimpsed the house as normal; dark varnished wood of the staircase ahead, kitchen door beyond, the lighter wood of the parquet floor seemed clear. I stepped forward and trailed my right hand against the wall until I felt the closed wooden door of the living room. I felt down to the handle and keyhole and my fingers brushed the key; good; they had done the same as me and closed the front living room, to make the house look empty. I tried the handle, just in case, but it was locked.

I stepped forwards to the space where the dining room door was. The door was open. I paused listening intently. Something was different; I could feel slightly cooler air, coming from the room. I stepped in, then stopped and stepped back. The last time I had been here, the dining room had been a mess, over-cluttered with furniture it was a minefield to get through. The back of the dining room led to the conservatory. Any light I shone in this room would be visible to the garden outside, but without it I was bound to bang into something.

I turned instead to the kitchen. The smell was stronger here; something burnt. There was a faint light in the darkness; it was the cooker, the gas fire was still on under a saucepan. 'mum?, Vik?' I whispered again. I stepped into the kitchen and crunched on something, not glass; it was quieter and felt more like grit. I moved over to the cooker. I needed more light, I couldn't see anything, but the windows of the kitchen looked out to the conservatory, and the back door was paned with glass. If I shone the torch it would be immediately visible from outside. Instead I pushed the pan off the fire and turned it up high so I could see slightly better. Then I lit the other rings. The fire illuminated the room with a steady blue glow.

The kitchen was a mess, all the cupboards were open and empty, and packets and jars were scattered across the countertop. It looked like the floor was covered in rice. My heart beating fast, I opened the cutlery drawer and took out the backdoor key. I unlocked the door and walked onto the patio. As I stepped forward, there was a distinctive crunch of glass; the light from the kitchen fire reflected in the glass panes of the conservatory, all except one pane in the door at the side. Someone had smashed it in.

Hurrying slightly now, I went back into the house and up the stairs. It was unlikely that whoever had done this was still here, but mum and Vik might be upstairs somewhere, hiding or hurt. I searched the whole house, shining my torch into every corner, but there was no sign of them. I even went onto the crawl space in the loft, but apart from some plastic crates of food and water, it was empty. They had obviously been taking precautions, but they were no longer here. In a way it was reassuring, I had been imagining them sick or worse.

Every room had been nerve-wracking to enter, wondering if they were inside, lying there. Finding the place empty was a relief in a way. Only, if they were ok, I couldn't work out why they hadn't called me.

I waited out the couple of hours until the sun rose, then went into the garden again. I could see the work they had been doing in the new vegetable beds, but their plants were several months behind mine; it would be a long time before there were any tomatoes or potatoes. I went around the edge of the garden, and at the side found several boards that had been prised off the fence and were lying broken on the ground. It didn't look like Vik's work; he would have been more careful and would have made a way of getting in and out that was neater, something he could secure.

I cautiously looked through the gap but couldn't see anyone. I stepped through into the neighbours' garden, which was rather overgrown, and saw the hole in their back fence. It looked like they had come in this way, through the back gardens, smashed the door to the conservatory, stolen the food from the kitchen, and left via the front door. I glanced around and saw a flash of red amongst the weeds. I bent down…it was a tin of Heinz soup. Maybe they had come back this way then. So who had gone out the front door? It must have been mum and Vik. But then, where were they?

I went back to the house, opened the side gate, and moved my bike into the garden. When the power came back on, I emptied the tin of soup into a bowl and put it in the microwave. I was tired and hungry. I hadn't slept all night and wasn't thinking too well. The knockers might come back…there was still food here, and it looked like they hadn't searched very thoroughly…I really wanted to be safe at home but I was worried for mum and Vik. Had they escaped? If so, they would surely come back to the house. I tried calling Vik's mobile, but again it went to voicemail. I left a message, explaining where I was, then decided against tidying up, and went to find somewhere to sleep.

I walked through the house and then looked at the living room door. It was locked, which on reflection, I found peculiar. Why hadn't the knockers opened it? I suppose it was dark at the time, maybe they had just focussed on the kitchen; the only mess was downstairs, it looked like they hadn't even bothered to go up to the bedrooms. Maybe in the dark they hadn't seen the door here or had been too busy carrying their spoils away and hadn't ventured further into the house.

I unlocked the door and stepped inside. In the morning light, it looked fresh and familiar. The old carpet and mismatched wooden bookcases, the cracked leather sofas, and oversized TV. It all seemed normal. In fact, it looked incredibly inviting. I locked the door behind me, grabbed a thick blanket from the pile, and snuggled up on the longer sofa. I was asleep within minutes.

I woke up to the afternoon sunlight streaming in through windows across my eyes. I had tangled myself thoroughly in the blanket as I slept but felt refreshed and alert. I listened carefully before I stood up, months of cautious living finally paying dividends; as I paused, I heard muffled voices beyond the door. I arrested the movement I had barely started and eased myself back down again, untangling the blanket from my legs as I did so.

6

Missing

Was it Vik and mum? I listened carefully… no, there were two female voices. I silently slipped from the couch and stood up. I crept towards the thick wooden door and tried to listen. The voices were speaking quietly and I could hear very little. I crouched down to the key hole and removed the key.

'So what do *you* think we should do then?' I heard one voice say.

'Leave it, there's no key, perhaps it's locked for a reason.' the second voice said impatiently.

'Maybe the key is on the inside,' said the first women, her voice rising, 'maybe there is someone inside, and they locked the door!' she sounded alarmed.

'Look,' said the second voice, sounding impatient, 'there wasn't anyone here last night, there isn't anyone here today, let's just get the rest of the food and go,' her voice became more muffled as I heard her step away from the door and towards the kitchen. Huh, they were just two women nervously searching for food. I relaxed back onto my heels, and then stiffened. Something wasn't right, they had come last night, but mum had stopped answering the phone in the morning.

I needed to know what was going on and where mum and Vik were. I listened carefully but didn't hear anyone else. I eased the key back into the lock and round and opened the door gently. The door opened inwards so the women didn't immediately notice and I was able to get a good look at them as they raided the kitchen. They were younger than me, both wearing jeans and jumpers, both with dark hair, one was slightly shorter, but they both looked thin, and when they turned slightly I could see that their faces looked drawn and tired. The shorter one was scooping up the packets and remaining jars, and placing them in rucksacks. The taller was going through the cupboards.

I stepped out into the hallway and moved to the kitchen door. 'Hi,' I said. Both women jumped, and looked shockingly scared. I had never seen that level of fear on anyone's face before. Then they took in what I looked like and some of the fear drained away. 'Don't be afraid,' I said, lifting my hands in a calming manner, 'I'm looking for my mum and brother,' I continued, 'they live here, have you seen them?'

'What?,' said the taller women; it was the impatient second voice I had heard from the sitting room.

'Have you seen my mum or brother?' I asked.

'Where did you come from?' said the shorter woman; the other, first voice. This was both of then then.

'I was in the living room, sleeping when I heard you,' I said, smiling slightly at the shorter one, 'you were right, I was just inside the door,' I turned to the taller woman again and repeated the question, 'have you seen my mum?'

'what?' she said again, 'no!'

They had backed together into the corner by the sink and both looked slightly nonplussed. They were in my house, stealing stuff, but I wasn't angry or threatening, I was smiling at them. I reached up to open an overhead cupboard and pulled out three mugs holding them in one hand by the handle. 'Coffee?' I asked.

Now they looked really confused. 'We're taking this stuff,' said the taller women aggressively.

'Yes,' I replied, 'I can see that, I don't mind, but I'd really like to find my mum and brother.' I moved over to the kettle which was behind them. 'Excuse me,' I said, indicating the kettle.

They moved aside and I picked up the kettle and filled it at the sink. Then I set it to boil and opened the cupboard with the coffee. It was empty. The shorter women opened her bag and pulled out the coffee jar.

'What are you doing?' hissed the other.

'Well, coffee sounds nice, I'm tired and hungry,' she said, as she pulled out a chair and sat down at the kitchen table. I opened the cutlery drawer, took out a spoon and the back-door keys as I did so. I spooned coffee into two mugs and then looked at the taller women. She stared at me and then nodded slightly, so I added the coffee to the third mug. There was a huge jar on the kitchen counter with some brown crystals right at the bottom. I opened it and put two teaspoons in my cup.

'Sugar?' I asked. They both nodded yes, and I added the sugar and poured in the boiling water.

'I really miss milk,' I said.

'Yes,' said the shorter women wistfully, 'I miss cereal in the morning and milky tea with biscuits.' I passed round the cups and joined her at the table as she continued, 'I miss bread too, and pizza and chips….' Her voice died away as I nodded.

'Look,' I asked, 'when you arrived last night was there any sign of an older woman, in her seventies?' I paused.

'Or a man, thirty-two, medium height, dark hair?'

'No,' she said, sipping from her cup and making a face, 'we came in because the front door was open.' This was news, so they hadn't smashed the glass door in the conservatory. When had that happened then?

'Was the conservatory door already smashed?' I asked, pointing out of the kitchen window.

She turned to look, 'Oh,' she said in surprise, 'We didn't see that last night.'

'I did,' said the other woman, 'when I went round to check the other rooms.' She came and sat down at the table next to her sister; it was obvious when they were sitting side by side. I must have looked worried, and when I didn't say anything she continued, 'Don't you live here then?'

'No,' I said, wracking my brains to think what might have happened to mum and Vik; if the door had been open, then maybe they had left earlier, when the smashed glass happened. But then they could be anywhere, they could be hiding out in one of the neighbour's houses or they could be trying to get to my place. 'I live near Watford.' I looked up and smiled with as much warmth as I could muster; 'I'm Zoe.'

I picked up a piece of paper from the pile on the side of the table. It looked like mum had been making notes to herself. Then looked round for a pen; a pot on the counter yielded a black sharpie. I jotted down my name and phone number, and put the names Nadia and Vik underneath. 'If you hear anything can you call me?' I asked.

The taller women frowned, but the shorter picked up the paper and put it in her bag, 'I'm Amy, and this is my sister Tina,' she said, 'I hope you find your family.' I smiled and stood up, walked to the back door, opened it and went into the garden.

I didn't know what to do. I didn't care about the women. I couldn't stop them taking the food, I definitely couldn't imagine fighting them...not like the youth I had hit in the park. This was different; they weren't a threat to me. But with the glass door broken, I couldn't really secure the house; I could lock all the doors, but anyone could easily get into the dining room from the conservatory. I couldn't really hide stuff either; there was so much of it, all the trinkets and ornaments, presents we had made for mum and dad. I looked around, overwhelmed; even the garden prompted memories; Dad, Vik and I playing cricket, accidentally lobbing the ball over the fence yet again… Mum showing me her cherries last year. I couldn't bear to think of people traipsing through, destroying all our stuff.

I walked round the patio, through the broken door into the conservatory, and then into the dining room. Scattered on the surfaces amongst other bric-a-brac, were photo frames. Mechanically, I picked up one of dad, opened the back, removed the photo and put the frame back. Then I went round and did the same for all the others.

I put the photos in the travel pouch I wore around my waist. I had made up a tiny survival kit, something we had discussed on the forums, just a few basic items in a travel pouch that belted around my waist. I wore it always when away from home. Inside I had a lighter, a safety pin, a coil of tooth floss, and a multitool in the shape of a credit card, one of the ones that contain a tiny knife, scissors, tweezers, file and pen. I also had a strip of hay fever tablets and a refresher bar for energy. I packed the photos away behind the energy bar and zipped the pouch closed. It was bulkier than before but not noticeably so.

I heard Amy and Tina leaving but ignored them. I went upstairs into Vik's room. It looked the same as always. I went into mum's. There was a picture of her with some friends, she was laughing and looked happy. I took the picture out of its frame and then looked round; as my eyes flittered from surface to cluttered surface, I absently noticed that things looked barer than usual.

I sat on the bed working out what was missing; my eyes drifted back to the dressing table…her hairbrush and hand cream and a couple of other things were gone. I opened the wardrobe; it looked slightly less crowded than usual. I couldn't really tell if anything particular was missing, but I was certain there was; it looked like they might have left on purpose, with time to pack up some stuff. I ran back downstairs and checked the top of the coat wardrobe; sure enough, mum's old black hat was gone. I was so relieved. They couldn't have been in that much trouble if mum had time to grab her hat.

I was still hungry, I went downstairs expecting the kitchen to be stripped bare, but when I looked in the cupboard, the old metal tins of rice and lentils was still there. Too heavy to take I supposed. I filled a pan with water and put them on to boil. The lentils should have been soaked, strictly speaking, but I didn't care; it was food.

When the lentil and rice mix was ready, I spooned some into a bowl, ate, and tried to decide whether to go home. It was getting on to evening and although I was locked inside a house, I felt deeply insecure. I didn't know who was around, whether there were still youths in the park, or even if the rumours about wild dogs were true. I should have asked Amy loads more things. I had let an opportunity slip.

I'd had a good seven hours sleep on the sofa; I was wide-awake, and was soon feeling bored. I sat in the kitchen doing old crosswords and reading mums notes. Eventually I let myself back into the living room for another nap to kill time. I set my phone to quietly wake me at 3am and dozed until I fell properly asleep.

At 3am I woke feeling groggy. I drank some water, ate some of the cold leftover rice and lentils then grabbed the bike from the garden and locked the kitchen and living room doors ready to leave.

I eased open the front door and listened carefully. It was silent. The lights were out, and the street was dark. I wheeled the bike up the road. Last time I had freewheeled down the hill, but this time I needed to go slowly. I crossed the road and walked the bike slowly down the other side, looking across at where I thought the car was. The night was warm and dry, the sky cloudless. As I stared across into the dark, I suddenly saw a flash of light a couple doors down from where I was looking. I stared into the dark and saw the flash again. I quickly moved to the concealing shelter of a hedge, ducking down out of sight.

There was definitely activity over the road. Lights flashed on and off and I could hear muffled talking. I was surprised I hadn't noticed them earlier, but my attention had been on the house a few doors further up. I couldn't see my car; it didn't help that it was small and black; not my preferred colour but I had bought it second hand for its reliability not its' looks.

I waited a while, then moved a couple of doors down into a driveway with a car and a hedge; much better concealment than just a hedge alone. The people opposite didn't seem to be doing much, I couldn't work out if they were waiting for someone or just hanging around. The lights I had seen were the screens of their mobile phones and there seemed to be a fair bit of banter going on, selfies being taken, and images being smirked over. It didn't look like it would stop any time soon. There did seem to be something in the driveway, but it was hard to see what.

I moved further down the road and propped the bike against a van. Then I worked my way back up the hill. I wanted to check the car, but the only way I was going to be able to get that close was if there was a diversion. The best thing I could think of was a fire. It hadn't rained for a while and the vegetation was dry. If I could get something burning at the top of the road, I could wait until they had moved away and have a quick peek without them noticing.

I made my way back up to the junction and slipped round the corner so I was out of sight. The fences here were constructed from wooden boards; dry and flammable. I felt along the fence with my fingers until I found a loose board, and tried to prise it off quietly. My fingertips gripped under the wood, but even tugging as hard as I could, it wouldn't budge; the boards were nailed on too firmly.

I stood, picking a splinter out of my finger…maybe at mum's house I could find something to burn. I let myself back in the house and looked in the cupboard behind the kitchen door. Sure enough, tucked away behind the odd bits and pieces, was a bottle that felt the right size and shape. I opened it in the dark and took a sniff; methylated spirits- perfect. On the way out, I picked up a couple of magazines from beside the phone. I couldn't see properly, but they felt like old phone books.

Back at the top of the road, I zigzagged back and forth with my hands outstretched until I bumped into the telegraph pole. I stacked the phone books into a tepee shape against it and doused them in meths. I soaked the pole too for good measure. Hopefully it was far enough from any houses not to cause any major damage. I pulled out my lighter and lit it; the meths ignited with a whoosh of flame that spread across the books and ran up the pole. I quickly turned and ran down the crescent and then more cautiously walked up the other side, back to the main road. I warily stepped onto the street trying to work out where I was. I had come out a couple of houses down from my car, but not as far as where I had stashed my bike.

As I stared up the road, I could see my diversion had been a complete success. The fire had flared up, bright enough to catch someone's attention, and draw everyone towards it, and although it had died down quickly, there was still a dull, orange glow, lighting up the surroundings and outlining several people. I could no longer see any lights around the driveway I had been watching. I moved closer, trying to be as stealthy as possible.

It wasn't until I was almost in the drive that I heard the phone, or rather the voice coming out of the phone. It was muffled and rumbling but distinctly a voice. I froze. I couldn't quite hear the words, but it meant someone was there. I moved forward, and craned my head over the bush between me and the driveway. In the light from the phone screen, I saw a large male figure propped up against a car, it looked very much like my car; it was a dark colour and the shape was right.

The figure holding the phone wasn't saying much, just nodding his head and occasionally mumbling 'uh huh,' or 'ok.' He looked big. I looked up the road and was alarmed to see, in the light of the fire, that some of the people were turning away and spreading out, searching. I weighed up my options and backed away towards my bike, cutting my losses.

I cycled home in the dark, along the empty main roads, reflecting on the last twenty-four hours. I hadn't found mum or Vik and was bitterly disappointed to have lost my car, but on the whole, I had come out ok. My car had always represented freedom, and now it was gone, along with all the spare kit it contained. But I could get another, there were still plenty on the estate, with the keys lying around nearby. The most important thing was that Mum and Vik seemed to have left under their own steam. I had to trust that they were ok and would get in contact soon.

Back home I waited at home for Vik to call, but after several days of continuing silence I had worked myself up into quite a state, imagining all sorts of things. I finally mentioned my fears to my group online and the first post back was immensely reassuring. 'Maybe they just lost your number' I was struck by the possibilities. Maybe they had lost their phones. If so, they wouldn't know my number but they could still be making their way towards me. I wrote my mobile number into a block of wood, and hung it on the front door; so if they arrived when I was out, they could contact me. I made sure my phone was with me at all times...I expected them to turn up at my place at any time, and was more determined than ever to stay where I was.

7

Meeting

Now that I didn't have anyone to speak to, I started to feel a bit isolated. I ended up talking to myself a lot of the time. Not in a crazy way, not shouting and yelling, but quietly just talking to myself. But after a while, the isolation really began to make itself felt. Talking to people online was only going to get me so far. I was talking to the birds in the garden, and the cats I saw in the evenings. Maybe I did need people after all.

I was still cautious about not being seen entering the house, but I began to walk more openly around the estate. I had a fair idea of which houses were unoccupied, but I now began actively mapping out which ones had people in.

There were remarkably few left, just a handful of households from the five thousand or so original population. A lot had died in the initial wave of the virus, and more had left to join family elsewhere I supposed. There were fewer knockers as well, most had come from the neighbouring estate, crossing via the tunnels under the railway line or over the bridge to get into Carpenders park. I went through the tunnel a couple of times, but I didn't feel as safe on the other side. There were more people over there, and although they seemed sociable, stopping and chatting to each other, I stayed out of sight as I didn't know how they would react to a stranger. They were a close-knit community, but I didn't know how they had managed to survive for three months. Possibly they had done quite well scavenging houses for food, and I knew there were allotments somewhere.

It was halfway through August, when something went wrong with the water supply. It happened over the course of a week. I didn't notice anything at first, maybe the water was a little cloudy, but I was boiling it in the kettle as a matter of routine, just to be safe, so I put the cloudiness down to limescale, but then it started tasting kind of off. The next day I opened the tap and the water that came out had definite particles floating in it. Something had gone wrong either at the water treatment plant or in the pipes that delivered the water.

I started using my lifesaver bottle to filter the water. It could take the cloudy water and turn it crystal clear. It was fast too; I could filter about half a litre in one go; just fill it up, push the pump a couple of times and the water would come streaming out the other end. I could replenish a 2-litre water bottle with clean water in just over five minutes.

I filled up a couple of extra bottles and took them with me on my cycle around the estate that evening. As I passed the first of the occupied houses, I slowed down and then stopped. I looked at the house for a full minute, but I had to start somewhere. I got off my bike and wheeled it down the drive to the front door. I rang the bell. I didn't expect an answer, but maybe they had seen me cycling round the estate before, because after thirty seconds or so, a youngish, blonde woman answered the door.

'Hi,' I said, I hadn't expected the door to open, and was a little off balance. The woman looked at me enquiringly.

'Hi,' she said, waiting for me to go on.

'I noticed you were still here,' I began, 'the water from the taps has gone a funny colour, but I have a filter that can purify water, removing any dirt and germs, so I wondered if you wanted some, um.' I trailed off holding up the bottle of water.

'Thank you,' she replied, as she relaxed slightly 'that's very kind; we've been boiling it, but it still looks cloudy and tastes weird.'

I handed her a bottle and asked, 'do you know anyone else who might need water?' I didn't want to pry too closely into her circumstances, but if felt good to be talking to another person. We chatted on the doorstep for a couple of minutes, she even invited me in, but I declined, I wanted to get round the estate before dark. The cautiousness had become ingrained, but I left with a wave and a smile, promising to be back the next day with more water.

Over the next couple of days I met everyone left on the estate. There weren't many of us, but that made it easier to trust each other. When people found out how few of us remained, they were shocked, and when I asked if I could tell people they had survived, they all agreed. I suppose all of us were a bit desperate for company, even those that were living with family must have wanted to see fresh faces. After a couple of weeks, once we had built up some trust, we decided to meet up all together in the primary school.

The school was roughly in the centre of Carpenders Park; up the road from the shops. I arrived early and found the broom cupboard. I swept away the glass from the broken front door and set out some chairs in the hall. I looked around trying to imagine how they might feel. With the broken glass swept away, the entrance was still fairly appealing; the path leading in might be knee high with weeds, but once inside there was a small welcoming atrium, decorated in primary colours, with posters of children's books on the walls.

The hall was accessed through a short corridor to the side and compared to the secondary school halls I was used to, this one felt very small, but there were so few of us that we would easily fit. There was a stage at the front, and the far wall had windows all the way along with two set of double doors at each end. Unfortunately, some of the windows were broken so I worked my way around the room, brushing away the glass and the debris that had been blown in by the wind. I opened wide the double doors; extra exits might make people feel more comfortable. It certainly made me feel better.

I looked around, would people talk to each other? I was desperate for conversation and I bet the others were too. But like me they might be a little nervous to start with. We needed an icebreaker. Spying some tables stacked in a corner, I began bringing them out. I took some large sheets of poster paper, and wrote a single question on each sheet placing them on the different desks. Questions such as; 'Would you be willing to trade food?' 'Do you think there is enough on the estate for all of us?' As people arrived, I handed them a marker and asked them to jot down some ideas as they waited. Initially people were cautious, standing in isolated pockets around the room, but after a couple of people started writing on the sheets, more joined in as they arrived, and a certain amount of small talk began as they wrote. People who had vaguely known each other, started to make conversation and the noise soon became quite loud, with the children running around laughing and adding to the din.

It was startling after the quiet of the last few months, and I could see that a couple of people were looking uncomfortable, so I climbed up onto the stage and waited until everyone had quieted down. 'Hi,' I said. 'You all know me, and some of you know each other, but let's do some quick introductions.' I sat down on the stage and indicated the two eldest in the room, 'This is Beryl and George.'

They nodded and smiled, and then realised I meant for them to say something. 'Um, good morning, I'm Beryl, this is George, and we live in a bungalow on Pen Avenue,' said Beryl.

A couple of murmured welcomes could be heard, Beryl seemed to have stopped, and it looked like George wasn't going to say anything, so I moved on, 'This is Helen and Brian.'

Helen smiled faintly and Brian said, 'Hi everyone, Helen and I are keen gardeners and we live in George Drive."

There were a couple more welcoming noises, so I moved to the last of the older couples.

'This is Robert and Sheila' I said, 'whom most of you know anyway."

Robert and Sheila stepped forwards; they were involved in several committees on the estate and were familiar faces to most people. 'Hi' they said together, smiling. 'Hopefully we can help each other out, until things return to normal,' added Sheila.

Then I looked at the two single adults, one was a tall spare gentleman, elderly but upright, the other a lady, short and somewhat stout. Both were wearing shirts and shorts, but somehow their outfits looked entirely different. 'This is Frank, and this is Cathy,' I said.

Frank smiled and said nothing, but Cathy looked around and said rather brusquely, 'I know I live alone, but I am not sharing my food, I have enough for me and think we should keep our stuff for ourselves.'

Several people looked uncomfortable at her plain speaking, but I noticed several others nodding in agreement. I didn't want to say anything, I sort of agreed with her, but said out loud, it sounded very selfish.

I looked at the five kids playing on the floor. 'So, who are you guys?' I asked them.

'I'm Adam, this is Heather and Andrew, and those are Rachel and William,' He said, pointing at them in turn. Rachel and William were both very young, maybe three or four years old.

'Are you twins? I asked. Their mother stepped forward to reply.

'No, William is four, Rachel is almost three,' she said, 'I'm Nina, I live in my mums house in Foxglove lane'

Nina was the lady I had met first, she lived in one of the houses round the back of the school. It was a bit of a warren back there and the gardens were tiny, she couldn't be growing food, so how was she keeping her family fed?

An Asian man and his wife stepped forward, 'we are Amin and Rabia,' 'and this is our younger son, Adam' they said. 'We live just down the road.' They had a sad look in their eyes and I wondered what had happened to their elder son, an accident or had it been the virus…? The people here were the lucky survivors; it would have been odd if none of them had suffered any losses.

'We also lost our youngest daughter,' said the last lady. 'Heather and Andrew are ours, I am Elizabeth, and this is my partner, Richard.' Richard smiled briefly, worry lines creasing his forehead, but Elizabeth looked around through kind eyes with a large open smile.

That was everyone. I wasn't quite sure what to do next; I stood up and paused uncertainly. After Cathy's statement, I didn't want to mention food. 'Is everyone ok for water?' I asked. There was a murmur of voices and nods and I smiled vaguely and then stepped off the stage. Most people were looking quite comfortable now, and after the glut of social interaction, I was tired and needed some peace and quiet. I sat on a chair and watched the kids play. Eventually one fell over and started to wail. It seemed that was the signal for people to disperse, and as people started to leave, I slipped away home.

For the next couple of days I carried on with the water deliveries. I knew where everyone lived, although I had been less specific about where I was; naming the street but not the number. I was also very busy in the garden. The crops were doing well. The Matina tomatoes were ripe, and I was able to pick four or five every day. The sweetcorn was swelling up nicely, and I spent a lot of time searching the runner beans for ripe pods so as not to accidently leave any to set seed. I even started experimenting with drying out some of the beans after picking so I could keep them through winter and have seed for next year. The first-early potatoes in the pots were mostly done, the stems had shrivelled up and dried out.

One sunny morning, I emptied all the pots onto a tarp and collected up a bucketful of small tubers, which were all that remained after my careful harvesting. The tarp now held a huge pile of old compost. I always used bags of fresh compost for the potatoes, as they were pest free and held water well. The potatoes that formed were much smoother and cleaner than they would have been in the ground; they could be cooked with the skins on, as there was little scab or slug damage.

I looked at the compost and the empty pots. I was going to need to grow another crop of potatoes but I couldn't just buy new bags of compost. I would have to re-sterilize the soil myself, and for that, I would need a microwave. The bramble around the side gate had put on a lot of growth and the only way I would be able to open it again, was if I cut it all down, which I didn't want to do. Instead, I took the wheelbarrow through the house, up the drive and across the road.

The first house I tried had a nice big microwave. It was heavy, but I managed to slide it into the wheelbarrow. I took it back to my garden, and using an extension lead, set it up by the heap of soil. I took an old ice-cream tub, filled it with soil, and put it in the microwave. Two minutes later and it was steaming hot. Then I looked around for somewhere to put it; all the pots still needed washing. I sighed and went to get the washing up liquid and a sponge.

The pots held about ten litres of compost and so each one would require five tubs of sterilized soil. That was at least ten minutes of microwave use. I set up an assembly line, with tubs of soil ready to go in, and washed the pots whilst I was waiting, but it still took ages. After an hour, I had filled only four pots. I was tempted to skip the sterilisation step, but the knowledge that the potatoes might be vital, come early spring, kept me going.

As I worked, I thought about the new crop. The weather had been pretty typical for August; summer storms had dumped a lot of water into the water butts, which had been fortunate, as they had been followed by a long dry spell. I anticipated that the autumn would run on late; last year the dahlias had continued flowering into November. I would take advantage of the long autumn by growing the leftover small tubers and keep them near the house to protect against any early frosts. However, the biggest problem was that potatoes had a dormancy period before they sprouted again and I didn't want the tubers to sit for five months in the soil before they started growing.

After I'd put in a couple of hours work I went inside and asked on the forums. I was out of luck; no-one seemed to have tried re-growing harvested potatoes. I took to google and quickly found some scientific papers on breaking potato dormancy. Luckily, being a science teacher, although they were pretty technical, I could just about understand enough to know I would need to lace the soil with ethanol which should get them to sprout in about a week.

I went looking for ethanol. It wasn't hard to find; most of the houses still contained their prior owners' copious alcohol collections and in the house opposite, I located a bottle of vodka. Back in the kitchen, I dipped a couple of potato tubers in a weak solution of water and vodka, laid them gently on a tray, and slid it into a cupboard. I filled some small 3-inch pots with sterilized compost, pushed a couple more tubers down into the soil until they were completely buried, and watered them with the vodka solution. I set the pots on the windowsill where I could see them.

Five days later, when I checked the cupboard, I was amazed to see tiny buds on the potatoes. The pots weren't showing any signs of life, but I waited. Two weeks later tiny green shoots were emerging from the soil. I rinsed all the small tubers in the solution and planted them in the waiting pots of sterilized compost. I arranged them around the outside of the house, setting up the drip irrigation system to keep them watered in the warm weather. I was busy and content. Delivering water supplies in the evening, gave me the opportunity to chat briefly with the other residents, so I wasn't lonely, and I was enjoying the challenge of trying to grow enough food to survive.

I hadn't organised another meeting. The families with kids were meeting up regularly; I often saw them running around the estate. However, I had no idea what the others were up to. But as I delivered the last bottle of water, a week after I had completed planting the potatoes, I got an unpleasant surprise.

8

Hiding

The bottle was for the elderly gentleman who lived on the far side of the estate. His name was Frank, and he lived in a detached bungalow near to the main road. He was a keen gardener and a member of the horticultural society, so I had known him slightly before the outbreak. Although polite, he rarely shared more than a quiet greeting and a polite thank you when I took him his water.

I left my bike propped against the low wall at the front and knocked on the door. It took a while to open and the face that appeared was definitely not Franks, it was a youngish man and he looked tough; the type of person I would normally avoid. 'Hi' I said thrown by the unfamiliar face, 'could I speak to Frank please?'

'Yo, Frank,' he turned away to shout inside, 'some girl's here, wanting you.' The man spoke like he was from the rougher parts of inner London, mashing his words together and dropping half the consonants. He turned back to me. 'Wha d'ya want?'

I took a step back, 'nothing, I was just checking on Frank, like I sometimes do.' I looked across at the bay windows but couldn't see anything through the net curtains. I was nervous and getting more so by the second. 'Are you a friend of his?' I asked, making conversation.

'Yeah,' he replied with a smirk, 'a friend.' I didn't like the way his eyes shifted from me and then up to my bike at the top of the garden. I waited a second and then backed away further, bending to pick a tiny weed seedling from the side of the path.

'Is Frank coming?' I asked, continuing to pluck weeds from the soil and backing further away as I did so. The man turned back inside to shout something and I bolted. Feeling utterly craven, I jumped on my bike and peddled away. I felt bad for Frank, but I didn't want to risk my safety. I would come back at night and see if I could find out what was happening.

As I peddled back, I kept a sharp look out; there were more open doors than usual. I tended to close them after I searched a house, but now I passed several open doors and even heard some voices as I passed. It was close to dusk, and as I cycled past one house, the lights suddenly turned on inside. There were people here! How had I missed this? To my sensitive ears the estate suddenly seemed alive with noise.

I had been using my front door ever since the meeting in the school, but now I entered my garden through the tunnel under the cypress. I hadn't used it for a while and there were crisscrossing webs that I brushed away with a shiver. Back in my house, I checked the internet and went on the forums; in my preoccupation with the garden, I had missed the big news. People were moving out of the city and camping in the fields on the outskirts of London. There were some photos in my local forum, taken at a distance, a field full of a tents and makeshift shelters.

I checked the boundaries of the garden and then went into the loft. I had toyed with the idea of sleeping in the loft previously, but hadn't seen the need. Now though, I suddenly didn't feel safe in my bedroom. I brought up the rest of the tinned and dried food and stored it in the crates in the loft. I had accumulated a fair few duvets and mats, and I made a bed of sorts between some of the cross rafters. Then I rigged the loft ladder so I could pull it up behind me and closed the hatch.

I sat, thinking about the garden. It obviously needed to be tended, but was there any way I could safeguard some of my crops? I could move some of the pots of potatoes into the garden opposite, next to the wood store. The wilderness was the best deterrent I could hope for, and would hopefully keep some of my food supply safe if my garden was plundered. I could rig up a water butt to collect water from the roof of the old greenhouse and rig some sort of irrigation... I could also harvest some of the bigger carrots and store them somewhere cool and dry. The loft would be too hot but perhaps beneath the cypress...If I could find some sand, I could create a clamp; that would store root veg for months.

I had some ideas but it all seemed a lot of work, and I was getting tired of working alone. I was dismayed at the thought of being completely alone again, I had got used to meeting up with the other residents, even if only to briefly hand over a bottle of clean water. I lay on the makeshift bed and stared up at the rafters, I could feel the light cloak of depression settling around me, weighing me down. I picked up my phone and called mum and Vik again, but there was no answer.

There was a power socket in the loft, so I hefted myself off the bed and opened the hatch. Wallowing in self-pity wasn't going to get me anywhere. I went down into the kitchen and got the kettle. The cold-water tank was also up there, so using my lifesaver bottle, I would have clean water and food to eat.

Waste would be a problem. I would need to go downstairs to use the toilet at least once a day.

As night fell, I curled up in my makeshift bed and tried not to think about spiders. I ran through all my plans and thought about Frank. Part of me really wanted to try to help him, but the rational part knew that there was very little I could do. Even if I went back and found him, I didn't know if he had let his visitor in on purpose; maybe he really was a friend. I was assuming he was being held prisoner, but the man had called him when I visited. Had Frank told him about my water filter? I hadn't told anyone about the specifics of the lifesaver bottle, but it was a very valuable bit of kit. And if Frank was in trouble was I in any position to help him?... Maybe he was locked in, in which case I would have to find the key, but how would I get into his house in the first place….The thoughts went round and round until eventually I fell asleep.

I did not go back to check on Frank. Instead, I focussed on moving the pots into the garden behind mine, setting up a watering system for them, and then disguising everything I possibly could. The summer weather and my copious watering had resulted in an unprecedented growth of all my plants, but particularly the roses, brambles, and grape vine. I had just let them all do their thing until I was sealed inside a wall of greenery on all sides. I had pushed the rose stems over the wall, and they had grown until they were a tangle of thorns that fell down almost to the ground. They stopped people from walking along the pavement and getting close enough to hear me moving around inside. Or at least that's what I had thought.

I had been preparing an area for more carrots, Carrots come in packs of a thousand seeds but didn't stay alive very long once the packet was opened. I was eating my way steadily through the current crop, and although I had been re-seeding where I was harvesting, I wanted to plant some more. They could be left in the ground over winter, and eaten raw; and I may as well use up the seed.

I slid my hoe forward and back, loosening the top layer of soil at the edge of the flowerbed by the wall. The apple trees were doing well, and although I had kept the base free of weeds, to reduce competition, I reckoned that a couple of carrots at the edge of the bed wouldn't really affect them.

As I worked, the footsteps on the road outside, that I had been half listening to, stopped. I paused, holding the hoe in the air. Had I been humming? It was something I often did when I was relaxed. I wondered if they had heard me; the footsteps continued and then I heard a cracking sound of wood breaking. I heard more banging noises and some grunts, some rustling, then silence.

The noise was to my right, at the back of the garden. I moved closer to the wall and crouched down on the path between the bed of sweetcorn plants and the greenhouse. I was well hidden but couldn't see anything. I strained to hear; from the silence it sounded like they were doing the same. I waited them out, and eventually heard a rustle, then shockingly, a deep voice rumbled out 'Ow, fuck, stupid fucking thorns.'

There was further swearing, and then the voices suddenly became quieter, as if they had turned away. There were movements and rustles, I hoped fervently that they wouldn't poke too deeply into the cypress; the tarp would surely give the tunnel away. They seemed to be moving away towards the other bungalow and sure enough, I heard glass smashing and banging as they broke in through the back door.

I relaxed a fraction and reached forward to pull out some of the weeds I could see amongst the sweetcorn plants in front of me, keeping low and quiet. For the longest time I didn't hear anything, and I wondered if they had already left, but after about half an hour, I heard banging again from the bungalow, they were probably trying to get out of the front door. If it was anything like mine, UPVC, they would have no trouble kicking through the foam panels. The banging stopped, and thirty seconds later I heard them walking back down the road. 'That was a complete waste of time,' said the deep voice.

'Yeah, sorry, I was sure I heard something,' said another voice, it was high and quick, a child perhaps. 'Ow!' said the same voice, sounding aggrieved. I listened carefully, but there was no further speech. It seemed the adult was not the talkative type.

The next morning the footsteps were back again, and again the morning after; they must have set up somewhere nearby. Where were they going every morning? The only thing past my house was the flats and then the alley to the cemetery.

A couple of days later I was woken at an unreasonably early hour by a magpie, rattling around on the tiles outside. It was five in the morning and dead quiet outside, except for the birds. I was still sleeping in the loft, which I had made a whole lot more convenient by adding blackout sheets to the Velux windows. I had strung fairy lights along the ceiling, and stapled sheets to the rafters to create a tent effect. And I had turned off the central heating, so I wasn't disturbed by the water pump, which was right at the foot of my bed. I wasn't quite sure what I would do come winter, but for now it worked well.

I went down for a hot shower and debated the wisdom of going out for a scout around. As I walked down the garden path twenty minutes later, I decided to pop over to check on the potato plants and see how much damage had been done to the fence. I climbed the ladder and scrambled over. The potato plants seemed to be doing fine, I could see the green shoots poking through in a couple of places, but I could also see the shiny slime trails of snails along the top of the soil. I made a note to grab the slug killer when I got back.

I crawled through the tunnel under the cypress and came up the other side. I peered out between the green branches and could see that about six or seven fence boards were missing, leaving a large gap open to the road. In a way, this was better, as I could see the road from the safety of the tunnel, but it also meant that as soon as I crawled out, I would be visible to anyone passing by. What I really needed was a way to look up and down the road from the safety of the cypress. Something like a periscope.

Leaving that idea to explore later, I exited the garden and moved out into the road. The weeds made it look desolate and the grey garage door opposite was broken open. I walked down the road in the morning silence and headed for the back of the cemetery. I made my way down a narrow alleyway between two bungalows. The tarmac was crumbling at the edges where the weeds were poking through, and there was ivy starting to peep over the fence on one side. Over the other, another plant, a wisteria perhaps, trailed long stems whilst old gnarled branches, laden with small apples, stretched out above. At the end of the alley there was a gate, which gave out into a wooded glade. It was propped open, half off its hinges. I paused and looked out through the trees, it was empty, but I could hear the gurgling of moving water.

I threaded my way through the trees and could almost instantly see the source of the noise; a small stream. The water ran shallowly along a gravel bed until it reached a small pool where it swirled briefly before streaming over a lip to a jumble of rocks just a foot below. At the side of the rocks were a number of discarded bowls and plastic bottles.

I walked along a path following the stream downhill, through a wooded area bounded by garden fences. The fences drew closer together until I was walking down little more than a narrow green passage between houses, then the water disappeared into a culvert and the path ended at a locked gate. I made my way back to the mini waterfall, crossed over, using the flat stones at the top, and followed the trail of discarded rubbish back towards the main part of the cemetery.

The trail soon reached the edge of the trees and the carpark. Parked in the car park was a massive green army truck. It was enormous, and dwarfed the small transit van next to it. I couldn't imagine what it was doing there. It didn't look like the truck the soldiers had brought previously, but it did look familiar. I couldn't place it though, so after a bit I turned my attention to the cemetery in front of me. The grass stretched away to the road and garden centre and was dotted with tents and barbeques, with camping chairs scattered between. From the occasional trees, lines were slung that supported plastic sheets and tarpaulins to create more shelters. There weren't a lot of them, maybe between fifteen and twenty, but they were large family sized structures. Nothing moved in the peaceful morning, and after staring at it all for a while, I quietly crept back home.

I sat at my kitchen table, eating porridge made with water; even with pieces of sliced apple and a lot of sugar, it tasted thin. I couldn't imagine how the camp was feeding that many people, and I was sure I recognised the truck. I went online and searched for video footage, and eventually found the answers.

It was a food truck, from the first attempts at delivering food to the city. It must have had immense quantities of food. Those first trucks had delivered army survival rations, because they were sent out before the government had reached an understanding with the large supermarkets. I read that there were twelve ration packs to a case and 48 cases to a pallet. A truck that big could easily still be feeding the hundred or so people in the camp. But it wouldn't last all winter. I couldn't imagine my amateur attempts at concealing my food would be proof against a more rigorous search. I sent up a quick plea to the universe asking that they would leave soon, and then tacked on another; that mum and Vik were safe.

9

Waiting

I built the periscope. Using some scavenged mirrors, drainpipe, and a lot of black gaffer tape. I used it to watch the comings and goings. There were disturbances pretty much all the time now. During the day, it wasn't so bad, but at night, there were people running down the street, glass smashing, screaming and yelling as different groups met up. At night, I sat in my loft, curled up in a ball, listening to the noises outside; trying to decipher what was going on. During the day, I carried on with my gardening, listening out for the interlopers, trying to stay invisible. I was grateful for the abundant growth that hid me from view.

They made it hard for me to tend to the garden and I sometimes daydreamed of poisoning the stream or at least blocking it further up. Then they would move on and life would go back to normal. The man and boy were regulars every morning, but there were also others; a trio of teenage girls would come by every afternoon, pursued by a gang of boys, all of them laughing and joking around. Lone women, looking bedraggled and tired would sometimes pass, searching for supplies or just wandering the estate. There were very few older people, or small children. In the evenings, the voices were often that of men, loud and rowdy. I guessed they were drinking the pub dry.

I really wanted to find out where these people had come from and why they were here and eventually I became curious enough to risk talking to someone. I set it up carefully, prepping one of the houses down a cul-de-sac, which backed onto an alleyway. One sunny morning I waited as one of the women wandered down the road, poking desultorily at the items in the gardens and trying the front doors of the houses. As she approached, I stepped into view, carrying a watering can, and started to water the flowers in the front garden.

When she ducked down behind the next-door neighbour's hedge, I pretended I didn't see her and began weeding the garden...a bit of a marathon task to be honest, but I wasn't doing it for real. I hummed softly to myself and eventually she stood up slowly. I started as if in surprise and then greeted her as if we weren't in the middle of the apocalypse.

'Hi,' I said, 'lovely weather today, isn't it?' brushing myself down as if to make myself presentable. I was wearing an old blue t-shirt and beige capris trousers, easy to run away in, but a very unthreatening outfit.

'Um, yes' she replied half turning.

'Are you part of the group camping in the cemetery?' I asked, crouching down and continuing to pull weeds.

'Yes,' she replied, inching forwards in order to see me over the bushy plants 'do you live here?'

'Yep, but I've not been here for long... I've come over from south Oxhey,' I pointed vaguely west, '...from over there... where did you guys come from?' I asked, returning the query.

Very soon she was talking along nineteen to the dozen, It turned out she was from inner London.

'We did fairly well on our own; we found food and stuff... we'd go into the back of shops and restaurants and get pasta and stuff we could cook at home, it was sometimes tricky because if you were unlucky you'd meet other people doing the same thing, who would sometimes nick your stuff off you.'

I nodded in sympathy.

'But later on, it was too dangerous to go out because of the gangs. We joined up with a couple of others; we had to contribute to get in, but they protected us... you just had to know the right postcodes to stay in...and make sure you got enough extra food to keep Xavier happy.'

'Xavier?' I asked raising my eyebrows slightly.

'Yeah, he runs our group, makes the decisions, people don't argue with him, he can be...' she shivered slightly.

'So why did you leave London?' I asked, turning the conversation away from the upsetting topic.

'People got ill, lots of people...about a week after the water went bad. We had a couple of nurses in our group, but even they got ill. They were sick and had diarrhoea. People called it crypto, but I don't know exactly what it was, only everyone started leaving, to try and find clean water.'

I nodded.

'Someone suggested the reservoir in Brent... the Welsh Harp; but there were already loads of people there, so we just kept going.'

'What made you stop here?' I asked.

'We saw the fields...we were going to turn off earlier, but then we saw the cemetery. Lots of people thought it would be spooky, but Xavier said it was perfect'

'To hide the truck' I said, nodding as if it was common knowledge.

Either she didn't realise that I knew more than I was letting on, or she didn't notice, because she answered without pause; 'Yeah, the truck was the big thing, Xavier didn't want anyone to see it.'

'So… are you staying…?' I said it with a friendly smile, but I didn't really care, I just wanted to know if they planned to leave soon.

'No,' she said, 'When they've finished the booze, we'll probably move on.' she sounded pretty dejected about it, but I was elated. I had found out everything I wanted to know and best of all they were leaving soon!

I stood up, dusting off my clothes and sighed, 'I wish I could make a find like that,,' I said, 'it's just so hard, always searching for something to eat…'

'You could join us,' she said unexpectedly, 'I'm sure Xavier would take you in, there are a couple of guys who are always looking to hook up, more girls are always welcome, and if you're cooking for someone, then you always get fed. Not much sometimes, but it's enough.' She said it earnestly, as if offering a good deal… as if hooking up to get food was perfectly acceptable.

I was simultaneously touched that she would make the offer and appalled that she would think it was ok. I tried to hide my shock but failed abysmally. 'Um, thanks…but that's ok… I like being on my own.' I said, I looked at my watch and clumsily made my excuses. Then I turned and bolted back inside. I left through the alleyway, giving thanks for my bungalow and garden all the way home.

Back in my kitchen, I went online to do a bit of research. Crypto turned out to be cryptosporidiosis. A parasite that was contained in oocysts that were found everywhere and could survive months in water sources. Normally it was removed during the filtration process. I had never heard of it before. I knew cholera and dysentery were a problem in third world countries, but in the UK, it was crypto that was the issue. It wasn't usually fatal but as I read further, I found it was the diarrhoea that was the problem; people died from dehydration. It was incredible, but it seemed to be true. People, especially children, were dying because they weren't getting enough fluids when they were sick.

A couple of days later I accidentally sprayed a heavy jet of water over the fence onto the road outside. It was a beautiful sunny day and the water trail gleamed wetly, giving me away, I rushed up to the loft, sealing myself in, peering out of the Velux window at the street below. I was waiting to be discovered, but as the water slowly evaporated over the next couple of hours, the street remained empty. No man and boy, no teenagers, no lone women or groups of men. They had gone. I waited till early next morning before I ventured out, but when I went to look at the campsite, I found the place empty. There was a lot of rubbish left behind, but the people had moved on.

It was a relief. The strain and isolation had been getting to me. Trying to work silently in the garden, never leaving the house, sleeping in the loft, much of the enjoyment disappeared when I was constantly on alert.

That evening I cycled round the estate, calling on all the people on my water route, but they had also gone. Only Frank was left, still in his home, looking a little frailer but still politely greeting me and accepting the water. I tried to apologise for running away that day, but he brushed it aside. 'It was much better that you ran, the young man was not quite as nice as I had hoped when I let him in.'

'Was he a friend?' I asked, 'Did you know him from before?'

'Yes, well actually no' said Frank, he suddenly seemed slightly embarrassed. 'He said he was a friend of my nephew, and he knew a lot about him, but I had never met him before.'

I nodded in sympathy. I was glad I hadn't had to deal with such a dilemma. None of my friends or acquaintances had come knocking at my door. I always claimed I was part hermit, and the situation was proving me right. It was nice though, that Frank was still around. The time right after mum and Vik disappeared, when I had been completely alone, still haunted me.

Frank and I methodically worked our way through all the houses on the estate searching for the others, but we drew a blank. We did find quite a lot of food rations that were obviously being horded by someone but had been abandoned when they left. These we split between us and stored away as an emergency reserve.

It seemed that we really were alone, but as the electricity and internet still worked and neither of us had anywhere to particularly go to, we decided to remain. Frank had cultivated his garden, much like I had. His visitors had eaten most of the available food, but the plants remained and he still had green tomatoes, tiny bean pods and various other immature veg.

I shared what I harvested when I visited in the evenings. I had a glut of everything at the moment, even the maincrop potatoes in the ground had done well. He, in turn, taught me how to store them properly for winter.

'It's like this, see?' he said, arranging the tubers on the trays, 'each one needs to be separate from the next, so disease doesn't spread, and air can flow freely.'

'I get it', I said, 'but where do you store them?'

Frank smiled and then led me back to his shed. Inside were banks of freezers, at least five, floor to ceiling on two sides. He opened a door. They weren't plugged in, so it wasn't cold, but the air inside didn't seem as hot as outside. 'They are mice and rat proof, and the insulation keeps the frost out,' he said, 'the only thing you need to do is check the veg periodically and remove any that look like they are going off.'

I was impressed. Frank was really prepared. I wanted to do something similar but couldn't imagine how. Frank's side gate was still useable but mine was now totally overgrown. I felt secure in my secret garden, but winter storage was going to be a problem.

I did a thorough audit of the bungalows surrounding mine, to find ones that were weatherproof with no broken windows. The row of terraced houses at the top of the road had solid wooden doors and, by dint of a crowbar and a lot of muffled swearing, I managed to lever a couple of them off their hinges. I used them to replace the broken UPVC doors on the bungalows and by the end of the week I had three houses, close to mine, that were secure. I used my sack trolley to move the doors around, which made it just about doable and avoided any houses with more than one step but even so, after that exertion I took a break for the next couple of days and relaxed in the hammock enjoying the September sun.

Over the next month, between tending the garden, harvesting food and visiting Frank in the evenings for my daily dose of human contact, I emptied and cleaned the freezers, moved them out of the kitchens into different rooms and tried to disguise them. It wasn't a lot, but hopefully, if we had visitors again, they might not find my food stores.

I won't lie; the winter was hard, really, really hard. It turned out that I had plenty of food. It wasn't particularly interesting eating pasta and tomato paste or baked potatoes with a bit of oil drizzled on, with an apple for dessert or a piece of Cornish fudge. But there was plenty. Frank and I had cooking competitions to try and pass the time. One evening I would bring over a dish, the next he would cook. He was a much, much better cook than I was. Some of the things I came up with really didn't work, but we ate them anyway; we couldn't waste the food. The chilli bottle selection I amassed actually came in quite handy for making my dishes edible. It was a good thing that Frank quickly grew to like the taste of hot pepper.

The thing that made it so difficult was the cold. I've always hated being cold and no matter how many layers I wore, if felt cold. The gas supplies from Europe had been fluctuating for a while and eventually they ceased entirely. We were still getting gas from government run platforms in the north sea but the fluctuating supply and power outages damaged a lot of boilers. Mine went first, Franks shortly after. By November I couldn't find any houses on the estate with working central heating.

One of the houses next to me had a wood burning stove, and if I closed the internal door, I could get the room nicely warm. I still had to go back to a cold house and bed though. Luckily, even after all this time, the electricity still worked. I could use the microwave to warm up my wheat bags. I amassed quite a collection but still, every morning woke to a freezing room.

I had eventually moved back to sleeping in my bedroom as it was slightly warmer than the loft. But one day, after a rather stodgy dinner stew of beans, potatoes and carrots, I was moaning to Frank about the cold when he asked whether I had a chimney.

'Yes,' I replied, 'but there is a gas fireplace which I've never used, the ignition doesn't work.'

'So use a match,' he said, with a slight smile.

I don't know why I had never thought about it before, but if the gas was still running, then the gas fireplace could be used. 'You're a genius,' I said, as I ran to put my coats back on, eager to get back and try it.

From that point on, the house was warmer than outside. I daren't go to sleep with the gas fire on, but it warmed up the house nicely during the day and I didn't have to worry about bills. Everything all seemed to work automatically.

The anticipated blizzards arrived in January. The first proper cold snap came at the end of November and although I fleeced all the plants and gave them as much protection as I could, by December the courgettes, beans and tomatoes were all gone. I had brought the pots of potatoes back around the house for warmth, and when the hard frosts hit I brought the pots inside and stacked them in the spare room on sheets. I didn't know how much photosynthesising they were doing in the dim light, but on clear days I could take them all out onto the front driveway to soak up what little sun there was. Then I would have to bring them all back in again when dusk fell.

The blizzard hit in the night and next morning the sight of the snow was glorious, blanketing everything in white and hiding the weeds and rubbish. I walked out as far as I could. Onto the main road, and up onto Merry Hill; the fields adjoining the east side of the estate. From the top of the hill I could look down and see the entire area. I hadn't been outside Carpenders Park for a while, but now it seemed like I could see miles and miles.

It was silent. Pre-outbreak there had always been sounds of traffic up on the hill; now there was only the faintest of breezes. The clouds were high, and the air was clear. It smelt clean and fresh. I walked around the fields in the general direction of Bushey, tracing large arcs and shapes in the snow and drawing dragons with my boots, until I stopped with a jolt; there was a footprint in the snow, a trail of footprints. I quickly turned, had I circled round and crossed my own trail? But I knew I hadn't.

I was about to, well, run away, wouldn't be putting it too strongly, when I noticed that the tracks were very small. I placed my foot alongside, the print was at least two inches shorter than mine, and I was a size five shoe. It looked like the print was made from either a small woman, or more likely, a child.

I decided to follow the trail for a bit. I scanned the fields in the distance but couldn't see anyone. The trail headed south, downhill towards the small wood that divided the fields from the golf course. The hill was churned up on this side with long wide bands running down the hill and lots of tracks all about. As the slope steepened the steps grew further apart, did that mean they were running? Suddenly, in the snow in front of me, there was an explosion of tracks, going in all directions. I paused to try and work it out. The snow was kicked up but I could distinctly see that there were another set of tracks; they were much smaller and much closer together. I moved on past the disturbance and the tracks resolved themselves into a trail of three people; the original set of tracks and two even smaller sets. All three continued down into the trees.

I had a small inkling even before I saw them, two boys and a girl, standing beside a bright red sled and making a snowman in a large clearing in the trees; Daisy, Toby and Lucas. I was unreasonable glad to see they were ok. I hadn't understood how affected I had been by all the deaths and disappearances. To see that they had survived was brilliant. The two boys were adding snow to the body, patting it into shape whilst Daisy was rolling the head of the snowman. It was large and looked very heavy. As she strained to lift it, I stepped out from the tree line and asked 'do you want a hand?'

All three of them looked up and shrieked, running over to the other side of the trees before checking whether I was following. When they saw I wasn't, they paused and stared. I took the opportunity to walk over to the head of the snowman and bent down to try and lift it up. It was really big and weighed a ton. 'Wow Daisy,' I said, as I lifted it and staggered over to the body 'it's enormous.'

'Hey,' said Lucas, stepping towards me 'that's our snowman.'

'Shhhhhh,' said Daisy, pulling him back, then she did a bit of a double take 'how do you know my name?' she asked belligerently.

'We met at the garden centre,' I responded, as I set the head on the body and twisted it so it was centred in place. 'I was getting a red robin shrub.' I gave the snowman a pat. 'There you go,' I said, then stepped back away from the snowman.

The three of them stepped forward in response and then Toby surprised me by saying, 'I remember, you're Zoe.' He came forward, quickly followed by Lucas and then Daisy.

'How have you guys been?' I asked, 'Were you ok when the people camped in the cemetery?'

'That was a bit scary,' said Toby, 'we had to hide for ages and our uncle wouldn't let us cook anything.'

'And it was Daisy's birthday, but we couldn't sing or have a cake or anything,' added Lucas.

I looked at Daisy 'Happy Birthday,' I said, smiling.

'It was ages ago,' she said, shrugging, 'what are you doing here?'

'I had to come out for a walk, the snow is so pretty, then I saw your tracks in the snow and followed them.' They looked at each other disconcerted.

'I hadn't thought of that,' said Daisy.

'Do you think Uncle Ben....' said Lucas nervously.

I looked at them all in turn. 'Did you guys sneak off without permission?' I asked, then answered my own question 'of course you did, well you better get home, your uncle's probably going mental.'

Toby and Lucas turned to look at Daisy, who uncertainly shook her head 'He thinks we're playing in the yard.'

'And if he comes looking for you? It's about lunchtime now…'

'I'm hungry,' said Toby.

'Me too,' chipped in Lucas.

Daisy looked mulish for a second, and then gave in. 'Ok but we need to give him a face and some arms.'

They quickly finished off the snowman with pebbles for his eyes, nose, and mouth, and twigs for arms. Then we headed back up the hill together, Daisy carrying the sled on her back like a backpack and Toby telling me all about their den and the go-kart they had made, and all sorts of things, until we were at the edge of the field in no time.

'How did you get out of the garden centre?' I asked.

'Uncle Ben turned the hole in the fence that you showed us, into a hidden door,' said Toby, 'we borrowed the key.'

I walked them back through the cemetery. Not a great place for making snowmen anymore; the ground was humped with discarded sheets and the rubbish that was lying beneath the snow. I could see why the hill had been much more inviting; especially for sledding. 'Should I come in with you?' I asked, it was time I met my neighbours, there were only Frank and me and them left, it seemed mad that we weren't helping each other.

'Oh no,' said Toby, 'if you come in, our uncle will know we were outside.'

'What will he do?' I asked curiously.

'Nothing really,' said Daisy.

'They just tell you off and make you feel bad,' said Lucas.

'And mum sometimes cries' said Daisy.

'Oh ok…try not to get caught then, and maybe next time, ask permission from your uncle…it might be wiser.

I left them at one of the paths, watching as they slipped over the bank towards the back of the garden centre.

When I got home, the tracks in the snow led straight to my door, so I set about creating a couple of false trails; walking up to the doors of several houses in the street and walking along surrounding streets and doing the same. It broke up the perfect white snow but at least I didn't see any other trails as I did so. It looked like my little corner of Carpenders Park was still empty.

After I warmed up, I went online to check in with the survival forum. There were fewer of us now, people came and went at random, and it was hard to know if they were really gone or just hibernating. Several people had posted how they were nesting up in a single room, rarely going out and bundled up in multiple duvets to stay warm. Others seemed to be better positioned, with log piles and real fires in the fireplace.

The snow stayed for a couple of days, then slowly thinned, it had almost fully melted when we were hit with another cold snap and more snow. I had to take a break from visiting Frank, as the roads were just too icy. I was lucky enough to find an electric heater, which I kept running all night to stave off the cold.

Then one evening in late January, when there were more of us online than there had been in a long while, a new poster appeared. 'Hi,' his first post read, 'I'm a representative of Hertfordshire County Council and we are letting everyone know about the settlement camps so that you can prepare to move to them when spring arrives.'

Before I even started to type a reply, someone else beat me to it and immediately typed back 'What settlement camps?'

Someone else typed 'Is there still a government?'

And a third person posted 'This is a closed group; how did you get access?' half a second later.

That was pretty much all my thoughts summed up before I had even hit a single key. The new poster replied after a pause 'further information will be posted shortly, please be patient, the council is working to fulfil its pledge of settlement homes and jobs for all.' The new poster logged out of the group and the speculation thereafter was rife.

After a bit I logged off and went back to the book I was reading. Settlement camps sounded ominous… and I didn't want to leave my home and venture out into the unknown. I was comfortable where I was and, yes maybe the last nine months had made me slightly paranoid, but I didn't want to raise my hopes that there might be an end to all this, that there might be a return to normal life somewhere ahead.

10

Decisions

The first snowdrops and dwarf irises started poking through the ground whilst the weather was still icy cold and grey, but I looked at the flowers as the promise of the spring to come. The days had warmed up a tiny bit when green spears of daffodil leaves started showing, but it was still weeks before the start of any warmer weather. I had returned to my evening meals with Frank and we both still had copious supplies. The storage freezers had done their work well; I had harvested seven crown-prince squash and still had three left. I had eaten roasted squash, squash soup, squash chips (not a success) squash pie and even tried a vegan squash cake that came out fine, although I did miss the buttercream icing.

The mystery poster from the council had been online a couple of times, describing the settlement camps and job allocations. It was all very mundane; the camps were just existing villages that had been cleared out by the army and assessed by the local authority council. You registered online, filling in a mass of forms, and then applied for whatever you needed, housing, job, food, school places. It was almost all done automatically; for example if you applied for housing, you would be placed in a queue for a camp place. When you reached the front of the queue you were allocated a camp. You could turn down the place but were then put at the back of the queue again. Once you accepted a place you could then look at the jobs available in that camp and apply. When you had a confirmed job you could then apply for other things.

The biggest advantage was that by registering, families that had been separated could find each other. Some of the online forms involved listing all family members and friends. The system flagged up all possible connections and allowed you to direct message them. It was a triumph of common sense admin and I admired the organisational minds behind it. One of the first things I did when I registered was to type in mum and Vik's names but there were no matches.

Still the idea was appealing. The camps used the existing infrastructure and had the workforce to run it again; supermarkets and schools, cafes, sports centres, hospitals and weekly rubbish collection. When I read about the last I was almost tempted to leave. I hated the chore of disposing of my rubbish and I was due to go out for a rubbish run again.

It was early in the morning on a grey wet day and I had just finished preparing dinner in the slow-cooker. I added the empty tube of tomato paste to the bag of non-compostable rubbish and tied it firmly. I swept the vegetable peelings into a box of compostable waste and added the cayenne pepper to discourage rats. Then I set out, bag and box in hand. The compostable rubbish was easily disposed of in the compost bins I had set up on the front driveway of one of the bungalows, but the bag would have to be stashed at the far end of the estate. I had found the keys to some lock up garages a couple of months ago, and was using the place as a rubbish dump. Even though I washed all the rubbish, and periodically chucked bleach around, it had become smelly and disgusting. I would really appreciate a rubbish collection service.

Frank was in favour of applying for a camp, but I wasn't sure. He felt we would be better off in an organised society whereas I wanted to see what I was getting myself into before committing myself. What I really wanted to do was to see the camps before I applied, see if they were really better than what we had. However the exact locations of the camps were secret, the government needed people to follow the system rather than just turn up so I couldn't just go and have a look.

I woke up one morning to find that early yellow daffodils had burst out all over the estate and the weeds were growing again in the garden. Spring felt like it had properly arrived. A couple of sunny days had me in the greenhouse thinking about starting new seedlings. The temperature outside was still only seven or eight degrees but inside the greenhouse it hit nineteen and felt like bliss.

I had tidied the garden completely over winter and was ready to start planting again. However Frank had other ideas.

'There's no point planting if you are leaving,' he said one evening, as we chopped some old, rather withered onions. We were going to attempt to make a risotto.

'But what's the point in leaving if we don't need to?' I responded, going down the well-trodden path yet again. 'If the government is getting things back on track then eventually people will come back home.'

'But what if they don't? Will you live here all alone? I won't be around for ever.' This was a new tack from Frank. He looked at me seriously 'I'm eighty-four you know.'

'Really?' I was shocked; I had put Frank in his late sixties or early seventies. Old yes, but not that old, but I really shouldn't have been surprised. I had met several people on the estate who were in their seventies and eighties and still ran the resident's association and community hall. Their energy was phenomenal. I began chopping the leeks that Frank had harvested from the garden that day, thinking hard.

I could see that I had been selfish. Frank was probably lonely for people of his own age. I was chatty and energetic but not exactly peaceful company. And I too missed the variety of talking to different people. I added the leeks to the pan where the onions were already sizzling nicely. Frank,' I asked, 'do you have family or friends in the camps?'

'Yes.' he replied simply. I added the rice and let it sauté for thirty seconds, stirring continuously to stop it sticking whilst Frank opened another of our stock of dodgy white wines. He poured in a good glug as I stirred it round. I waited and eventually he continued. 'My nephew and his family were listed as being in one of the camps in the Chilterns, and two of my partners' nieces' children made it to a camp in Kent.'

'You have a partner Frank?' I asked astonished, how did I not know this stuff? I was a rubbish friend.

'I had a partner,' he responded sadly, 'he passed away last January,' He added the vegetable stock to the pan as I continued to stir, 'we were together 56 years.'

I racked my brains for something tactful to say, 'I'm so sorry…. I can't believe I never asked.' I stirred the rice slowly 'How did you meet?'

Whilst Frank regaled me with tales of his late partner and the things they would get up to in their rather exciting youth, I rethought my stance on leaving. I would have to go, if only to accompany Frank to the Chilterns to be with his family.

Once we had decided to leave, we were suddenly very busy. We filled out all the forms and soon had allocations at the

Chiltern site. I was still cautious so listed my home as mum's house. Carpenders Park was my safety net; my fall back if the camp didn't work out. The forms were comprehensive; I told them what was needed to get the house and the job, and kept my application essay simple and short. I was naturally cautious; the new Government didn't need to know my every secret.

The job was hard to decide on; I was torn between teaching in a school and working on a farm. I had a feeling that large-scale crop growing would be nothing like the gardening I was used to, and I was missing teaching desperately. I wanted to be back in front of a class, I missed the energy and the banter, the adrenaline that came from performing for demanding teenagers, where every second you had to be on the ball. Frank found it easier, everyone had to have a job allocation but people who were retired pre-outbreak could pick a simple admin job, Frank chose a position in the library.

The army were providing transportation from pick up points to the camps. There were no pickup locations inside the M25, the nearest was at 11am every Tuesday on the A41 where it bypassed Berkhamstead. Google maps said it was 15 miles; a five-hour walk. I reckoned that at my speed it would be more like ten and that would be the direct route via Watford. If I bypassed all the populated areas it would take even longer.

We decided to break the journey into two parts, do most of it in the first day, rest overnight, and arrive at the pickup in good time the next day. We used google maps and I had the OS Explorer maps for the Chilterns East and Chilterns North, which showed most of the footpaths we would need. We were missing a section but I laboriously print screened the missing area from the OS mapping tool online.

After examining the possibilities, we settled on Bovingdon as our stop. It had a garden centre with large greenhouses which we hoped to camp at. We didn't know if there would be empty houses which we could stay in so decided to prepare in case we had to camp outside.

I took out my hiking rucksack and my camping gear. We decided to only take the one tent – mine. Our packs would be too heavy if we carried two of everything. Instead we divided the load between us and just about managed.

I collected the camping stove and some rations from my loft, along with the remaining box of Cornish fudge and the painkillers. The guidance said not to bring very much as we would be given everything we needed when we arrived. I didn't even bother with a change of clothes, only some spare underwear and a favourite t shirt. I would wear thermals with my technical jacket and trousers to stay warm.

I took the photos I had collected at mums and a USB with everything on my computer. I packed the lifesaver bottle and after debating a while, I stuffed in all my spare seed packets; I might have a garden in my new house. After packing, although my bag felt heavy, I had some room so I unpacked the seeds and wrapped them instead in my favourite blanket in a dry bag and stuffed it in the top; cosy and familiar it would help me feel at home.

I booked the pickup and then went back on the forums. There was still very little information on the settlement camps, just the usual propaganda from the government about 'places for all' and a new snippet on a Peoples' Charter that the government was producing. The survival forum was very thin now. Most people seemed to have left or were no longer posting, but as I read the recent posts, I got the impression that not everyone was wholly convinced by the new system.

There was some talk of the restrictions of having to apply for specific jobs. People had got used to being independent and a lot of the original forum members had been self-employed; their own bosses. They weren't relishing having to go back to working for someone else. I on the other hand, would be only too happy to get back to work and not have to worry about being responsible for everything.

We had timed it well; the pickup was on the Tuesday and it was Sunday. We still had a lot of stored produce and food. The dry goods would last for years so we cached them in my loft in the plastic crates and hid them under the spare duvets and blankets. However, I didn't want to leave the remaining veg stores and apples to rot in the freezers. In the end, I planted the potatoes in the empty beds and covered them with fleece, just in case I had to come back. I also scattered the remaining carrot seeds from the open pack in the side borders and hand pollinated the apple trees that were just coming into flower. I couldn't believe that all my work preparing the garden was going to go to waste.

I took the remaining squash, carrots, and apples to the garden centre and left them in my wheelbarrow in front of the gates. I tied a brightly coloured scarf to the metal railings and hoped someone was still there to see it. Once that was done, there was only one thing left to do. I was still hoping that Vik and mum would come and find me, so I left messages for them in the kitchen and written on the front door, then I went for one last bike ride around the estate to say goodbye.

Sunday evening Frank and I ate our last meal, we splurged on all the good stuff; we used most of the remaining oil to fry proper chips and ate it with a tinned steak pie we had been saving and at the end of the meal Frank pulled out a surprise from the fridge; A trifle!

'I had a small carton of UHT milk in the larder,' he said, as he spooned it out into two bowls.

'You're amazing Frank,' I said, smiling hugely, I loved trifle. I hoped that the settlement camps had milk and eggs. It was amazing how much it was needed in everyday recipes, cakes, scones, even cereal in the morning. Pre-outbreak I had loved brewing my own rich smooth coffee, drinking it sweet and milky; I had tried to get accustomed to having it black, but it wasn't the same; the strong milky cup we had that evening was the nicest I'd had since the summer. We arranged to meet in the morning, early, by the tunnel under the railway. Then I went back to have my last sleep in my bungalow and say goodbye to my home.

We were lucky; although it was freezing cold, there was very little wind and the sky was clear. It was 6am, the sun wasn't up yet but it was light enough to see and as I walked through Carpenders Park, I said a sad goodbye to all the houses that had become so familiar. I reached the bridge and there was Frank, waiting already.

'Morning,' I said.

'Good morning Zoe, how are you?' he asked.

'Great,' I said, 'it's a beautiful morning. I paused, 'I still can't quite believe we're leaving.'

'I know,' said Frank, 'I've lived here for over fifty years.'

'We can always come back' I said, 'I've locked everything up and turned off the gas and water, the house should be ok.'

'Of course you can,' said Frank, 'But the camp sounds well run and I'm sure we'll meet lots of great people.

'Yeah,' I nodded, 'I'm sure it'll be fine.'

We stepped cautiously through the gloomy tunnel out into South Oxhey but there was no one around. We walked briskly up the road between south Oxhey and Oxhey village, with the golf course either side of us, then along a residential road until we reached a main street into Watford.

The houses were mostly nice detached properties but if you looked closely, you could see the smashed window or door that indicated it had been broken into and ransacked. The junction was blocked with the wreckage of a car crash, people had obviously tried to go round them and been trapped by the metal railings, blocking the road further, and forming lines of abandoned cars in all directions. We turned right looking for the track to the cricket club. It was overgrown but remarkably free of rubbish. It wasn't the path that google had suggested, so I guessed that people leaving London would have used the main streets instead. We reached a small bridge and jinked right onto a footpath that lead us up onto the old dismantled railway line; the Ebury way.

The walking was flat and easy, and within fifteen minutes we had reached Croxley industrial park. I had been a bit worried that people would be camping here, but a quick google search had assured me that apart from the mail delivery office most of the warehouses were small businesses or factories, not food warehouses. Soon the heath appeared on our right and as soon as we could, we crossed inside and stopped for a short break.

The morning sun was rising and, as we sat quietly, drinking from a flask of hot chocolate, rabbits began popping into view. It was a lovely scene, apart from the morning in the snow, I hadn't been out walking since the outbreak. Frank and I sat peacefully, watching the rabbits play. Suddenly the morning quiet was shattered by a series of deep barks and yips. A trio of dogs raced towards the rabbits, following them as they scattered.

We watched as they raced around until, very quickly it seemed, one of the dogs had a rabbit in its mouth. The other dogs quickly ran in until all three were tugging at it. The rabbit was making sharp screaming noises, then it went quiet. Frank and I looked at each other and simultaneously stood to leave. The dogs dropped the rabbit and stared at us.

This did not look good. The dogs were standing over the bloodied corpse and they did not look friendly; their bodies were rigid, tails up but not wagging and as we stood there, one of them began to growl, its lips pulling back to show its very sharp, pointed teeth. We stood unmoving.

'Um Frank, 'I whispered, 'what do we do?'

'Nothing…let's just wait them out.'

We stood there frozen in position, but then a second dog began barking and snapping it teeth. I took a step back. Then another.

'Frank!' I said.

Frank stepped back also, whilst the dogs continued to snap and growl, but then the third dog looked down at the rabbit and picked it up. Immediately the others were distracted. We continued to back away as they worried the rabbit between them. When we reached a path we turned and walked rapidly away, not quite running, but not far off.

At the other side of the heath we climbed the steps up to the footbridge, crossed over a small river and the canal, and then stepped down onto the towpath.

'Feral dogs,' I said shakily.

'I thought you were being overdramatic when you mentioned them,' said Frank.

'I was, I've never seen any evidence of them before,' I swung my walking stick; it seemed rather flimsy 'let's just hope we don't meet any more.'

The weeds hadn't started into growth yet and the towpath was passible. We walked until we could see the railway line above us then started looking for a path to Croxley Green. The map got a bit complicated at this point and we had quite a few false starts, but eventually we found a track that crossed over the railway and we headed up past a large secondary school until we were back on paved roads in the town centre.

The road we needed was straight ahead, beside us loomed a tall stone church with enormous stained glass windows high up in the wall. They were unbroken; an odd sight in this new world, I looked closer and saw that the whole building seemed sound. There was a bench in the garden behind, and although it was in the cold shade, Frank sat for a bit whilst I had a poke around. With the flask lid of hot chocolate in my hand I wandered around the whole building.

It was incredible, all the windows were above head height and the walls reached up at least three stories, dwarfing the surrounding houses, which were not small by any means. The stone arch of the porch had enormous, solid wooden doors behind, and the edges of the building were all thick solid stone; the place was a fortress.

As I made my way round back to Frank, I passed a tiny walled courtyard. The door opened and someone stepped out behind me. I whirled around, but it was a lady, in her late fifties perhaps with greying hair. 'Hello,' she said, 'can we help you?'

'I was just admiring your church,' I replied, my brain racing, 'We were just taking a break on our walk.' I stepped back so that I was now visible to Frank from his seat on the bench.

'Would you like to come in and see the inside?' she asked.

'That's ok,' I said, she seemed harmless, but we were carrying everything most important to us and who knew how many people were inside and what they would do. Frank came up beside me and nodded to her.

'Good morning,' he said, with his impeccable manners 'thank you for your kind offer but my companion and I should be on our way.'

As Frank was speaking, a man appeared at the end of the lane beside us. His waxed jacket looked almost new, but his wellies had mud splashes almost all the way to the top.

'Good morning Anne,' he said to the lady, nodding to Franks and me, 'here are the eggs, some kale from Tony, leeks from Anita, and Judith put in some of her carrot cake.'

He looked at us appraisingly as he passed over the small open crate he was carrying, with an egg box, the veg he had mentioned, and a Tupperware container that looked like it was big enough for at least half of a good sized cake.

'Thank you John,' said the lady, 'These visitors were admiring the church, I was just inviting them in to look around'

I looked at Frank, these people seemed ok and it would be good to talk to others and get a feel for what was going on outside. We had been isolated so long; I had just assumed that society had completely collapsed except for the settlement camps. It looked like I was wrong.

'We wouldn't want to impose,' said Frank, with his most charming smile.

'Not at all, we love having visitors; it's so unusual nowadays to see an unfamiliar face.'

She turned to go back through the door and Frank and I followed. The courtyard was bare except for a narrow stone bench that ran around two sides. In the third was a big iron studded oak door. Anne lifted the latch and the door swung open silently.

Inside the church was split down the middle into two areas; one side filled with dark wooden pews, the other had a long U-shaped table with a white tablecloth that could easily seat thirty. The far end was laid with places for a meal.

'We all try and eat lunch together,' said Anne, indicating the table. 'Meals are much more varied when everyone adds a little something.'

I looked around, there were signs of projects in progress all around, the pews were filled with bric-a-brac; half sorted into piles. In one corner was a half built wooden frame, surrounded by woodworking tools, next to it was a bookcase with books stacked up beside it, ready to be shelved. A pile of knitting sat on a chair, it looked like a church, but also a bit like a junk yard. And over it all the morning sun shone through the east facing stained glass window, spilling colour across the stone walls.

'it's amazing,' I said, 'we're from Carpenders Park, there isn't anything like this on the estate, everyone just slowly disappeared until it was only us left.'

'Oh dear,' said Anne, 'and now you are off too?' It was a subtle probe but not unfriendly.

'The government has set up settlement camps, we're going to the one in the Chilterns so Frank can join up with his family,' I said.

'And you?' she asked, 'do you have family there?'

I thought of Vik and mum, wondered if they were ok, had something bad happened to them? Had they caught the virus or crypto from contaminated water? Were they even still alive?

'I don't know where they are, hopefully they will find me.'

Frank coughed politely, 'I think we really must be going, thank you so much for your time.' I gave one last look at the stained glass window and then we turned and headed out. I had a lot to think about; if these people could function well as a community, then there would be others doing so as well. Maybe we didn't need to stay at the settlement camp, if it didn't work out then at least I would have options.

We walked up the Croxley Green road in silence; 'Perhaps…' I began speculatively 'if we hadn't had the knockers…'

'I don't think so,' said Frank, following my train of thought easily after so much time together, 'we were too spread out and most people didn't know more than their immediate neighbours.'

I wasn't so sure, Carpenders Park had only five or six entrances; if we had worked together, we could have barricaded them and shared resources. Maybe if we had looked after each other, it wouldn't just be me and Frank, walking to the settlement camp.

11

Attacks

At the top of the green, we took the country lane to the west. It was narrow, with high hedges and after ten minutes, houses began to appear. We walked through, staring at the enormous detached houses. It was deserted and somewhat bleak; a reminder that even the wealthiest hadn't been immune from the virus and it's fallout.

The road turned northward and ambled alongside a wood before reaching a T junction. Out to the left were green fields, falling away into the distance, in front of us, a field sloping upward and to the right, a row of red houses. We needed to keep heading north but up ahead was the M25. There were a couple of options, at the red houses we could turn onto a footpath that would take us over a footbridge, or we could continue east on the road and use the much wider crossing further along.

We had debated heavily when we planned the route, Frank was in favour of the car crossing as it was wider. I preferred the footbridge as I felt it would have been less used and less likely to be blocked. We had agreed to postpone the decision until we arrived at the red houses. Now we were here; red brick houses on the right, and on the left was an old flint cottage, it looked very picturesque in the winter sun, but as we paused, debating whether to take the path, dogs began barking from behind us.

We looked at each other and then began to run. Not far, not even a hundred meters, just down past the cottage and up to the hedge to the field. But as we ducked behind the hedge, Frank began to make a weird groaning noise.

'Frank!' I grabbed his arm, shocked at his appearance. He looked grey and there was sweat beading on his forehead. His eyes were closed and his right hand was clutching his left arm. He sank to the ground behind the hedge and began scrabbling in his pockets. 'Frank, what do you need?'

'Spray bottle,' he mumbled. His face scrunched in pain as I quickly searched his jacket pockets. Finally I found it. He took a puff, his hand shaking and falling quickly to the floor. I grabbed the bottle before it rolled away.

Oh god, what had happened? 'What can I do, Frank?' he shook his head and just sat. We waited together and after five minutes he suddenly pulled himself upright a bit more and shook his head. 'Sorry Zoe, my heart isn't as good as it was,' he said, in a voice that was almost normal.

'Do you have some pills or something?' I asked, 'statins or aspirin?'

'I had all sorts, but I've been running low for a while,' he replied.

'Oh Frank, why didn't you tell me, I could have looked out for some.'

Frank gave me a slow look 'I looked, everywhere. I found lots. I had enough for the entire winter.' he paused for a couple of deep breaths, 'I filled it out on the form and the camp has stocks of all the pills I need, plus they have a doctor and can transfer me to a hospital if need be.'

Why hadn't he told me? And then I remembered our long conversations where I had determinedly argued against leaving. I suppose he had been trying to tell me, in his own way. I kicked myself; I had delayed for no good reason, if we had left a couple of weeks earlier we would be there already. I had probably caused untold damage to Frank's heart. I was a science teacher; I knew that a heart attack resulted in heart muscle tissue dying from lack of blood and oxygen.

The dogs had stopped barking and we stayed there a good long while, drinking hot chocolate and eating our mid-morning snack. I debated what to do; should I leave Frank and go alone to get help? Should I go back to the church at Croxley green? We had come more than halfway and had less than five miles to go. We had all day; we could do it very slowly, half a mile then rest, then continue.

I looked at Franks backpack; He wouldn't be able to carry it, and there was too much for me to put it all in mine. 'Frank,' I said, 'How about I set off with your backpack, take it up to the footbridge, and then come back for you?'

Frank nodded tiredly, I could walk a leg with his backpack, stash it, walk back, collect him and my pack, then when we got to the next stop he could rest whilst I moved the backpack to the next place on the map. It would mean I would have to do each leg three times; tripling my distance, but all the cycling and gardening seemed to have made me much fitter.

It was a slog; I would go to the edge of the next field, drop the pack, trudge back to Frank, and then set of again. We took plenty of breaks and Frank didn't look any worse, but it took us almost five hours. I had been tempted by all the cars at the pub we passed near Sarratt but as I hadn't a clue how to start a car without the key, it seemed easier to just keep going.

We were too tired for anything to go wrong; too tired to stop and check for people at the little hamlets we passed. There was a horrible uphill slog by some woods near the end and then the last road seemed to go on forever, between hedgerows and houses. We almost missed the nursery when we got there; it wasn't a garden centre at all but a massive trade nursery behind some houses. I was almost tempted to stay anyway but even in my state, I could see the flickering lights of a TV from the front room of the main house. There were very definitely people here.

We stumbled further down the road, but it was all large detached houses and the open green of the village. Eventually we found a thick hedge and pushed our way into a garden. I set up the tent whilst Frank brewed some tea; I was desperate for a strong coffee but couldn't risk the smell. I blew up my thermarest and got Frank to lie down in the tent, whilst I scouted around.

The house was empty. It joined with the building next door that looked like it might once have been grand old stables but had been modernized recently. The whole plot was almost entirely surrounded by tall brick walls, some very old, the rest recently built. There were also sumptuous new-build houses at the back of the plot, and I could see a swimming pool and Jacuzzi through the French windows of the largest building. Unlike elsewhere, these houses were locked up tight. I was loath to break in, but we needed running water. In the end, I resorted to prying open the French doors that led to the swimming pool, and as I was there, I turned on the Jacuzzi. To my surprise it worked.

I went back to check on Frank who was sleeping soundly. I hovered over him, unsure of what to do...night was falling rapidly and it was getting very cold. We would be better off in the house. I leaned over him and shook his shoulder gently, 'Frank?' I whispered, 'Frank, are you ok?'

'Zoe?' Frank opened his eyes and his face screwed up in pain.

'Frank, we need to move inside' I said.

He sat up slowly, and then crawled out of the tent. He lent heavily on me as we walked round to the house at the back of the plot. I got him settled into a large upstairs bedroom and went to collect our stuff.

When I returned for the final time, I checked the water in the Jacuzzi. It had warmed up nicely and it seemed like the filter was still working as the water was clear and smelt fresh. The temptation proved too much. I deserved a treat.

As I lolled in the Jacuzzi in my spare t-shirt, letting my stiff muscles relax, I wondered what tomorrow would bring. We were about four miles from the pickup point. I could go out early, take Franks pack, return and then we could set out together. I packed up the tent and everything else we wouldn't need next morning into Franks pack. Then I set my phone to wake me at 5am and fell into bed.

Ten hours of solid sleep later I woke stiff and achy but fully rested. I checked on Frank who looked much better, and let him know I was going before slipping out of the building into the night. I had taken a good look at the map before I left; the first part was easy, staying on the main road until I got to a T-junction, then I needed to jink right and then left again. After walking a good few minutes I stopped; I had missed the turning. I backtracked and continued northwest, again missing my turning and only realising when I checked my luminous compass and saw I was now walking southwest.

Luckily the sky was beginning to lighten otherwise who knows how long it would have taken for me to get there, but eventually I arrived at the junction with the A41. I stashed Frank's bag behind the nice big sign that said PICK UP POINT 6, then headed back. The return journey was much quicker but by the time I got back I was ready for breakfast. Frank had tidied up so the place looked immaculate again and had warmed up army ration breakfasts; sausages and beans, I fell on mine in delight and we were ready to leave by nine.

The final leg was much quicker than the previous day, Frank seemed to have regained some of his former strength, but I was careful to keep it slow. It wasn't as sunny and there was a cold wind, so we took fewer breaks but we were there by half ten. By the time we saw the green of the army land rover we were freezing. I had half expected there to be others waiting but we were the only ones there. As they pulled up, a soldier jumped out with a riffle covering us both, looking extremely competent.

He took barely five seconds to ask us our names before he was striding up onto a vantage point and searching into the distance with binoculars.

The driver turned off the engine and got out more slowly. although he was wearing army fatigues and carrying a gun, he was young, he looked like one of my students, although he must have been at least eighteen. Or did the army recruit at sixteen? I could never remember.

He ticked us off a list and patted us down, but only in a cursory sort of way, 'sorry sir, ma'am, but it's just procedure.' Frank collapsed into the back seat and I grabbed our packs and waited in anticipation to see where we would be taken.

We sped down the road for about ten miles and then took a couple of left turns. The signs had been removed but I recognised the area from some Duke of Edinburgh camping trips, we were near Wendover woods. The trees lining the road were stark, not yet in leaf this early in the year and I could see the army base as we passed. Further on there was a new chain-link fence on the left and then we came to a roundabout with a gate across the road and the chain-link fence continuing on the right, parallel to the road. There was a guard at the gate who waved at the soldiers in the land rover and pulled the gate open.

Inside was the settlement camp. I don't know what I was expecting, tents maybe, or barracks-style housing, but it was just a town. It looked familiar…was it Wendover? I was sure I had been here on an expedition with the kids at school. There were residential roads leading into the town centre, but it looked tidier somehow; there weren't the usual post-outbreak weeds and rubbish around. And as we approached the centre, the difference to other towns we had walked through became even more apparent.

It looked like a normal town pre-outbreak; there were people about on the grey streets in the cold wind, scurrying between shops, going in and out with bags full of goods. People were calling out to each other, stopping to exchange news. They turned to stare at us as we passed, curious but not hostile, some with welcoming smiles.

The Land Rover pulled up beside a clock tower and we got out. Beneath the tower was an arched doorway and on the doors was a large round sign; 'Chiltern Camp Parish Council'. One of the soldiers pulled open the right-hand door and we walked into a tiny room with windows round two walls. Most of the space was taken up by a large counter that divided the room into two. Behind it a large bearded man looked up and beamed at us. He stood, 'Welcome to our Chiltern settlement camp. I'm David, have you been here before?'

'No,' I said reflexively, then realised he probably meant had I been to Wendover before, I dithered, should I say something?

'No,' said Frank, as he sank down in a chair by the window. He still looked frail.

David looked concerned and picked up a file from his desk; he opened it and glanced down, paused, then picked up the phone on his desk. He pressed a number on speed-dial. 'Don't worry Frank; we'll get you to a doctor as soon as possible. How are you feeling?' he look up as he spoke, blue eyes gleaming warmly behind round metal framed glasses.

Frank pulled a face 'Ok, I'll be fine once I get my pills.'

I shook my head. 'He had a heart attack on the way here,' I interjected; I hoped it was true that they had hospitals and medical facilities, Frank really needed some proper medical help.

'Oh,' said David, 'It might be best if we take you straight to the medical centre.' he called one of the soldiers over, Frank stood, slowly. The soldier opened the door and stood back, it was the younger soldier and he had an odd look on his face as he ushered Frank back into the land rover. David looked at me appraisingly and glanced down at the file in front of him. He picked up a pen, tapping it on the form. 'Ok, on your form you said you were a science teacher and have some food growing experience?' he phrased it as a question.

'Yes, I used to work in a high school, and I grew some carrots and potatoes last year,' This was a bit of an understatement, but I had grown cautious when talking about food.

'That sounds fine,' said David, looking down at the forms on his desk 'and I see you've been allocated a house in Manor Crescent, which is convenient as it's right next to the school.

Quite nice houses with good sized gardens. As a teacher you will be working for the council, so you'll have the place to yourself.'

To be honest it sounded perfect 'That sounds amazing,' I said 'what's the catch?' I was joking but David looked up sharply.

'There is no catch; we're just providing what the government promised 'A place for everyone." He seemed a little put out.

'It seems fantastic,' I said hurriedly, 'I can't believe how much you've managed to achieve, I'm really grateful to be here.' He seemed mollified, but I was surprised at his reaction. Maybe there *was* a catch somewhere; I would have to look out.

The phone rang and David picked it up, he listened carefully, nodding in response to whatever he was hearing. His features in neutral radiated bonhomie, with ruddy cheeks and crinkles in the corners of his eyes. Eventually he put the phone down and smiled at me, the crinkles deepening. 'That was the receptionist at the medical centre,' he said, 'Frank had been allocated a place in the care home off the high street, but we're going to keep him in the hospital temporarily, whilst the doctors monitor his condition.'

'Great.' I responded, 'How is he doing?'

'It's too early to say, but he'll get the best care there' replied David.

I could feel my shoulders relaxing as some of the tension I had been carrying for the last twenty-four hours drained away.

12

Benefits

I walked over to the house marked on the map. I wasn't expecting very much; I had assumed that the town would be full of refugees like me, and resources would be short, but when I reached the street and checked the address again I looked up at a gorgeous new home. A yellow brick, three-bed, semi-detached property. It was one of the smaller houses on the road, but it fit me perfectly.

I unlocked the door with the key I had been given, and stepped into luxury. The door opened straight into a bright open plan living room with stairs against the far wall. The light oak floor was shiny and clean, and the house smelt fresh with the distinctive odour of furniture polish. There were fresh flowers on the mantelpiece and a huge TV on the wall.

In the kitchen, there were groceries on the table; tea, coffee, sugar, bread, eggs and a small sponge cake, and when I opened the fridge, there was milk and butter. I was in heaven. Upstairs the double bed in the master bedroom was made and the bathroom was pristine. It was perfect. They had even attempted to neaten the garden; the lawn had been trimmed back and although it looked yellow and patchy, I knew it would green up soon.

I opened the back door using the key lying on the kitchen counter. As I stepped out, I could see, only a couple of meters beyond the wooden back fence, there was a chain-link fence that stretched out across the back of the gardens. I was intrigued; the map showed that this was the edge of the town with only fields beyond. What was the extra fence for?

I pulled a patio chair into the sun and sat, stunned by my amazing new home. It was so lovely; did all the new arrivals get such well-kept houses? And who had done all the cleaning and decorating? They had done a remarkably good job. The weak sunshine warmed my face, as I looked around. The garden was north facing but had potential, the area next to the house was a shady patio but the fence at the far end would get full sun most of the day. As I sat making vague plans for flowerbeds, I heard the faint sound of footsteps, which slowly grew louder. They seemed to be coming from behind the fence. I stood up, walked over to the bottom of the garden, and peered through a tiny hole in the wood. Between my garden and the chain-link fence was a narrow alley of trampled down grass and walking along this alley were two soldiers in full uniform, carrying guns. Large guns, rifles perhaps, or automatic weapons. I didn't know what they were, only that they made the soldiers look formidable. I returned to my seat reassured; there would be no knockers here.

After a while, I began to feel the cold and returned indoors. I made a cup of coffee with real milk and slowly ate a piece of the cake as I read my way through the welcome pack David had given me. The largest document was a glossy brochure from the government explaining the 'jobs for all' pledge. It was a nice idea, but I wondered what would have happened if there hadn't been a teaching job going at the school. Would I have had to move to a different camp? Or would I have been given a completely different job? Some of the papers related to the house; there were no bills to pay as everything was provided by the council. It made sense; if I had to pay bills, they would just have to pay me a larger salary to cover my expenses. As it was, I could easily get by on the ten grand salary that went with the job.

I really wanted to go online to check in with the guys on the forum. I took a last gulp of coffee and moved to the living room, I hadn't seen a computer on my quick tour, but there must be one. I searched the house, going back through the rooms checking all the cupboards and drawers, but there was nothing, not even a laptop or tablet. That was odd. How would I do my planning for work? I sat back at the kitchen table and looked through the notes I had been given; maybe the school would issue one. The pack did indeed contain a list; the school would issue stationery, calculators, and planners, but it didn't mention a laptop anywhere. I shrugged in annoyance and pulled out my phone. I clicked on the internet but only got a blank page; there was no signal. It looked like the outer world would have to wait for an update.

The doorbell rang. I froze for a second and then relaxed… I was in the camp and safe from knockers. I walked out of the kitchen and through the large windows in the lounge could see a smiling woman, waving at me. I opened the door.

'Hi,' I said rather warily.

'Welcome to Manor Crescent!' she replied 'We've all been so excited to have a new arrival'

She thrust out the dish she was holding, and I automatically caught it.

'Uh, thanks,' I said, 'would you like to come in?'

I stepped back, into the house and looked down at the dish; it looked like a pie of some sort.

'It's apple pie' she said, seeing my look, 'made from the apples from our tree.'

I loved apple pie. 'Thank you,' I said, 'I'm Zoe.'

'Oh, yes, I forgot to introduce myself, 'I'm Irina.' she replied. She had black curly hair and guileless eyes and looked about eighteen, but I guess she must have been older.

I ushered her in and we sat down in the living room. I was still in my waterproofs and fleece, and felt a little self-conscious when I compared myself to her casual elegance; a soft cream jumper and figure hugging jeans.

'Would you like some tea or coffee?' I asked, trying my manners back on to see if they still fit.

'Oh, no thank you, I won't stay,' she said, 'I just wanted to say hi, and welcome you to the neighbourhood. It's always exciting when someone new arrives.'

'That's very kind of you,' I said, 'have there been many new arrivals?'

'Oh yes' she replied, 'well, we only arrived a couple of months ago,' she smiled reminiscently 'My husband and I. We were so grateful to reach somewhere normal again. I felt just like you probably do, excited and a little overwhelmed,' I nodded, 'but don't worry, everyone is very friendly' she said, leaning forward and looking earnest.

'Thank you, that's good to know,' I paused and there was a little awkward moment whilst I dug around for something to say. 'The house is really lovely,' I finally said, 'did yours look this good when you arrived?'

Irina looked around and I saw her eyebrows lift just a little. 'The kids did a really good job on this place,' she said, 'ours wasn't quite in such good shape, but I suppose they didn't have as many workers back then.'

So many questions… 'The kids?' I asked.

'Yes... the kids sometimes do chores... for extra credit.' She paused looking suddenly uncertain, 'Anyway I ought to get going, I just wanted to stop in and say hi.' She stood and I followed, 'Please feel free to knock if you need anything, we're just next door.' She pointed to the left and beamed at me.

I smiled back and walked her out. I closed the door behind her and watched from my window as she walked away. I was pleased that the neighbours seemed friendly, but didn't really want people popping over all the time. I wasn't exactly great at small talk and unless she was a keen gardener, I didn't think we would have much in common.

I took the apple pie into the kitchen and sat down again with the welcome pack. I read through some short leaflets on refuse and recycling schedules, library opening hours and services, and the shops and how to pay for goods. This last leaflet was very interesting. It seemed they had discarded normal currency and were using a special settlement camp currency called the Chiltern pound. There was no physical currency; instead, I had been issued an account, which I could access on special terminals in the library, and a card to pay for things in the shops.

I had been up early and walked a lot of miles already, but after a deliciously simple lunch of fried eggs and toast (with butter!) and another strong cup of coffee I decided to go out and explore. The first thing I did was to walk round to the school. It seemed ok; a sprawling site of large interconnecting buildings made of red brick. Very clean and tidy and quiet.

I walked down to the main road, popping into the local Tesco to pick up some fresh food. I was astonished to see that they had a range of ready meals and even fresh fish and chicken. There wasn't any red meat but to have chicken and fish was a small miracle in itself. I wondered where they were getting it. Was there a camp by the sea somewhere, trading fish for whatever it was that grew in the surrounding fields? Was there a factory producing ready meals and shipping them out across the country to the settlement camps?

There weren't any prices on the produce, which I found strange, but as it was my first day and I was celebrating, I decided to treat myself. I used my payment code to buy a rainbow trout, some new potatoes, and some cereal. I took the food home so the fish wouldn't spoil, then went out again. I walked down the high street, popping into the library and admiring the rather large collection of fiction and romance novels. As I was there, and there was a terminal free, I logged on using the code in my welcome pack. Hopefully, I could get online and talk to the group.

A screen with just a couple of option boxes appeared; payment account, member requests and council notices. It seemed that the terminal only had limited functionality. I clicked on payment account and was shocked to see that the food this morning had cost over thirty Chiltern pounds. With no house bills or rent, I had thought that my salary of £10,000 was perfectly adequate, but if food was going to be so expensive, then it might not be as generous as I had thought.

I exited the library slowly, walking down to the cricket club and out along the fields until I was blocked by a gate across the road. I stood staring through the gate for a second; either side was the same chain link as behind my house. I pulled out the map and worked out where I was. I had started up at the north east corner of the town and was now right on the southern point. The chain link fence must circle the entire town. If I hadn't known how easy it was to get through chain link fence, I would probably have felt very reassured by the wall. As it was, I turned back and walked up past a pub and a preschool where I could hear children shrieking with laughter. At the roundabout I turned toward the station but the station road was blocked off with more chain-link gates and soldiers.

They were the first sign of the army I had seen within the town, but they seemed approachable and smiled as I slowed to a halt. The train service at Carpenders Park had slowly fizzled out sometime during the first couple of weeks of the outbreak. But the presence of soldiers indicated that perhaps trains here were still running.

'Hi,' I said, as I looked up at the soldier who towered over me, 'Can I ask you something?'

'Of course Ma'am, how can I be of assistance?' he replied. He had no obvious weapon, although I imagined that with his physique, he would be able to deal with most forms of trouble without breaking much of a sweat.

'Are the trains working?' I asked.

'They have some special trains running, to move goods around the country,' he replied, 'unfortunately they don't have a passenger service yet, but hopefully that will appear sometime soon.' he smiled, and I was struck again at the niceness of everyone here. They all seemed so pleasant and friendly.

'Thank you' I said. I was surprised and pleased, I had assumed that movement around the country would be impossible, but if there were trains then it might be possible to one day visit my cousins near Newcastle, or friends in Yorkshire and Scotland.

I turned away and, back at the roundabout, took the next left, walking for about ten minutes along a residential road. It was long and tree lined, with large houses of varied design. There were smaller streets running off it to the left and right, all with neat grass verges. It was all very civilised. There were signs of life in many of the houses, the only jarring note was the bare driveways; there seemed to be an absolute absence of cars.

The road curved, so I took a footpath to the right and up another long road, eventually meeting a large street, this looked like the main artery into town. Walking south, I came to a petrol station and then the health centre, where Frank was.

I walked into the foyer and over to the reception desk. The staff bustling around looked professional and competent and the young girl at the desk, no more than twenty or so, turned to me almost immediately.

'Hi there, how can I help you?' she asked, blonde hair bobbing as she spoke.

'Hi' I replied, 'my friend Frank was brought in this morning, can I see him? How is he doing?'

The receptionist glanced down at the clipboard. 'Oh yes, the nurse left a note that he wasn't to be disturbed. I'm very sorry.'

'Is he ok?'

'Yes he's fine,' she replied, he's just resting right now'

I looked around; the health centre seemed well resourced and organised; at least the small area I could see from reception. I could come back later.

'Can I leave a message?' I asked.

'Sure' she handed me a pen and a post-it. I scribble a quick note, saying how wonderful my new home was and that I hoped he felt better soon. Frank and I had been looking after each other for so long that if felt weird leaving him to someone else, but it looked like he was in good hands. I exited through the automatic glass doors then I took the next left, back up to the school and my new home.

I unpacked and opened the closets. I had only the clothes I had arrived in but, when I opened the cupboards in my new bedroom, I found a whole new wardrobe. Some of the millions of forms we had filled out online had asked for our body measurements and I could see that everything on the hangers and shelves in front of me seemed to be in my size. There was a rather nice black suit for work, I couldn't tell if it was brand new, but it certainly looked in perfect condition. There were also a rail of stark white shirts, which I didn't much like; I preferred to wear colourful T-shirts or polo neck jumpers under the jackets of suits, but I certainly wasn't going to make a fuss. For casual wear, there were jeans and thick jumpers, but no dresses or skirts, which I thought was odd. Not that I would wear dresses, but I liked the comfort of a long skirt, especially in the summer.

I would buy some more casual wear later; in the meantime I found a pair of pyjamas to lounge around in and went to watch TV while I waited for dinner. I flicked through the channels; all the programs were re-runs, but it was relaxing and mindless and I settled in to a pleasant evening.

13

Questions

The school day started at 9am, so I arrived at eight hoping that they were expecting me. I waited at reception nervously, trying to work out why the school felt so cold. Eventually it came to me; there was no artwork on the wall, no posters or photos, nothing celebratory at all.

The headmaster of the school, Gordon McAteer, seemed to be like most headmasters; piercing glance, firm handshake, busy. He gave a quick welcome speech: 'We're glad to have your expertise, we've missed having a science teacher, hope you settle in ok, please come to me if you need anything…' and then a second teacher, introduced as 'James, my irreplaceable deputy,' took me off for a tour round the school.

James had a little more personality than the head. He had a dry wit, explaining that the students were a little challenging, especially those that had come from outside.

'Does that mean there are students that were living here when the outbreak occurred?' I asked, 'people for whom the camp was their home before?'

James looked a little disconcerted, 'Ah, um, yes,' he replied, 'most of the original residents now home school their children, but about half the current cohort were studying here pre-outbreak. We try not to discriminate between the two groups.'

'And were you a teacher here before the outbreak?' I asked.

'No, none of us were, it's a fresh start,' replied James, as he walked briskly on. He opened a door to a large hall 'this is the gym, and also where we hold assemblies….'

A fresh start…I wondered why they had needed that, had the school been that bad, pre-outbreak? I would have to check Ofsted as soon as I could get online. There hadn't been a computer at the house, but I could no doubt use the computer in my lab. 'So where are the science labs in relation to where we are?' I asked.

James paused for a second. 'We don't use the labs as such; the students have fixed rooms. Apart from assembly and lunch they stay in those rooms all day and the teachers rotate amongst them, switching lessons when the bell goes.'

I frowned, I hated moving between rooms, it was hard to set up lessons, and even harder to keep track of where everything was. 'Do the kids behave during the gap- the time after one teacher leaves and before the next arrives?' I asked.

'Oh yes, we have teaching assistants who deal with discipline issues.' He said it so confidently that I was reassured, it was very different to what I was used to, but I was sure it would work out. I relaxed slightly; it would be great not having to deal with behaviour all day long.

The school only had about ninety students; in a building designed for a thousand, I could see why they had changed the system. They had two classes for each year group, so the classes were tiny, some only had six or seven students, others had ten or twelve. The only time they were all together was in assembly, which, oddly, occurred every morning and seemed mostly to involve listing students involved in work projects.

My timetable had me teaching only three lessons a day, but I had to create the resources from scratch. I had been looking forward to creating a new, more relevant syllabus; focussing on human biology, ecology, growing food, exploring the physics of things like bridges and boats and solar power, and discovering the chemistry of water and how it is treated to make it clean. I wanted to make it more relevant and useful, so students would finish school with a good basic understanding of things they would need to know, rather than cramming their brains with tons of knowledge that they would immediately forget.

Instead, I was given another government pamphlet, this time with a science curriculum explained in excruciating detail. The instructions were clear, I was to teach the specification, and at the end of the year, the students would be tested. It was expected that they would all pass. I read it and winced, it was enormous and full of dry facts. There wouldn't be time for experiments or discussions or exploring topics in depth, just to get through the content would require every minute of every lesson to be spent transferring information.

The rest of that day, I shadowed the maths teacher. She was good, but she also had a syllabus to get through and I could see that a lot of the students just weren't getting it, the lessons moved on too quickly. The teaching assistant at the back of the room didn't seem to help much; in fact, he didn't work with the students at all, just wrote up notes, and took kids out when they began fidgeting too much. I could hear him shouting at them through the door and sat wincing. I knew some schools pre-outbreak that had believed in zero tolerance, but this was something else.

The next morning I went into school, ready to teach. Oddly there weren't any computers in the classrooms, so no

PowerPoints or videos during the lesson; just old fashioned 'chalk and talk' as it was called – using the board for explanations and writing tables for the students to copy and fill in. I had planned lessons that would be as interesting as possible with such limited resources, and was glad to start with a class of the youngest kids, aged 11 or 12. They were sweet and friendly and I knew the lesson would go ok. However, the teaching assistant for the class made me nervous. His name was Malcolm and when I entered the classroom, I could see the glower on his face as he looked at me. The lesson was going well and the children were involved and interested. We had a real buzz going and they began calling out answers. Almost immediately, Malcolm was standing beside them frowning. I stopped, and walked over.

'It's ok Malcolm,' I said, 'a little bit of calling out when they are enthused and engaged is alright. I allow it in my classroom.

He frowned at me, 'But the school doesn't.' he replied dourly.

I was speechless. I wasn't used to being challenged in my own classroom, but maybe this was what having a behaviour specialist was like. I turned back to the class and was relieved when the bell went.

During lunch, I was sitting in the staffroom, looking through the work the students had done in class. I was pleased; they had produced some nice work and it looked like they had followed the lesson pretty well. I looked up from the books as James came in through the door and walked straight towards me, 'so… Malcolm says you are having some trouble with the behaviour of year 7?' he enquired.

I was taken aback, 'No, not at all, they were a delight to teach, they were so enthusiastic; they just forgot to put their hands up occasionally.'

'Hmm, well if you can't cope, let us know and we'll provide some extra support until you get them under control,' replied James, 'we prefer things to be calm and orderly here, it gives the students stability.' He paused and looked out of the window, 'and when a teacher can't control the class it removes that stability.' He looked back at me and smiled, but I felt alarmed. How had I managed to give such a bad impression on my first day?

'I'm sorry, I was just trying to get them involved,' I said, 'I'll make sure they put their hands up tomorrow.'

After lunch, I had a year 11 class; 15 and 16 year olds, who I was supposed to prepare for exams. I knew nothing about them and was slightly anxious. I arrived at the classroom before the students and introduced myself to the teaching assistant, Jonathan. He smiled reassuringly; dressed in a grey suit, and with a firm handshake, he looked stern but fair. I felt relieved; between us, we should probably be able to handle any behaviour problems. The bell went and I stood at the door as the students came in. They immediately split into two groups, some at the front, others right at the back with a gap in the middle. This was typical; the naughty kids would always try and sit at the back. I would let it slide for now, just see what they were like. I took the register, writing the names on a seating plan and started the lesson with a sketch of the digestive system. My drawing was basically just a squiggly line, starting at the mouth and ending at the rectum. I began writing the first label but was arrested by a muffled giggled, coming from the front of the class. I glanced sharply over my shoulder to see a lanky, slightly dishevelled boy with overly long hair grinning at me. I checked the seating plan.

'Alex,' I said, humour in my voice, 'shall we agree that I can't draw, and get on with the lesson?' it was true, my diagrams were pretty awful, but they got the information across. Alex sobered up quickly and looked over his shoulder.

'Sorry Miss,' he said quietly, as Jonathan looked up sharply from the back of the room.

I turned back to the board, only to be interrupted again, this time by whispers behind me as I wrote. I looked back, but the front row were all quiet, diligently copying the diagram. Instead it was the kids at the back this time, two girls giggling and whispering, and surely those were phones in their hands? I looked at Jonathan but he didn't even raise his head. I checked the seating plan.

'Sophie and Imara, please could you hold up your books.' I said.

'Why?' came the response from Sophie.

'I'd like to check you are doing the work.' I replied, still with the same light tone and slight smile.

The two girls looked at each other and then held up their books. From where I was, they looked completely blank. I looked at Jonathan but he was still not paying any attention.

'Perhaps you would like to sit closer, so you can see the board,' I said, 'you are supposed to be labelling the digestive system.' My tone was slightly cooler but not antagonistic. I didn't know anything about these kids and there might be a reason they weren't writing.

'Thanks, but we're fine.' said Sophie.

'Yeah, we're ok here, aren't we sir?' added Imara, looking across at Jonathan.

'Yes you're fine' he said, not even looking at them, he finally raised his head but it was me he frowned at, 'Miss, please carry on.' He returned to writing in his notebook as I stared at him nonplussed. I looked around the class and from the front row got a tiny shake of the head from the girl sitting next to Alex. She looked at me with a worried gaze; her big grey eyes trying to send me some sort of message. I looked back at the two girls, determined to get control of the classroom, but was interrupted from the front; the girl next to Alex had put her hand up. I check the seating plan.

'Yes Freya?' I asked.

'Please Miss,' she said, 'what's the word below the pancreas?'

I looked at her speculatively, had she interrupted me on purpose? It definitely seemed like she had. I turned to the board to complete the diagram, answering her as I did so. There were undercurrents in the classroom and I needed to find out a bit more about the teaching assistants' role before I challenged the status quo. Otherwise, I would end up with another reprimand from James.

After work, I went to visit Frank, but yet again, I was turned away at the door. I walked down the high street feeling low. It was almost dark already. I did my usual route around town, but at the train station, the friendly soldier had been replaced. 'Ma'am you shouldn't be out at night, we prefer that camp civilians stay at home during the evening,' he said frowning, his hand shifting grip on the automatic gun hanging across his chest.

I stepped back, alarmed. This was news to me, nothing in any of the literature I had been given had mentioned a curfew. I began to feel the stirrings of apprehension. This was not turning out as I had hopped. The house was nice, but the job was throwing up some issues, and although I had been given clothes and household goods, the cost of food was prohibitive…And now it appeared I couldn't even walk where I wanted. I just hoped Frank was getting the care he needed.

In the staffroom the next day, I sat on the edge of a group of teachers and soon enough, the maths teacher asked how I was getting on.

'It's okay,' I said, 'but I'm a bit confused about the teaching assistants, and why there is such a distinct split between the kids at the back and the front.'

'Ah' said Stephen, the English teacher, 'I was puzzled too when I arrived, but it makes sense. The school used to get the most trouble from the refugee kids, so that's why the teaching assistants focus on their behaviour.'

'But they sit at the front and work hard,' I said.

'They sit at the front to be as far away from the teaching assistant as possible,' said Stephen with a laugh, 'not because they're interested in learning.'

'Well I found them much quieter than the kids sitting at the back.' I said.

'Yeah, they're used to being on their own,' he replied, 'they don't talk much because they have trust issues.'

'Oh?' I said.

Stephen continued looking intent, 'what you have to realise is that these kids were out on their own, looking after themselves for months and months. They resent being told what to do and don't really want to be in school. That's why we have to be strict with them.'

I thought back to my interactions with Alex and Freya, at the work the front row of kids had diligently completed, and then compared it to Sophie and Imara and the others at the back. In the end, the two girls had written just the date and the title, nothing else.

'So what should I do if the kids at the back don't do the work?' I asked.

'The original residents' kids? They've probably covered the topic already. I would leave them be, their parents have their education under control and wont thank you for interfering.'

There were a couple of rueful nods and murmurs of agreement from the other teachers. This was sounding worse and worse. There seemed to be a distinct discrimination against the refugee kids going on, and it looked like I was expected to teach with half the kids ignoring me.

The bell sounded and I walked to the year 11 classroom, Should I do what Stephen had suggested, and ignore the lack of work done by the kids at the back? It went against the grain, but everyone had seemed in agreement that it was a waste of time trying to discipline them. And James had made it clear that the teaching assistants dealt with all behaviour issues.

The year 11 students were sitting at their desks by the time I arrived.

'Books out,' I said, 'the title is Enzymes.' I looked along the front, Alex and Freya had their heads down, writing, along with the two kids next to them; Ruth and Mark, but the pair of pretty blonde girls behind them were whispering.

'Taz and Leila,' I said, 'please stop talking now and write the title.'

'I've written it already,' said Taz.

'Shhh,' said Leila, clutching her arm.

Jonathan stood up, 'Taz! Outside!' His voice cracked like a whip, and Taz sprang up, and was out of her seat and outside the door so fast I barely had time to see the look of dismay on her face. Jonathan slowly followed and I could hear him beginning to reprimand her as I called the register.

Leila silently pushed Taz's book forward slightly and looked at me. I leaned over my desk, sure enough, there was the date and title, neatly written and underlined. Jonathan's voice got louder. He was almost shouting now, his sharp voice sending words through the door. I heard him say 'ungrateful' and 'lazy', and had enough. I hadn't asked him to take Taz outside and she hadn't done anything wrong. I had made a mistake.

I set the first task and walked to the door. Opening it, I popped my head around I looked at Jonathan and Taz. 'That's enough, Taz, please come in now.'

'I'm not done.' said Jonathan, dismissively. 'She answered you back and needs to be reminded why that is unacceptable.'

'Well I need her in class to do the work; perhaps you could do this later.' I said, opening the door wide and ushering her to come in.

Taz looked at me, then at Jonathan and back at me. She hesitantly stepped towards the doorway, and when Jonathan was silent, walked through, hurrying back to her desk. I smiled nervously at Jonathan and waited for him to enter. I could see why he was in charge of behaviour; he looked intimidating and unyielding. He shook his head.

'You're too soft on them,' he said.

'I'm sure you'll help me toughen up.' I replied, I hoped my tiny act of defiance wouldn't be reported to James. I would have to be extra careful in class. I didn't want a repeat of what had just happened.

Every morning as I left my house for work, Irina would be doing the same, waving and wishing me good morning. Every evening I would come home, eat dinner and then try to visit Frank. Every day I had been turned away. If felt a bit like I was stuck in a time loop. It was time to break out and do something different. It seemed that if I really wanted to see him, I would need to be more than just persistent. So on Saturday I set my alarm for 5am and walked over to the medical centre. I took my torch and my multi-tool and walked round the whole building, peering in through windows and trying all the doors. They were all locked.

I waited in the dark, invisible in my navy waterproofs, hoping that someone would take a smoking break or something, like they do in films, so I could slip in behind them, but nothing so dramatic happened. I just got steadily colder and colder until the sky lightened and the morning dawned. I tried again at the front desk, kicking up a bit of a fuss, and asking to see a manager but got nowhere. In the end, I stopped, as the receptionist was starting to look a bit scared and I felt bad.

Instead, I went home, had some breakfast, changed into non-threatening jeans and a baggy jumper, and went back to the Parish office. David was still there but this time he frowned when he saw me. 'You've been disturbing the staff at the medical centre I hear,' he said, 'what's the problem?'

I was surprised he knew so much, but shouldn't have been, I had seen how organised they were when I arrived.

'I would like to see Frank, we've been here over a week and nobody will let me see him,' I said.

'Ok, let me check it out for you,' he picked up the phone and speed-dialled. 'I have a query about a Frank Tipson, came in last week Tuesday…' he listened intently and then looked up at me inscrutably. 'ok… uh huh… well that wasn't handled very well,' he said. He listened further then said, 'I'll take care of it, but next time you need to inform everyone on the council, not just Doctor Peterson.' He rang off and looked at me again.

'Why don't you sit down,' he said, indicating the chairs lining the wall as he moved round the counter towards me. He looked at me as we sat, 'I'm very sorry Zoe, but Frank didn't make it through that first night, he had another heart attack and passed away in the early hours of the morning.'

I stared stunned, I had been going there every day and all the time he had already been dead? 'But why didn't they tell me?' I asked, 'I was there, every day, they said he was resting…'

David shook his head in sympathy, 'Well, we have a counsellor who informs the patient's family, and Frank had listed his nephew as his next of kin. He was informed Wednesday morning and the cremation was last Friday.'

I still didn't understand 'but why didn't they tell me?' I asked again, 'the receptionist saw me every day and said nothing.'

'The receptionist isn't allowed to pass on information like that, as I said, it is the counsellors job to do so.' David looked slightly annoyed for a second 'I will definitely bring this up at the next parish meeting, it shouldn't have happened and I'm very sorry.'

I didn't know what to say so in the end I said nothing. I stood up, 'Thanks for your help, David,' I said, as I left. I went home. I climbed the stairs and sat in the smallest bedroom, which I had turned into an office. I stared out over the garden to the fields beyond. Frank was dead, the whole journey had been for nothing; he hadn't even met his family before he died. Tears prickled at my eyes and I sat there a long time as they rolled down onto my cheeks. Ever so often I lifted an arm and scrubbed them away with my sleeve, but they kept falling. He couldn't be gone.

Sunday I woke up and cried. I ate breakfast and cried, and then I went for a walk. I avoided crying on the walk but as I passed the health centre, I started to feel a new emotion; anger. Frank had been fine when we arrived, he'd had a heart attack on the way, yes, but with the right medical attention he should have been ok. What was going on in that place? Why had they let me think my friend was alive for a full eleven days after his death? What sort of place was so strictly controlled that they couldn't tell people someone had died?

I recalled my encounters with the staff, they had been efficiently polite, I had thought, but looking back, their silence had been odd, especially that last morning. Why had she looked scared? I wasn't that intimidating. My feet halted as I decided to go in.

'Good morning,' I said to the receptionist, who was the same one who had been on duty the day before. 'I'm very sorry about yesterday.'

'That's ok,' she responded, the apprehensive look on her face switching to relief. 'I fully understand.'

I looked around the reception area, 'Is there any way I could see the doctor who was treating Frank?' her smile faded 'or perhaps the nurse who spoke to him last?' I put on my most pleading smile.

'No, sorry' she said, 'look you can't, you need to go, you're going to get me in trouble again.'

'What?' I said, I looked at her in puzzlement; she had that scared look again. 'Who can I ask then?'

Her response wasn't what I was expecting. She looked around, but the room was empty, even so, she leaned forward across the counter and whispered 'You're a teacher, ask the kids at the school, they know.'

I stared for a second, then turned and walked out. Why would the kids know? And how did she know I was a teacher? Was there no privacy around here? I walked slowly home, something was going on, I could feel it, and I had no backup plan, no secret way out, nothing to keep me safe.

14

Help

I settled into my teaching timetable, working hard to curb some of my natural enthusiasm and make my lessons calmer and more orderly. To be honest I thought they were boring, but James came in to observe and said I was improving nicely.

After the receptionist's cryptic statement, I thought carefully about which student to ask. I spent a week looking around during lessons, trying to suss out what the kids were like. I needed someone who had their eyes open. I debated asking Freya; she had helped me in my first lesson with the class, but during break times I had often seen her talking with Alex or the other kids. I needed someone who I thought would keep my questions to themselves.

The year 11 class were learning about ionic bonding; I had set them the task of drawing the electronic structure of the first twenty elements, boring and repetitive, but required. I circled the room and when I reached the quietest and most inscrutable of the refugee kids, I crouched down to look at her work. 'Ruth, I need help' I said quietly.

I continued to look at her work as she turned her head to look directly at me. Everything this kid did was purposeful and thought out. She was small with light brown hair drawn back in a ponytail, her skin was pale from winter, but she had freckles across her nose. She wore the school uniform, grey trousers, white shirt, and burgundy blazer. She looked unremarkable but in lessons, I had glimpsed a quick intelligence and her occasional comments conveyed a great deal of worldly experience. I looked back at her, but she made no response. I looked down at her work, put a couple of ticks, and moved on. I hadn't really expected a response, not with the enforcer, Jonathan, in the room, watching everything and making notes.

After school, on my evening walk, at the northernmost end of the route up by the grid of residential streets, I found myself walking behind two youths. I almost didn't recognise them in normal clothes, but it was Ruth and Mark. They looked older out of uniform and were walking slowly; deliberately slow in fact. I wasn't speeding along, but even so, I was drawing closer. They timed it so I caught up just as we reached the small footpath that cut between two roads. They paused on the footpath, half-turning.

'Hi,' I said, not knowing what else to say.

'What do you want?' said Mark, taking his hands out of his pockets and turning to face me full on. It was an aggressive stance, with very little of his usual polite student demeanour. I was taken aback, but quickly recovered.

'I need to know what's going on and someone said to ask the kids in the school. I picked you Ruth, because you look like you know.' I spoke to Ruth rather than to Mark. He might be bigger than both of us, but I knew who was in charge.

'Where did you come from?' asked Ruth.

'Carpenders Park, near Watford,' I said, 'I would have stayed there, but Frank's family was here.'

'Who's Frank?' she asked.

I paused, thinking carefully before speaking, trying to frame my words to capture our relationship. 'Frank was eighty-four and also lived in Carpenders Park...He and I became friends over the autumn and winter, and we travelled here together... Frank died the night we arrived.'

'Oh,' she said, there was a wealth of comprehension in her voice. 'How much do you know?'

'Nothing! I don't know anything,' some of my frustration was leaking through. I swallowed. 'I need to know what's going on. Why does this place feel wrong? Why is the school so strict? What's with the soldiers at the gates? Why does it feel like they are watching me all the time?' It all came out as an incoherent muddle. Stumbling and stuttering, I ground to a halt.

I stared at them in mute appeal but got nothing back but a nod. 'You have good questions; we're not supposed to have the answers. We'll check back with you.' with that Ruth stepped back and then they both turned and walked briskly away. The encounter was over. I had no answers and a whole load of new questions. Had I made a mistake asking her for help? But my gut told me no. Besides, I needed to trust someone.

I watched them disappear out of sight ahead and wandered slowly home, 'we're not supposed to have the answers' she had said, as if she did, but was wary of telling me. What type of trouble could she get in for just answering questions?

I had to wait until the next week to find out. Both Ruth and Mark gave me no indication during class that they wanted to talk so I left them alone. I continued to teach and began to reach out to the other teachers, hoping to make some connections. I was cheerful and friendly, and every afternoon, in the meetings that seemed to proliferate the timetable, I made copious notes and made sure to ask relevant questions to show I was listening. In truth, I would have been driven out of my mind with boredom if I hadn't been assiduously writing, occasionally breaking off to draw vines and flowers in the margins during pauses in the tedious explanations of policy and procedure. However, I must have impressed the headmaster, Gordon, because he walked over one morning as I was prepping my lessons.

'Good Morning Zoe,' he said, peering over my shoulder, 'how is it going?'

'Fine, thank you, Sir,' I replied.

'You seem to be very diligent in your preparations,' he said, 'it's a work ethic, we appreciate.'

'Thank you, Sir,' I said, feeling simultaneously patronised and pleased. I worked hard, and I liked it to be recognised.

'There was some trouble when you arrived, I recall,' he said, 'but things seemed to have worked out nicely.'

'I like the efficiency, Sir,' I said, 'how well-organised everything is.' It was true, it was one of the things that had most impressed me when I arrived. I didn't need to add that I found the restrictions stifling and the meetings mind-numbingly dull.

'That's good,' he replied, slightly absentmindedly as he looked around at the rest of the teachers His gaze focussed back on me 'We need people to step forward and take positions of responsibility within the school,' he said, 'we're looking for someone to administer the exams and analyse the data produced.' He smiled as if conferring a favour.

I winced internally, that would be an enormous job, the extra administration alone would eat up all my free periods, and I knew that senior leadership in schools were apt to ask for reports at very short notice. If I accepted, I would be opening myself up to working even later into the evenings and weekends. However, it was important that I kept on the good side of management here, and if I had a position of responsibility, I would naturally be associating more with people in charge and might therefore find out more.

'Of course,' I said, 'I would be glad to help.'

Gordon, nodded, pleased, 'Excellent, I'll set that in motion.' He turned abruptly and I wondered how soon I could get out of there.

The forms for the new job arrived the next day. The school receptionist handed them to me with a smile.

'Moving up in the world I see,' she said. The receptionist doubled as the headmasters PA and was part of the inner circle of management. There were several forms, but also a letter detailing a significant pay rise. I was impressed; I hadn't negotiated a pay increase and therefore hadn't expected it.

When I did eventually get a miniscule nod from Ruth, I was ready. I'd had a week to clarify my questions. Although I had lots of minor questions; about the school, the source of all the resources, the council, at heart all I wanted to know was whether it was worth staying.

As we stood on the same footpath, Mark handed me one of the town maps. He indicated the allotments at the northern edge of the town. 'All the students are expected to work in the allotments after school and Saturday mornings,' he said, 'can you find a pretence to meet us there?'

'I could bring some seeds,' I said, 'I have spare packets.'

'No, don't do that,' said Ruth quickly, 'seeds are like gold-dust, keep them,' she paused, 'and don't let anyone see that you have them,' she added.

'Perhaps I could ask for compost to make some raised beds in my garden?'

'Perfect,' said Ruth, 'we have plenty, left over from autumn.' she looked around, flashed a rare smile and they both quickly walked away.

I wanted to set up Saturday so I would be above suspicion, so at lunch, I made a point of engaging Stephen, the English teacher, in conversation. He had been open and informative before, and was also a keen gardener. We had already exchanged several reminiscences about dahlias and other plants we had grown pre-outbreak, and I knew that although it was still only the middle of March, he had begun working on his garden.

'Stephen,' I called, as he passed by with his tray of food from the canteen, 'Can I ask a question?'

He detoured around a sofa and took a seat next to me at the table. 'Of course, what's up?'

'I'm thinking of setting up some raised beds on the patio, I'd like to make a shady fern garden,' I said. 'Do you know where I could get some compost to improve the chalky soil?'

'Good idea,' he said, suddenly enthusiastic, 'I don't think anyone has tried a fern garden yet; you should be able to get a wide variety of plants from the surrounding houses.'

'And the compost?' I asked again.

'Oh, that's easy…the allotments have loads.' He took a bite of his sandwich and after a pause continued, 'You need a permit from the council, and they need to approve your gardening project, but David is pretty laid back about issuing them.'

I finished my last gulp of coffee, 'Great' I said, with a large smile, 'thanks so much.'

In the afternoon I got permission to leave at 4pm….I didn't really need to, but James had a habit of making snarky remarks if he noticed someone had left before five, even though he knew that everyone worked late into the evenings at home.

I walked briskly down to the clock tower. David was behind the counter as always and greeted me with a jovial bonhomie that was new to our dealings. 'So I hear great things about you,' he said with a huge grin, 'helping the school, making friends, Gordon is very complimentary about your skills.' I smiled weakly. I wasn't quite sure where this was going.

'So… have you thought about coming to some council meetings?' he continued, 'we would appreciate someone with your talents.'

…And mouldability I thought, I had been pretending to be utterly compliant and it seemed to be paying dividends.

'Wow, really?' I said, trying not to overdo the enthusiasm. 'I'd love to help if I can, everything is working out so well here,' I paused 'I feel bad about Frank, but to be honest, I hadn't known him for that long, it was just the uncertainty that made me upset.'

David seemed to buy it. His smile, if anything, grew wider. 'So, what can I help you with today?' he asked.

I blinked; I had expected him to know already. 'I wondered if I could get some compost from the allotments' I said, 'I'd like to make some raised beds in the garden.'

David picked a form from the top of his pile…was it just coincidence that it was there? Or had he had it ready…did he know what I was there for? I was getting paranoid.

He spent a few seconds filling it in and then signed it and passed it across the counter. 'There you go, good luck with the fern garden,' he said, confirming that someone had passed on my conversation with Stephen.

'Thanks,' I said. I paused, hand on the form, 'David, if I wanted to go back, to pick up some seeds and plants from my garden back in London, would that be possible?'

'David's smile grew fixed, 'I'm sorry Zoe, but it's just too dangerous to let people go wandering around the countryside, and we don't have the manpower to escort people wherever they want to go.'

'Yes, but if I was willing to take the risk…'

'No, I'm sorry…it was in the forms you signed when you applied, once here, you committed to staying for at least two years.'

I nodded, I had read that, but hadn't thought they would keep us locked in like prisoners.' I picked up the form off the counter and turned away.

'Thanks David.' I said as I left, looking down at what he had written.

David's signature was striking; bold and angular it crossed half the page. An idea stirred and as I walked home, I glanced at the paper in my hand several times; it might be useful to have a perfect copy of David's signature.

I didn't have any tracing paper, but I had studied Geology at university, and part of the course had been field surveying and making geological maps. I had devised a way of copying maps by using a lightbox rigged from a lamp and a glass cupboard door. The kitchen in my new house had similar glass doors and I carefully took one off its hinges. I propped it on a couple of stacks of exercise books and placed the lamp in the space beneath the glass. I placed the form on the glass pane and covered it with a sheet of plain white paper from school. Then, I placed the lamp underneath so the light shone through and highlighted the signature. I traced it carefully, so I had several copies and then tried to work out where to hide them. Eventually I stuffed them in the gap between the TV and the wall.

Saturday was raining heavily. The grey morning made me oversleep and I felt sluggish when I eventually woke up. I had a very brief shower wondering what time the students finished at the allotment. There was an umbrella by the front door and, wearing my waterproofs, I picked it up and stepped out into the rain.

The allotments were accessed via a track off the main road, next to the northern entrance to the town. As I approached the gates, the soldiers stood more rigidly to attention, staring at me, so I waved the form at them and hurriedly turned left and walked down the track. The plots beside me looked well-tended, but there was very little growing; some leeks, kale... I could see some students rolling out some white fleece over some beds. The chain link fence jinked north around the allotment site before continuing west. At the entrance was a large shed, with all the tools used on the allotment. I entered, the sound of the rain loud on the galvanised zinc roof, and showed my form to the lady sitting at a desk behind a computer monitor.

'I just love gardening,' I gushed, 'can I wander around; take a look at what you're doing?' I did my best brainless, naïve and innocent impression. I felt bad using it, but there was no doubt that it worked; people found it easy to write me off as harmless. I needed to speak to Ruth and I didn't want her watching me too closely.

'Well,' she hesitated, I beamed at her, 'I suppose so,' she said.

There were twenty-four plots, which had been subdivided so each was split into eight smaller areas. There were students everywhere; even the younger ones seemed to be helping. Some had family with them, but others were grimly working in the rain, silent and alone. I strolled around, grateful for my waterproofs and umbrella. Although they all had jackets, I could see that some students were wearing wet jeans. They must have been freezing. I began to be concerned.

'Morning Miss,' it was Mark; he at least seemed to be wearing appropriate clothing. He was double digging the soil, which in this weather seemed like madness.

'What are you doing?' I asked, 'Isn't that difficult?'

'It's what I have been assigned' he said, 'They assign tasks based on ability, I'm strong so I get the grunt work, it's probably what I'll be assigned full time when I finish school.'

I was appalled, Mark was bright in class, he had a natural scientific bent and picked up concepts easily, but his future career was limited to labourer? It seemed a waste of his potential and must have been incredibly frustrating for him. But maybe I had got it wrong; maybe it was a temporary assignment.

'What do you mean, assign?' I asked.

'Everyone in the camp is assigned a job,' he replied, 'you were lucky; teaching is a council paid profession so you get a nice house and good salary, and as long as you do what they want, you can have a nice life here.'

Mark dug his spade deep into the ground, then paused leaning on it, looking around the allotment at the kids working away. 'Young people from outside aren't so lucky, we are assigned jobs the other kids don't want, manual jobs in the farms or in the chicken factories.'

'Ok,' I said, 'start at the beginning... I keep hearing references to the council and the soldiers seem to answer to David. What exactly is going on?'

'You're better off asking Ruth,' he said, 'she can explain it better.' He looked up across the allotments and at the far end I saw a small figure steadily working away; Ruth.

I meandered over, careful to talk to several other students, asking what would be planted in the beds they were tending, talking about how the courgettes I had grown had turned into marrows when I wasn't paying attention. How the slugs seemed to maliciously go after crops rather than the weeds. I didn't need to pretend my interest, but I kept my goal in sight. By the time I had reached Ruth she had finished hoeing the bed. 'This way,' she said, indicating the path to the back of the allotment.

At the end of the path was a water tap. Ruth began to clean her hoe, 'We checked up on you, found your posts on the survivalist forum.'

'Why do you need to be so careful?' I asked.

'There was a boy who arrived with us, he wasn't careful, and he disappeared,' she replied, as she ran water over the mud clogged end.

'Do you know what happened to him? Was he kicked out of the camp?'

'No-one leaves the camp,' she said, emotion sliding into her voice for the first time. 'Did you know anyone on the outside who had ever been inside one?' she asked.

'No, but I didn't socialise much,' I said, 'in fact I only met two people on the way here and those were the first new faces I had seen for six months.'

She nodded in acknowledgement, 'When you arrived did David ask you if you had ever been here before?' she asked, scraping the dirt from the end of the hoe using a metal strip sticking out of the ground under the tap.

'Yes?' I was puzzled, what did that have to do with anything?

'He was checking if you knew where you were. You must have said no, to have the freedoms you do.'

'I don't think I have much freedom; everyone seems to know what I am doing; I feel watched all the time,' I said, glancing around.

'You're here with me though,' Ruth pointed out, 'of your own inclination…. that's freedom.'

She paused for a bit, using the brush hanging from the tap to clear the remaining mud as she ran it under the water. I followed the hose along the ground; the source of the water was a large water tower outside the fence. My gaze rested on the fence, and as I absently watched, two soldiers came into view, walking in the narrow alley between the allotment and the chain-link fence.

I quickly shifted my gaze to Ruth, 'Ok, explain it to me, what's going on?' I paused expectantly, Ruth picked up the now clean hoe and began walking to the other side of the allotment, in the few minutes we had been talking, everyone had finished up and had disappeared. We walked back alone.

'I arrived here with a friend, Michael. He had been injured whist foraging in the city, his hand was crushed in a door…. By the time we got to the camp it was really infected, he had a fever and was delirious. He was taken away to the medical centre and, just like your Frank, he apparently died in the night.' she swallowed. 'I don't think they treated him at all; they use an awful lot of synthetic opioids here, I've seen the inventory lists. I think they euthanised him, I imagine they justified it to themselves, they were putting him out of pain… even if they had fixed his hand he would never have been as strong. They don't take in new people unless they can contribute.'

I looked at her as we walked past the tidy vegetable beds, it sounded incredible; something an emotional teenager would make up, an outrageous conspiracy theory in a typical small town. But then I really looked at her, her eyes looked sad but not irrational. I had been going to say something bland and commiserating but instead, prompted by the bit that had interested me, asked, 'inventory lists?'

'Things arrive from the other camps all the time, and there are lists that keep a record of what they have and how much they use. An enormous database showing stocks of food, medicines, clothes… everything, even books, are tagged' she replied.

I remembered that David had gone through my bags when I arrived, a security check, he had said, but he had taken photos.

'And have you noticed there are no computers here? No cars or bicycles, no phone signal for the major networks?' when I nodded, she continued, 'that's the main method of control, the council have them, normal residents don't. 'Have you also used the money system? The Chiltern pound?' she asked.

I nodded again, and she carried on. 'There isn't any way of changing the old currency into or out of Chiltern pounds, so the council control the flow of wealth in the town. Only adults who are paid by the council can earn Chiltern pounds. The council employees spend those pounds in the shops and facilities in town, which is how other people earn money. Only adults are issued with account numbers. That means kids have absolutely no money. It also means you can't take any of it with you if you leave. It stops people from moving between camps and increases the government's control.

'How do you know all this?' I asked fascinated.

'Some of it we've just picked up, but the details...we found a computer in the Heads office at school, we were lucky, the password was on a post-it note on the monitor. Mark poked around a bit'

We were walking slower and slower, but were approaching the end of the allotment rapidly. 'Hold on,' I said, 'I haven't collected my compost.'

Ruth pointed at the wheelbarrows lined up against the shed, then the enormous pile over to one side. 'I'll do it, it will look like you've made me do extra work, and give the right impression,' she looked at me 'scowl or something, look a bit bored or impatient.'

The rain was stopping so I closed my umbrella, propped it beside me and put my hands in my pocket sighing. I leaned against the shed and crossed one heel over the other, I let my eyes settle in the middle distance and my features relax into an expression of vacancy, then I began to hum.

'Oh,' said Ruth, her eyes widening then narrowing quickly as she stared at me. Up to that point, I don't think she had comprehended how much I had been faking everything.

She pulled a wheelbarrow down and continued. 'What we've worked out so far is this...the government sent the army to local councils to help distribute food. Because Halton Base was located just outside Wendover, the town got a lot of protection. The residents got sick but had food and resources.' She was walking away into the shed as she spoke. I debated whether to follow but a minute later she reappeared with a spade.

'This area of the Chilterns has a lot of rich people; they moved to Wendover for protection, co-opted the local council, and persuaded the base commander to help build the fence around the whole town. The soldiers patrol it, and no one was allowed to enter unless they had been vetted by the doctors.' As she said this, she was lifting compost into the wheelbarrow, appearing to be working hard but actually spilling most of it back into the pile.

'The call for survivors went out in January and they carefully set up the program to encourage anyone they needed and then, when they arrive, they are encouraged to stay.'

I nodded, 'the nice house, clothes and food to draw you in, the Chiltern Pound to make you stay, as you can't take any of it with you'

'And the soldiers to remind you how much better off you are inside.' She added 'You haven't been here long enough yet, but periodically, people attack the fence trying to get in, and the soldiers fight them off… but it's all staged, we've seen the strategy plans'

'But what about Frank?' I asked, 'why did they let him come?'

'To get you,' she said, 'we needed a science teacher and I've seen your file, you're earmarked for the council, they want you as a scientific advisor…not for actual science advice, but to liaise with new arrivals and get people to do whatever they want. You could make their lies sound plausible and sincere.'

'But I wouldn't have done that,' I said, 'there's no way I would put myself before others, lie to people.'

'They must have thought you would,' she said shrugging, 'if you were eased into it.' The wheelbarrow was almost full; we were running out of time 'Did you put anything on the entry essay on the form to make them think that?'

'No,' I said, standing upright and starting to pace back and forth, 'I described my strategy of hide, wait and stay safe, I even put some of my experiences with the knockers in my essay.'

'Knockers?'

'The people who came knocking on doors asking for food; I hid from them.' I understood suddenly how this could be construed, it wasn't exactly altruistic. 'but....'

'That might have been it' she said.

I was disturbed, had I been so selfish that they had thought I would join their little village fiefdom? Encourage others into what seemed remarkably like the medieval system of serfdom?

The wheelbarrow was full and the woman from the shed was coming out, holding a clipboard in one hand and locking up with a large bunch of keys. She glanced at Ruth and then looked at me as I picked up my umbrella, passing it from hand to hand clumsily as I tried to pick up the wheelbarrow. My little act worked... the lady stopped me with a wave of her clipboard. 'Hold on, the kids have nothing booked for this afternoon, let her take it to your house, it will give her something to do.' She unlocked the door, walked back inside and picked up the phone. She said a couple of words, scribbled something on her clipboard signed it with a flourish and walked out again. She pulled it out from under the clip and handed it to me...it was a work order.

'Just sign it when you're satisfied and give it to her' she said. 'I've put her down for an extra two hours so feel free to use the entire time'

Ruth made a noise under her breath 'Thanks,' I said, taking the form and giving the gatekeeper a big smile. Ruth picked up the wheelbarrow and paced beside me, lagging slightly behind. I was puzzled for a second by the glare she was giving me but hoped that it was for the gatekeepers benefit; I had unwittingly just given her two hours more work, and she might not have understood that I just wanted time to go over what she had told me. The clouds broke and the sun peeped out. I began to hum again. The gatekeeper didn't suspect a thing as we walked beside her back to the road.

I mulled over what I had just learnt. I didn't know who to trust and I had been told a great many unpleasant things. I walked home in silence, and when we arrived, she dumped the compost in the garden and made to leave.

'Where are you going?' I asked.

'I need to return the wheelbarrow' she replied, I could see she was tired, but I'd had time to think and I needed more answers.

'You have time, take a break' I said gently. 'Come inside and join me for lunch' I hadn't really planned it, but I couldn't let her go back, cold and wet and probably hungry.

'Ok, I'll have missed lunch and they only give you cold leftovers if you are late.'

We went inside and I took out some eggs, butter, and bread and put the kettle on. Ruth's face was mostly impassive, but I could see she wasn't unaffected by the sight of the food.

'What do they feed you at the hostel?' I asked curiously.

'Whatever people don't want; the leftovers from the shops, stale bread, and old veg they make into soup…'

'What happens to the food from the allotment?' I asked as I cracked two eggs into a frying pan.

'It gets boxed up and goes to the council who distribute it amongst the residents. It's supposed to be fair, but the best stuff go to the council members and to the military commander, then to employees of the council, then to the shops..' she trailed off as I added a knob of butter and some salt and pepper to the pan and the smell rose into the air.

'Perhaps you could butter the bread' I suggested.

When the eggs were done, I glanced at Ruth, emptied both into her plate, and cooked another for myself. We ate and chatted about life before the outbreak, and then it was time for her to go. As she lifted the wheelbarrow once more, I asked one more question; 'Are you going to try and escape?' She looked at me silently but didn't respond.

15

Escape

It was nearly mid-March, I had been at the settlement camp for just under a month, and I had decided I wanted out. My fern garden was going well, as was my attempts at monitoring the patrols around the town. I had their pattern sussed, and had been working on the fence, loosening some of the boards so they would swing sideways to make a hole. I made sure to have a predictable routine, which involved a lot of time alone; when I left, I didn't want anyone to miss me. I joined the gym, and went Mondays, Wednesdays and Fridays, building my running stamina and strength.

I was preparing to attend my first council meeting as an observer. I dithered between work clothes and casual wear, deciding in the end to go for a mix of the two; black trousers and a jumper. I arrived early at the church hall where David was setting out chairs and tables.

'Hi David' I said.

'Hi Zoe, if you wait just a second I'll grab you a seat.'

He turned and placed a chair at the far end, 'The meetings are open, but you're the first person to attend in months. You should be able to see everyone from here.'

I sat, waiting, as people drifted in, they looked at me but didn't offer greetings, just sitting at their places and murmuring to each other. David handed me an agenda and the meeting started. I watched as they smoothly worked their way down the list, organised and efficient, working out alterations to rubbish collections and library hours, and ending with a discussion of a planned festival. If I hadn't heard Ruth's explanation, I might have taken it at face value, but as it was, I could see that they were staying away from certain topics and glancing at me when certain points were raised.

Afterwards there was tea and chocolate biscuits, a very rare treat. I was introduced to a lot of smiling faces, but there was one name I recognised.

'Zoe, may I introduce you to Dr Peterson,' said David, 'He is the director of our medical facilities and chair of the council.' I looked up at a tall spare man, with grey hair combed sideways.

'Pleased to meet you,' he said, 'I apologise for the mix up with your friend.'

'Um…' I was silenced by a wave of grief, 'that's ok, it was a genuine mistake.' I said, 'Do you know what happened? I haven't been able to talk to anyone about it.'

He looked at me sharply, 'As far as I am aware, Frank Tipson had a heart attack in the night and died. What more do you want to know?' I paused, confused, looking at his cold grey eyes. What did I want to know exactly? I wasn't sure, but I wanted more details than they seemed willing to provide.

'Thank you Dr Peterson,' interjected David, 'I'll talk to Zoe.'

I watched as the doctor walked abruptly away, reminded yet again why I didn't want to stay here.

The next day, at school, I stepped up my research. I explored fully, giving the excuse that I was looking for demonstration science equipment. I found a lot of old prospectuses and some newer paperwork. It looked like the school had actually been a great school, pre-outbreak, but the surviving teachers had protested against Gordon's ideas. I found the minutes of a set of meetings hidden away in an old computer lab. The staff had written to the council, the letter was signed by at least six people and one of them was the ex-head of science.

I wanted to know what had happened to my predecessor, so I asked the Wendover kids. I waited till lunch time; the Wendover kids tended to go home for lunch, the refugee kids were assigned school cleaning duties. I had searched the science labs for old exercise books and had eventually found a couple belonging to existing students. As we were leaving the classroom, I fumbled my pile of stuff and dropped the two books in front of them. Naturally they picked them up.

'Hey miss, where did you get these?' said Olivia, a good-natured rather dopey kid from year ten. Millie, beside her, was leafing through the second book.

'I remember this,' said Millie, we did this last year.'

'Yes' I said, 'I was trying to see which topics you had already covered with your old teacher…'

'Mr Webster,' filled in Olivia, 'he left at the start of the year.' she giggled and turned to her friend, 'Do you remember?' she said, 'when the soldiers came into school because my dad had got all the stupid teachers transferred…'

'Shhh!' said Millie, who was unfortunately not as indiscreet as her friend.

They both giggled as I took the books and we walked our separate ways. 'Transferred…' compulsory relocation to a different site maybe… or maybe they had ended up somewhere else. I now knew what happened to teachers who couldn't cut it here.

I was searching for the technology department, and I eventually found it down a corridor, locked behind a set of double doors. I broke the glass to get in; by this point I had few scruples left. The woodworking rooms had mostly been stripped of tools, but in the supply cupboard I found a pair of electrical pliers.

I was ready to leave. It would be fairly easy to get away. As far as I could tell, I wasn't being watched in my own house, and the soldiers weren't watching the area outside the fence at all, their eyes turned inwards when then walked the circuit. But as I pondered the ways and means, a slow conviction began to dawn on me, I was going to take all the refugee students with me, they were my kids… my classes… the way they were being treated was wrong and somehow we would all get out together.

I think Ruth thought I had resigned myself to the situation, but a couple of weeks after we had talked, I put a note in her physics exercise book. It was risky but I sketched out a spacecraft in orbit with a stick figure showing in a round window. I drew an arrow pointing to it and put a couple of fancy equations beside it. The words I used were oblique:

'The bigger the mass, the greater velocity required to escape orbit. This spaceship has the ability to reach a much greater velocity and carry a much larger mass than the design shows'

Then I added some questions beneath;

1) Calculate the <u>maximum load</u> the spacecraft could carry on its' trip to Mars.

2) The vessel must leave before the hot season starts on Mars; calculate the <u>shortest time</u> it can be ready to launch.

3) The ship needs to carry enough fuel to reach the correct velocity. If it will take <u>eight hours</u> to reach its destination how much fuel does it need to have stored?

I hoped Ruth would be able to decode the invitation and respond.

I was not disappointed. The paper was returned with '50 x 14 = 700kg' next to question one, and '60x60x72 = 259200s' under question two. Question three filled up the rest of the paper with some very complicated maths using the formulas I had given and a doodle of a stick figure walking under a clock. I interpreted her answers; fourteen students wanted to escape, they could be ready in three days and she had got the message about walking for eight hours.

We met up that evening at the usual footpath. I got straight to the point. 'What's stopping you from leaving?' I asked. It really didn't seem that hard to me, there weren't that many guards and the fence seemed easy to get through.

'We're watched closely, we can't just go where we want, like you,' said Mark impatiently.

I looked around at where we were and raised my eyebrows 'but...'

'Our evening duty at the allotments start at 6pm,' said Ruth, 'after school we have to be back at the student hostel by 4pm, that's why we don't stay for any of the after-school clubs. We eat and have to be at the allotments by 6pm.'

I glanced at my watch; it was 5:40. 'So what happens if you are late?' I asked.

'It's very simple; the gatekeeper at the allotment takes a register on the computer, it automatically updates at the hostel; if we are marked late, we don't get our next meal.' Mark sounded pretty angry about it.

'No-one is usually late more than once or twice, it's a very effective punishment,' said Ruth, 'If we are booked for a work order then the forms end up at school and the headmaster's PA enters them into the system. The hostel always tracks where we are supposed to be.'

'And the forms have to be signed to show what time we finished,' added Mark, 'if we finish a job early we have to get back to the hostel and hand in our forms; otherwise we miss the next two meals.'

'And if someone doesn't turn up to where they are supposed to be then the soldiers at the army base are alerted and they send men around the perimeter checking.'

'A couple in our year tried escaping,' said Mark, 'they were caught cutting through the perimeter fence. The next day they were assigned chicken factory jobs even though they were months away from reaching sixteen.'

'Chicken factory?' I asked.

'The hostel overseers laugh about it sometimes, but it sounds horrible, the workers are locked in all the time there,' said Mark.

I shivered; this is what they had to look forward to. I glanced at my watch again 5:45, 'I have David's signature, I'm sure I can do something with that, I'll get you out somehow,' I promised. Then let them walk briskly ahead. It sounded like all their time was regulated, but then I remembered; I had been able to get Ruth assigned to wheel my barrow of compost home. All it had taken was a bit of feigned helplessness. It might be possible to get the students assigned to work for me. If we picked a long hard job at a weekend, I could get a work order that freed them up for the whole day.

I needed a reason to get them to my house and in the end it was Stephen who gave me the idea. We were marking exercise books in the staffroom, waiting for the day to end. 'What are you working on in your garden Stephen?' I asked, trying to make conversation.

He looked up, a smile on his face, 'I'm thinking of ripping up the decking and putting in a pond,' he said, 'there's a garden centre and aquarium shop just outside town with plenty of supplies.'

I was intrigued, 'How are you going to get there?' I asked.

'David has arranged for a pass for me, and a jeep from Halton camp.' He rubbed his hands together 'I could get a large pond liner and a waterfall feature...there might even be some koi carp still alive...' His eyes stared into the distance dreamily as he listed all the things he was hoping to find.

Stephen was becoming more of a mystery to me, he seemed a nice guy; pleasant and friendly. A good teacher; caring about the kids work and conscientious, but he seemed to be totally ok with the strict regime and unquestioning of the status quo. I didn't understand how he was so placid and content. But Stephen wasn't my problem, I was interested in his familiarity with the camp procedures.

'Oh, a garden centre! Can I come?'

For the first time Stephen looked slightly uncomfortable, 'well, you have to ask David, he arranged it all, although I don't think people are supposed to know that I'm going off site.'

I smiled, 'ok, don't worry, I won't tell as long as you bring me back a nice fern.' I turned back to my marking, maybe I could use Stephen's trip somehow. He was ripping up his decking, maybe I could rip up my patio, that would be a backbreaking job, and moving the rubble would require a lot of bodies. The only problem was that I'd have to be sure that the right kids were assigned the work.

In the end, Mark swiped a blank work order from the gatekeeper at the allotment. I was trying to find the right way to ask David, I didn't want him to say no, as that would have scuppered the plan completely and I was dithering about how to approach him. But one afternoon, I found the work order in Ruth's exercise book, with the names of the students filled in. I stared at it in surprise and then quickly shut the book, looking around the staff room to see if anyone had noticed. I took it home and traced David's signature onto it using the remade lightbox. The next morning I popped the completed form in the PA's in-tray when she wasn't looking. The names were read out at assembly and, as simply as that, it was sorted; we were leaving on Saturday.

I examined the maps I still had in my backpack, there were many paths, but one option stood out; the grand union canal. The disused Wendover arm of the canal ran alongside the school, up northeast to Tring, where it met the main canal. This then curved in a huge arc down to Watford. The vegetation on the banks of the canal would shield us from view and we couldn't possibly get lost. If we made it out past Halton without being seen, we would find it pretty easy to get to Tring which was only 5 miles away. The full loop would be over twenty-five miles, which was too far to walk in one day, but if we could get bikes we could easily cycle the whole journey along the towpath. The difficulty would be getting to Tring and finding bikes before we were missed.

Saturday morning saw me up and dressed early. The weather was cold and grey, but it wasn't raining. I had packed everything in my backpack and was sitting waiting in the kitchen when the doorbell rang. I walked through the living room and opened the front door, expecting Ruth or Mark, but was surprised to see David with a whole load of students behind him looking petrified.

'Zoe,' he said.

'Hi David,' I said weakly, suppressing the urge to search for Ruth or Mark amongst the sea of faces. 'Wow, it's early, have you come for breakfast?'

He wasn't smiling, 'No, I've come to see what's going on, apparently I signed a work order?'

I opened the door wider and stepped back, there wasn't anyone else with him, no soldiers or other adults, maybe I could contain this.

'I'm sorry David, what work order? And why are all these kids here?' I turned to them, finally spotting Ruth and Mark, 'hey guys, I'm making pancakes, do you want some?' I turned and walked back through the open space, hoping they would follow.

'Zoe,' David barked, not moving 'Why is there a work order with your address on it, listing fourteen kids and signed by me?'

I stopped in the kitchen doorway and turned back to face him, 'Really, David, I don't know,' I said earnestly, 'I have no idea what you are talking about, is it some sort of mistake?'

David looked at me and I stared back at him, trying not to break, not to give away any hint of my furious thoughts. What could I say? He knew it couldn't be a mistake; there was no getting round the forged signature. Would he believe someone had set me up? How could we still get away. There was no way we could whilst David was watching. Unless we incapacitated him. Could I hit him? It was out of the question, David was a big guy, and loud, and anyway he hadn't ever done anything to me.

Suddenly my mouth started talking, it wasn't planned, the words just came out. 'David, what is going on? Why are you so mad?'

'This is ridiculous, stop lying and tell me what this is…' he strode forward into the living room waving a form at me, it was the work order.

'David, what am I supposed to have done?' I said, in my best helpless, innocent voice, stepping back as if in fear.

'You faked a work order,' David yelled, as he followed me into the kitchen, 'what are you doing with these kids?' If he hadn't realised yet what we were doing, he must just have come over as soon as he had seen the form, without any plan or idea what was going on. The kids streamed in after him and I heard the front door snick closed.

I was now standing in the kitchen on one side of the table, David was on the other side, and between him and the kitchen door, spread out, were Ruth and Mark and the other twelve kids. Some of them were carrying backpacks, all had dark coats and scarfs, mostly in either green or brown or black and looked prepared for the cold weather. In the warmth of the house the sight was incongruous. I stepped over to the stove. I hadn't been kidding, I had spent the time I had been waiting making pancakes. I used the spatula to lift the top pancake from the stack warming on the pan and placed it on the top plate of a pile waiting on the counter. I popped open a bottle of golden syrup and drizzled the sugary treacle over one side, before folding it and offering it to David, 'David, I really don't know what you are talking about, but have some breakfast, you might feel better.'

He knocked the plate out of my hand onto the table where it spun wildly. His eyes searched around the room and settled on my backpack, he looked at me, then at the kids, dressed for the outdoors and finally put two and two together.

'You're leaving.'

'Yes,' I said, 'is there something wrong with that?' I wanted him to admit out loud that this whole place was a fraud, it pretended to be all fine and friendly and normal, when it was anything but.

'Zoe, you can't leave,' he said, 'the soldiers won't let you, it's too dangerous out there.' He sounded calmer now, like the normal David, calm and sensible and highly credible. I ignored him, picked up the pancake and started eating.

'Would anyone else like some?' I asked, a series of nods had me dishing out the food to the nearest kids whilst David watched nonplussed.

'You came here because you couldn't hack it out there,' he said, 'here you have everything you could possibly need or want,' he gestured around, 'we have given you a beautiful home... a garden...'

It was at this point that Ruth, who was passing the plates of pancakes back to the others, decided to make her voice heard, 'but we don't have any of this, where is our home? Our gardens?'

David's voice turned rough 'You don't deserve any; you are just stupid rat city kids who happened upon this place and we were good enough to take you in.'

He reached out and dashed a plate from her hand then grabbed her arm. I heard all the hidden venom and bile that I had guessed had been lurking under his usual bonhomie. 'You think we don't know how you survived in the city, scavenging and stealing? Well there is none of that here; we turn parasites like you into useful members of society. We have fed you and educated you, now you owe us.'

He shook her and Ruth gasped in pain. I found myself instantly and awesomely angry. 'Let her go!' 'Now!'

David looked at me in surprise. I wanted to hit him with a violence and urgency I found disturbing.

'I am taking these kids somewhere better, where they are not treated as slaves.' I said, 'We're going and you are not going to be able to stop us.'

The words came out as if I was watching someone else, even as I spoke I was thinking furiously, surprised at the words coming out of my mouth. 'I didn't put everything on my form,' I said, slowly and ferociously, 'I have a black belt in a Japanese martial art...I know how to fight... I have climbed the Himalayas, scrambled alone over mountains in Spain and Scotland.' I stepped closer to him and reached across to the knife block, 'I have walked the streets of London at night,' I paused, my voice rising, 'I walk alone and I know how to defend myself.' As I spoke, I drew a knife and pointed it at his face, desperate to make him believe me. 'If you do not let her go, I will *hurt* you.'

The funny thing is, I didn't feel stupid saying it. I meant it; I really, really wanted to hurt him. And I think he saw it. Saw how fiercely I was holding myself back. He let her go.

'Sit down' I said.

'You can't,' he began to bluster.

'SIT DOWN' I yelled, I was shaking and sweating, and the adrenaline was pouring through me.

He sat, still blustering. 'Mark,' I said, 'there's some gaffer tape in my backpack.'

Mark didn't need telling twice. He had David trussed up and gagged in no time. It looked like he had done it before.

I pulled out a chair and sat down, feeling drained. The kids had all stopped eating, but now they started passing out the pancakes and syrup. They seemed awfully inured to what had happened. I was still shaking. Ruth sat down opposite absently rubbing her arm. 'That was brilliant, thanks Zoe.'

I nodded but didn't say anything.

'Are we still going?' she asked.

'Yes, let's eat and then we'll go as planned.'

'What about him,' she asked, motioning towards David.

'We'll leave him where he is, someone will find him eventually.' I didn't really care, as long as he couldn't get out and raise the alarm.

I got up and checked the gaffer tape, but he was bound tight. There was no way he was either going to free his limbs or get the tape off his mouth. Even if he tipped over, it was a sturdy wooden chair and wouldn't break. I still had the knife in my hand and I slowly slid it back into the block. Then for good measure, I took a tea towel and draped it over his head, covering his eyes. That would make doing anything a million times more difficult and he wouldn't see where we went.

I looked around at the kids eating. I taught most of them and although I knew some better than others, they were all good kids. Apart from Ruth and Mark, there were five other students from the year 11 class: Alex, Freya, Leila and Taz, and Jack, a good-natured bright boy. There were four kids from the year below; Kai and Eddie; a pair of smiling boys who always had a cheeky greeting when I saw them on the way into school and Drew and Mateusz, who I knew less well. Ruth had also brought along Alisha and Jasmine who were inseparable twins from my year 7 class. Liam was the only one I didn't teach; at only ten years old, he was in the primary school. I looked at Ruth as she introduced him. 'He's young, but sensible, he won't hold us back,' she said in response.

We moved into the garden and waited for the soldiers to pass on their circuit. Once they had gone, I opened the slats of the fence and slipped out into the alley. Using the pliers I started to unwind the wire, glancing left and right nervously. It seemed to take forever, but less than ten minutes later, everyone was through. We ran sideways along the fence to the hedge that bordered the school, then followed it north round the edge of the field until, there in front of us, was the canal.

'Do we have to cross?' whispered Drew, who, with his long legs, had arrived first. He had pushed his way between two bushes and was looking out over the canal. I could see the towpath on the other side, but the water looked dark and deep, with brown leaves and twigs floating on a dirty scum on top. It looked uninviting and it was far too cold to let people get wet.

'No,' I said, 'there should be a crossing at the end of the field.'

Kai and Eddie immediately set off at the front and I followed, scrambling over the little hillocks of grass and trying not to get scratched by the arching stems of bramble that reached out from the mess of hedge plants that had grown up along the side of the canal.

I tried to move quietly, the only sounds the rustle of our coats and the quiet query of concern from Alisha, when Jasmine tripped and fell. I reached the end of the field and saw a wide path beyond. Mark and Drew pushed through the hedge, stepping up onto the path on the other side. Holding back some of the whippier branches they helped everyone through. There was a small footbridge over the canal; we crossed and then we were on the towpath.

Once on the flat gravel path I started running, I sent Drew and Freya up to the front to set the pace, Mark at the back.

The kids seemed to be in good shape, I was the worst off, my attempts at building stamina at the gym had improved my ability slightly but I needed all of Marks silent encouragement to keep going. Ten minutes later we were in Halton, it was still very early, so we slowed to a silent walk and stole through, crossing the main road quickly and fearfully, before continuing on.

We continued alternating between jogging and walking for another mile until we could see, between the trees, that we had reached another urban area. Had we reached Tring? I stopped and spread out the map on the ground, I needed the break, and I wasn't the only one. In this age of google maps it appeared that I was the only one that could reliably read an ordinance survey map, but it confirmed that we hadn't yet reached the A41. Another ten minutes put us at the main road.

I took out the map again as we rested under the carriageway. It felt like a secure hiding place, but I could see that the others were still tense. If David got loose somehow and sent soldiers after us, they would catch us easily. The map showed a couple of options, we could follow the canal in a big loop around, north of the town or we could follow the side roads in and hope to find a bike shop.

'Are there people in Tring?' I asked as the year 11 students gathered around the map.

'No,' said Alex knowledgeable, 'the survivors all moved to the settlement camp, we had some in our class.'

I looked at Ruth, 'they didn't come with us?'

'No, they were rich kid survivors, with families, not city refugees like us.'

I had wondered how Ruth and Mark had picked the fourteen, now it was obvious; they had picked city kids without any ties to friends or family in Wendover. It must have been hard organising them all; persuading them to trust me, in retrospect, my job had been much easier.

'Ok, we're going into Tring,' I said, 'we need to leave the towpath.'

We walked the lanes to the big Tring junction and then followed the road into town, finally reaching the town centre. Everyone was tired and we needed a break. The shop fronts were all broken with the insides open to the elements, they appeared to be stripped clean but poking around ahead of us, Kia and Eddie found a cafe that had tables and chairs still inside.

We trooped inside and collapsed into the chairs, I paused a second and then stood up, 'Where are you going?' asked Mark.

'We should have a lookout,' I replied; I was still cautious, especially in an unknown town.

'Good idea,' said Ruth, 'Jack, Liam, Freya...' they quickly stood and ran out, Jack and Liam turning left out the door, Freya turning right as if they knew exactly what to do. Maybe they did, apart from how they behaved in school, I didn't really know much about them. Freya had already surprised me with her athletic ability, she seemed tireless. I was relieved, the kids might not be tired, but I was exhausted. I hadn't done so much running in my entire life.

Then Ruth unexpectedly asked, 'where are we going?'

I looked at her confused, hadn't I explained?... No, I was going to have discussed it over breakfast, but couldn't because of the arrival of David. They had all been blindly following me ever since we had left, not knowing where we were going or what they would find there. I was touched by their trust.'

'We're following the Grand Union Canal all the way back to Watford,' I said, 'then walking down to where I used to live. I have a lot of food stashed and a food garden started. We can set up there, settle in, and hide. No one will find us. We'll be safe and can craft some sort of life for ourselves.'

'What are we doing here?' she asked.

'We need bikes,' I said, 'we'll be much faster on a bike along the towpath. When we've had a couple of minutes rest, we can spread out and try and find a bike store or something.'

'Great!' said Alex immediately, looking much happier. Most of the others also seemed to perk up although Alisha and Jasmine looked nervous. Maybe they hadn't ridden much before.

Leila and Taz immediately stood up and were off, running out of the cafe, 'back in a sec...' called Taz. The rest of the kids continued lolling on their chairs, tired from the fast pace we had set. Less than a minute later, the two girls were back.

'There's a bike store round the corner,' Leila said, dancing in round the tables.

'And it's still full of bikes,' said Taz, giving Leila an exuberant shove. Now they were out of the settlement they seemed to have suddenly come alive.

We had struck lucky. I had been fairly sure we would; this was cycling country and Tring was a nice commuter belt town, probably with a cycling group and dedicated cyclists who spent weekends cruising up and down the canal and in and around the Chilterns. My main worry had been that the bikes would have all gone, but Taz reported that they were all still there.

When I got to the shop I understood why; they were chained to the racks with some sort of high strength security wire. I stopped, unsure what to do, but Jack set to work on the locks. I couldn't see what he did, he was so fast, but one after the other, fifteen bikes were lowered off the walls and very quickly had new owners.

I was aware of time passing and wheeling my bike out of the shop, I called to the others. We rode off, quiet and purposeful, back to the canal. This time Alex took the lead, it was obvious he was super comfortable on a bike. Alisha and Jasmine were wobbling in the middle, receiving encouragement from Mark. The rest of us spread out as we cycled along the towpath for almost an hour, stopping every ten minutes or so to let the slower members catch up.

We rode along the towpath through the town of Berkhamsted and into Hemel Hempstead. A couple of times I glimpsed dogs in the distance, but our numbers kept away any unwanted company and there was no sign of pursuit. There were boats tied up along the riverbank but no signs of life inside. We passed a play area and stopped to rest; sitting on a concrete plinth around a stone sculpture, but the cold eventually forced us on.

Twenty minutes later, we reached the M25 where we collapsed in a huddle on the towpath, too tired to cycle any further. The massive concrete structure arched over us as we sat and ate lunch. After eating the sandwiches I had made, I pulled out my phone. I had had no signal for the six weeks I was inside the camp and was looking forward to getting back in touch with the outside world. I turned my phone on and let it load. WhatsApp messages from friends and family began to pop up along with email notifications; it felt immensely good to be connected again. Then a notification for a missed call appeared from an unrecognised number and a notification for voicemail. I dialled, there were eight new messages. I opened the first and heard Vik's voice.

'Hey Z, where are you? We're at yours but it's all locked up. Sorry we have been out of contact so long. It's been quite an exciting time. Hope you are back soon. Bye'

They were alive! I felt such relief, but it was typical of Vic not to explain anything. Where had they been all this time? I listened to the other messages which got steadily more and more worried, the last one was from two days ago.

'Hi Z, I don't know if you are getting these, but I hope you are ok, we're still with Catrina and Ben, please let us know if you are ok. Bye'

I was confused, they hadn't said where they were staying; just that they were staying with some people called Catrina and Ben. I didn't know who they were talking about but I immediately texted back, 'Hi Vik, great to hear you guys are ok. I've been in an area without signal for the past six weeks, should be home soon. Zx' Halfway through sending the message my phone died, but at least I knew they were ok.

I felt a surge of joy and gratefulness; my family was safe and we had reached the M25; the army didn't venture inside, they had said so themselves. We were safe.

16

Disaster

The kids were sitting around talking and eating, and I had the map out, trying to work out how far we had left to go, when, overhead on the motorway above us, we heard the throaty roar of motorbikes. We looked up, paralysed for a second by the unusual sound.

'Scatter! meet at Carpenders Park.' I yelled as I grabbed my bike and belted along the path. Some kids followed me, some went the other direction, and I noticed some scale the tall spiked metal fence beside us, up and over in a second. Then I was racing away, a bunch of us flying along the towpath.

I glanced behind just in time to see Leila and Taz bounce off the path and into the trees. There was a building up ahead; a lock, but the roar of engines was getting louder. The trees disappeared and glancing to my right, I saw something moving on the road parallel to us. I was too far to see individual vehicles, but close enough to see them veer of the road and cut across the field heading towards us. The others were pulling ahead of me, Alex and Alisha and Jasmine. 'Wait,' I yelled, but they were too far away.

I skidded to a stop in the shadow of the lockkeeper's cottage and scrambled off my bike, not pausing to catch it as it fell into the water. I jumped up onto the wooden arms of the lock gates and ran over to the other side, grabbing at the white rail to keep my balance. I pushed through the bushes and then was running, slicing through brown grasses, panicked by the soldiers behind. Ahead, less than a hundred yards, I could see a line of trees, I plunged towards them, but before I could check, slipped down into waist high water into another canal.

The freezing water made me gasp and splash. I stopped moving almost immediately, petrified by fear. I listened intently at the sounds in the distance but heard nothing close by, no one had followed me; I was alone. The motorbike engines were moving north and south along the towpath. Shielded by the lockkeeper's cottage, no-one had seen me cross the canal.

I ducked down in the water so I was hidden by the tall grasses, then rose up again, staring across the field despite myself. I could see the bikes racing along the towpath... they were going to be caught; Alex was in front, far behind, Jasmine and Alisha were peddling furiously. I held my breath as the soldiers gained quickly. When they got close, they didn't do anything sophisticated, just shot straight past the bicycles on the outside knocking them into the canal. The kids had no chance and there was nothing I could do. I watched a couple of soldiers get off their motorbikes to fish Jasmine and Alisha out of the water whilst the other two sped after Alex. I turned to look for the motorbikes going south but they had disappeared out of sight behind a line of trees.

I looked around me, suddenly aware of the freezing cold. I was far enough away to be practically invisible, but if they started searching, I would be quickly found. I knew I had to get out of the water, already my teeth were chattering.

I scrambled up the bank and rolled into the trees, they were thin and leafless and beyond them was another field, open and exposed. I lay on my front, hidden in the thin dry stems of last year's grass, shivering in fear and shock and cold. Ahead was a bank with a much thicker covering of vegetation. If I could get to it, I would have a much greater chance of staying hidden.

I pulled my backpack off my back and pushed it ahead of me crawling after it, but I couldn't see where I was going and it was far too slow, I had to trust that they couldn't see me through the thin vegetation lining the second canal. I scrambled to my feet, crouching, and ran through the grass towards the bank of brambles. I shoved my way up the bank then froze as I glanced back; I could see clear across the fields. How had they not seen me already? I could see them as clear as day. I almost fell in my haste to hide, and crouched down amongst the brambles and bushes. Looking out into the distance, I watched the soldiers milling around, rounding kids up into a line.

I watched as they began to spread out into the surrounding fields, searching. I had to move or I would also be caught. I began to inch backwards, slowly shifting my weight from leg to leg as I moved up the bank, shuddering with cold and fear. I stared out over the fields and willing them not to look my way. Eventually I reached the trees at the top and fell backwards onto gravel; I had stumbled onto the railway.

Standing I shook uncontrollably, my teeth chattering, and shudders of cold wracking my body. I looked up and down the track; I was completely hidden from view. I mentally gathered myself and began to run along the wooden sleepers, trying to put as much distance as possible between myself and any pursuers, I was wheezing and squelching with smelly canal water, tripping every few seconds over the sleepers. I stopped every couple of hundred yards to catch my breath, my legs shaking. I was almost completely spent but after ten minutes the tracks slipped down into a cutting and I could see a tunnel ahead.

I stumbled into the tunnel dead with exhaustion. The shivers had abated with the warmth generated by running but I had never pushed myself so hard before. The day seemed to have gone on forever, the argument with David, leaving, the run to Halton, Tring, then the cycle ride, that panicked sprint across the fields, falling into the cold water and the slow crawl up the bank then the last ten minutes of running and tripping. I sank to the ground and sat, unable to move even one pace further.

Soon I began to shiver, I was sitting in the shade in the cold march temperatures, soaking wet. I was going to be seriously ill. I opened my backpack and emptied the contents out around me. I hadn't brought much; I'd left the camping gear behind, as it was too heavy, although I had my lifesaver bottle and my torch and some other bits and pieces. I had some flapjack and a packet of butter and my dry bag. I opened it up and was glad to feel that the blanket and seeds inside were still dry.

I packed up all my stuff except the flapjack and blanket and stood up, I had to keep going; if I sat around cold, I would get hypothermia. Already I was starting to feel a dangerous lassitude. I rubbed my hair with the blanket and then wrapped it around my head like a headscarf, tucking the ends in around my neck. I began walking into the dark, eating the flapjack, I felt sick, but I knew I needed the energy.

The light began to fade and from my pocket, I pulled the torch. I turned it on, but nothing happened. I gave it a shake, but it was soaking wet. It needed drying off. I stumbled along on the gravel, dragging the back of the torch across the wall so I walked straight and didn't trip over the rails or sleepers. The time stretched on, and in the dark, I heard scurrying and scratching.

I was utterly exhausted but I couldn't stop. I began counting my steps like I was marching; one… two… three… four… it was an old trick which I used on long treks. The numbers gave me rhythm, kept my feet plodding on, way past tiredness. one… two… three… four…, five… six… seven… eight… each number just a single huffed syllable. Mindlessly matching my steps to the rhythm of the words.

Eventually there was light ahead, I didn't know how long I had been walking for, maybe about ten minutes, I kept plodding along and eventually the tunnel became a deep cutting, which gradually became shallower and shallower, I knew I should make a decision, stop somewhere, get some dry clothes, but I was too tired, I just kept walking. I passed under a road, ahead was a station and glancing to the right I saw a gate, I stared at it unseeingly for at least five paces then veered off the gravel and walked towards it. I stopped, stymied. It was padlocked shut.

It was a blue metal gate, sturdy and tall. I didn't think about it, just climbed up onto the long bolts which secured it in place and reached up to hold the top. I pulled myself up, stepping onto the locking bar in the middle, then I sat on the top, swung my feet over and lowered myself gingerly to the ground. I landed in a heap, my legs collapsing under me, but I was out.

I was in a back street, sitting on the tarmacked road, staring up at the sign on the building beside me …. holiday inn. My eyes closed and a picture of my favourite beach formed. I jerked awake, and struggled to my feet, swaying. It took a long time to get started again, but once I was walking, I kept going. I had no idea where I was, but I followed the road round, walking in the middle of the street, surrounded by large glass buildings. I kept walking ignoring all side streets until I came to a massive junction and realised I was in the centre of Watford. In front of me was the shopping centre. I crossed the road and walked through an area of broken glass, I was in Debenhams.

By this time I wasn't thinking at all. I walked around in a daze looking for women's wear. I found a load of clothes, size 12, some still hanging on hangers, others scattered across the floor. I collected the warmest things I could find; vests and light fleeces and eventually ended up in homeware; I stripped off, used the fluffiest, softest towel I could find to get dry and then changed.

I was absolutely shattered, and although the store was trashed like most other shops, there was still a lot of stuff around. Homeware had a display bed, with a duvet. I couldn't resist. I climbed in, just for a second, snuggling under to get warm. I tried to think what to do. I hadn't seen anyone on my walk through Watford, although to be truthful I hadn't been looking. Debenhams felt cold and empty. The shopping centre was silent, just the cooing of doves, trapped inside and flapping around.

I sat, cocooned in the duvet and closed my eyes trying to visualize where I needed to go… if I cut through the centre I could walk down by Tesco… under the bridge and up through the park… that would put me on the road back home, from there I would be an hour away….. I yawned, snuggled down flat, and fell asleep.

17

Regroup

I opened my eyes… what had I done? I couldn't believe it. In a place I didn't know…lying in plain sight. I jumped up out of the bed, grabbed my backpack, and quickly made my way out. I had been incredibly lucky that the place was empty.

When I reached the open air, I stopped in surprise, the sun was shining down out of a blue sky, the clouds had disappeared, and the world was bright and airy. It was mid-afternoon and as I followed the road home, I felt my spirits lighten; maybe some of the others had escaped, and would be at Carpenders Park when I arrived. As I walked up through the overgrown park, full of rubbish and south along the road back through Oxhey, I thought of what it had been like pre-outbreak, and I was reminded of Frank and our optimism as we had set out for the camp.

Unlike my last journey however, this time I twice saw people in the distance. And instead of hiding as usual, I waved, in case any of the students had made it this far. Surprisingly people waved back, but neither time was it anyone I knew. I took the tunnel under the railway line into Carpenders Park, looking around eagerly, had anyone made it here? But there was no sign of anyone; the weeds were growing up through the cracks and drifts of dead leaves piled up against the sides. It was just as it had been when Frank and I left.

I walked wearily up the long slope into the station itself. The barriers were open and as I walked through, I could see through the glass windows that there was something propped against the rail outside. My hopes rising, I walked out onto the platform. In front of me was a brand new bike. 'Hello?' I shouted as I looked up and down the platform hoping desperately to see that someone, apart from me, had made it to safety. I heard a slight noise to my right and ran around the side of the building only to pull up suddenly; rising from a bench with a look of hope on his face, was Alex.

He jumped up and I rushed forward arms outstretched, 'Alex!' I said, then I checked, teachers didn't hug students, it was ingrained deep in me, but what the hell, I was so happy to see him I gave him a big hug anyway. 'Are you ok?' I asked, 'how did you get away?'

'I outran them' he said, 'just kept going along the path. After a minute I saw a bridge so I went up the slope into a town, it was easy to lose them after that. What about you?'

'I crossed over the canal at the lock, and made it to the railway line. How did you find your way here?' I asked.

'I ended up in Watford, eventually I found a railway station, I heard you yell something park and when I checked the board, Carpenders park just a few stops down the line.'

'Clever' I said, 'well done' I paused, not wanting to ask, 'Have you seen any of the others?'

'No,' said Alex, looking down and hunching his shoulders, we were both silent for a second, then he straightened up, 'but I could go look, now that you're here?' he stared at me, expectantly, waiting to be told what to do.

I looked at him, he didn't look tired at all, and if there was even a chance that any of the other were in the area then we needed to look for them, but we needed to be organised; leave messages that the other kids would understand and plan a search. And I needed to get to my bungalow and check that it was still secure.

'Ok, some of the others might find their way up here,' I said, 'we need to leave them a message so they can find us'

I looked around; opposite the entrance was a large board with the overground line stations drawn on it. There was a lot of empty white space. I rooted round in my bag until I found my sharpie.

'Can you draw?' I asked Alex.

He reached for the pen 'what do you want me to put?'

'Draw a bike,' I said, 'and then fifteen stick figures,' he drew a rather good picture of a bike and then 15 stylised stick figures, some big, some small, some in pairs, they were recognisably us. 'then put large ticks above you and me' Alex ticked a tall thin stick figure, and a shorter one with a round face and holding something small, perhaps a pen. I took the sharpie and beneath the drawing wrote:

'WAIT HERE'

'I'm going to walk home, it's just up the road' I said, 'I'll check that everything is as I left it. Can you quickly cycle round the estate and meet me there? I walked around to the back of the board and quickly sketched out the estate, drawing in the locations of the station, school, shops, and bungalows. Then I pointed to my house. 'I'll be here.' I said.

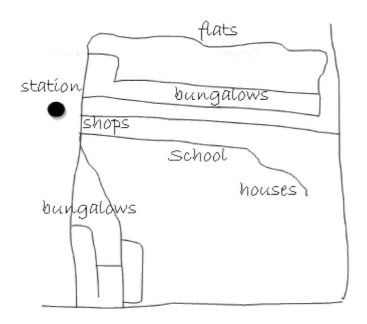

I wanted to tell him to be careful, to explain all the possible dangers and to urge caution, but although Alex often gave the impression of carelessness, he had managed quite well on his own. I didn't want him to see my worry so I stayed silent as I watched him wheel his bike through the barriers and freewheel down the slope. Then I picked up my backpack and followed him.

I walked past the shops and the pub up towards my house; everything looked exactly how Frank and I had left it six weeks ago. The weeds were a bit taller and some of the trees and hedges were breaking out into leaf, but it was the same, familiar Carpenders Park. A warm feeling of security filled my chest and displaced some of the anxious worry. As I approached my house I pulled my key from my pocket, eager to get inside, but as I entered the drive I stopped in surprise;

there, sitting with his back against the door, was Mark. He looked up as I approached and gave a tired smile.

'You took your time,' he said, but the tired relief in his voice made the words less confrontational than usual.

'Mark!' I said, 'you made it! Where's Ruth... and the others?'

He stood up and I could see a long graze running down the side of his face, 'Freya and Matty are hiding round the corner,' He gave a sharp whistle as I looked around. I could see movement over the top of the hedge. I walked round and there was Freya, supporting Matty, who had his arm around her shoulder. Matty looked in terrible shape, he was shivering and mumbling, his foot was dragging along the ground wrapped in a bloody bandage and when he got closer, I saw that he was soaking wet.

'Are you ok? What happened?' I asked, over my shoulder, as I ran back to the house to unlock it and let them in.

'I'm fine, Matty was injured in a stupid accident,' said Freya.

The house was untouched, everything as I had left it. I moved into the kitchen and quickly turned on the heaters and the stove. 'Sit down and get warm,' I instructed. I went into my bedroom and removed the bottom drawer on the bedside table. In the space underneath was a shallow plastic box. I walked back to the kitchen, removing the three sets of keys from inside.

'Mark, apart from that,' I indicated his face, 'are you injured at all?'

'No I'm fine, but we need to do something about Matty; he fell into a swimming pool full of glass and cut his leg.'

I handed him a set of keys, 'two doors down, across the road, red wooden door, there were a family with teenagers there, you should find some clothes to fit.'

I turned to Freya, 'Are you ok?' I asked, she looked uninjured, but I needed to be sure.

'I'm fine, we were lucky,' she said.

'What happened?' I asked as I took out my lifesaver bottle and began the process of filling it up from the hose that connected to the water butt outside.

'We jumped over the fence and into the area under the motorway,' she said, 'but there wasn't any cover there, so we ran through and climbed over at the far side. We found ourselves in a small village, just five or six houses, but they were big and empty.' She paused and I could see the fatigue in her face. 'We got in to one of the houses at the back where there was a pool in a big glass conservatory. The glass was all broken, that's how we got in, but when Matty slipped into the pool, none of us realised it was full of glass. It took us a while to realise he was bleeding. Mark bandaged him up, but he lost a fair bit of blood.'

I filled the kettle with the water and moved into the hallway, opening the loft... 'How did you get here?' I asked.

'We found a bike in the shed and a two wheeled trailer in the outbuildings of the small farm over the road. We put Matty in the trailer, hooked it up to the bike, and took turns cycling. Mark knew your address.'

It sounded like they had had a tough time. I started passing down some of my supplies from the loft, blankets and duvets and a couple of the first aid kits I had stashed away. There was a knock on the door; it was Mark, back with clothes, and he had found the freezer with the food stash.

We covered the single bed in the back bedroom with some of the spare blankets and then Mark picked Matty up from where he was resting in the kitchen. 'I'll get him changed and see if we can clean his wound.'

Just as he was moving Matty across to the bedroom there was another knock on the door; a jaunty rat-a-tat tat. He froze and Freya looked at me wide eyed. 'What?...'

'It's Alex,' I said, as I moved towards the door, 'sorry, I should have mentioned it.'

I opened the door, hoping that Alex had found some of the others; I knew Alisha and Jasmine were caught, but seeing Mark, Freya and Matty had let me hope that some of the others had maybe gotten away also. Alex was standing on the doorstep alone, but then jumping in from either side came Leila and Taz. 'Look who I found!' he said happily.

The girls pushed their way past Alex and hugged everyone they could get their hands on. It was chaos for a few moments, but then Mark pushed them away so he could tend to Matty.

I took the four of them into the kitchen and went out into the garden to get some peppermint leaves. The house hadn't been disturbed at all, there wasn't even much dust particularly, but the garden was well into spring. The garlic from last year had sprouted and weeds were springing up all around. I picked a double handful of peppermint and returned to the kitchen to make peppermint tea, but the kettle was empty.

'Mark needed the water,' said Freya, 'I'm just getting more,' I could see she had my lifesaver bottle and was alarmed for a second; if she broke it we would have no way of getting clean water. But she was using it perfectly. She'd obviously been watching carefully earlier.

I re-boiled the kettle and made the tea. It was warming and reviving so I took a cup into Mark and Matty.

'How's he doing?'

Matty was changed and sitting propped up in bed. His left tracksuit leg was rolled up to his knee and Mark was gently dabbing at a long cut with a towel. Beside him was a bowl of steaming water.

'Better' he said, 'the cut is long, but it's along the muscle rather than across, it should heal ok if we can hold it together. Do you have sterile strips?' he asked.

I was impressed by his knowledge of first aid, it was much better than mine. I put the cups down on the bedside table and went to get the first aid boxes.

Frank and I had raided the pharmacy and collected all the medical kits we could find around the estate. Then we had collated the supplies and outfitted two cases with all the best bits. I had surgical strips in abundance. I passed the kits to Mark who, for the first time, looked impressed. 'Good, can you get Freya?' was all he said. I wanted to help but I barely knew Matty, He would probably be more comfortable with Freya.

I went back to the kitchen and looked at the food Mark had brought from my food stash. I put the pasta on to boil, and waited with Alex. Soon enough Freya came back into the kitchen.

'He seems ok for now. Mark is just finishing up.' She said. 'What happened to everyone?'

'I definitely saw them catch Alisha and Jasmine,' I said.

'And Eddie and Kai were running back along the towpath, the soldiers would have caught them pretty quickly if they stayed on the path,' said Freya.

'Jack climbed over the fence with us, but he didn't follow us into the village, I think he climbed the bank up to the motorway,' said Mark, walking into the room carrying the bowl and bloodstained towel. He carefully poured the water down the sink and then refilled the bowl and left the towel to soak.

'Did you see where Ruth went?' I asked, 'or Liam or Drew?'

'I think I saw Liam go into the water.' said Taz.

'There was a boat tied up on the opposite bank he might have been aiming for.' added Leila.

'Ruth wasn't tall enough to make it over the fence, I didn't see where she went,' said Mark. He slumped in down onto the floor by the heater. He hadn't changed or dressed his own cut.

'Right,' I said, looking at him assessingly, 'let's sort you out, and then you guys can decide where you want to sleep.'

I rescued the bowl from the sink and got a fresh towel. Whilst I cleaned up Marks graze on the side of his head, I explained about the three bungalows that were prepped and secure. Leila and Taz decided to take the first, Freya decided to stay with me to take care of Matty, and Mark and Alex agreed to keep the one he already had the keys for.

We tidied up and then, although I was still exhausted, I left the house to go for a walk around the estate and up to the station, see if anyone else had made it back. As I walked past the familiar front gardens and houses, I savoured the joy of being home, but mixed in with the happiness was worry and guilt. It was my fault they had been caught, I had led the escape and I had stopped when we had been so close to safety. Stopped because I was tired, and stayed to eat and play on my phone. If we had just walked a bit further we would have been safe. I had to correct the mistakes I had made; I had to get them back. There could be no celebrating being home until we were all here, together.

There wasn't anyone at the train station, but as I walked around the estate, I noticed that a couple of houses seemed to be occupied. There were lights on and I could see shadows of movement through the windows. I made a note to go back the next day and see if they were inclined to be sociable. Back home Freya was feeding Matty and the rest had left to sort out their new homes. I found my phone charger and plugged in my phone. I was shattered so I left all the things I should have been doing and went to bed.

The sound of movement in the house woke me next morning. I lay there for a second thinking of the things that needed to be done. We needed to get the garden started as soon as possible; there were six mouths to feed now, and the dried goods would run out eventually. I wanted to see who else was living on the estate and I wanted to try to locate the others; find out where the soldiers had taken them. That last point seemed impossible. I had no idea how we could track them down. I wondered suddenly if my message to Vik had been sent. It hadn't so I resent it and then, groaning with muscle fatigue, got up.

The day progressed pretty well. Matty stayed in bed, resting, but the others helped weed the garden as we waited to see if anyone else would turn up. The carrots seed I had sown before I had left were now delicate seedlings about an inch high, we had returned just in time to put down some slug killer before they were all eaten. The potatoes had also started to sprout under the fleece. I felt the pot method would be better, so I got Freya and Alex started on sterilising the potting compost and dug up some of the potatoes for replanting. Leila and Taz started pruning back the rose to give the fruit trees more room and Mark, giving me a sardonic look, picked up a spade and started digging a new bed. I was waiting for a message or call from Vik and it made me anxious, I drifted from task to task, but by lunchtime the garden was looking much better.

Sitting down to lunch of pasta and tomato sauce I took out the seeds from my backpack and lay them on the table. Everyone perked up at the sight.

'Wow Miss, where did you get those?' asked Alex.

I smiled, 'You can call me Zoe, it seems silly to call me Miss' I spread out the seeds, 'I picked them up from the garden centre at the start of the outbreak, I was growing food already, so when the food shortages started I was ok.'

'Where is the garden centre?' asked Leila, 'can we go and get more stuff?'

'I think there are people living there,' I said, 'a family with three children, I've met the kids a couple of times but not the adults.'

'Should we go and have a look?' said Taz.

'Eventually,' I said, 'first let's go talk to the people living round the corner; they weren't here when I left. It could be people that have returned, or it could be people that have moved out from London.'

I took Leila and Taz with me, they were friendly and open and unthreatening, I filled up a couple of bottles of filtered water as gifts and then we walked around past the school up to the houses in Foxglove. The house I had seen lit up the previous night had been Nina's house. She and her two children had disappeared after the travellers from London had camped in the cemetery, but I wondered if she had returned.

I left Leila and Taz at the top of the garden and walked down and knocked on the door. It remained closed. 'Nina?' I called, 'Is that you?'

There was a noise from inside, then the curtain at the window next to me was pulled aside. Nina's face stared out at me. I smiled and gave a small wave and her face disappeared as she walked round to the door. It opened slowly. 'Hello?' she said weakly.

I was struck immediately by how thin she had become. 'Nina, it's Zoe,' she looked at me blankly, 'we met in the summer, do you remember? ... when we all met up at the school ....and the kids were all playing in the hall?' I paused before each sentence waiting for a response, but it wasn't until I mentioned the children that I got one, and it wasn't what I was expecting. Her eyes welled up with tears which dripped down her face, she stared at me, unmoving.

'Nina,' I asked, 'Where are William and Rachel?'

She turned around, still silently crying and walked back into the house towards the stairs. I quickly waved at Leila and Taz to come in and followed her up.

At the top of the stairs she turned right and walked into a brightly painted room with two small children's beds. Lying in the centre of the beds, unmoving, were two small shapes. I walked closer, horrified, it was William and Rachel, but pale copies of the chubby, lively kids they had been. Although they were dressed in clean, colourful clothing, their faces and hands were thin, the shapes of their skulls showing through, their chubbiness had gone and they lay there, their chests rising and falling faintly. As I stared at William his eyes opened 'mummy,' he whispered. I stopped, I had thought they were dead and the relief hit me like a sledgehammer.

'Nina, what happened?' I asked appalled.

'There wasn't any food,' she said brokenly, 'we went with them because they had food and I didn't have very much left in the house, but then a couple of weeks ago they ran out and we were kicked out. We walked and walked; it took us almost a week to get back here, but all the food was gone. I've been looking but I haven't found anything, not even in the gardens. We tried eating the grass but William was sick.'

Leila and Taz were standing in the doorway. Leila looked as horrified as I felt, but Taz looked odd, if anything she looked angry. 'Would you like to come with us?' I said gently, 'We have food,' I reached forward to pick up William as she nodded. He weighed very little and I could feel how thin he was. Leila moved forward and picked up Rachel.

Taz picked up a bag and stuffed in some toys and blankets and then we all, slowly and carefully, made our way downstairs.

Outside Nina blinked in the sunlight and swayed. 'Taz!' I said. I was holding William and couldn't catch her if she fell.

Taz grabbed hold of her shoulder, a bit roughly 'useless woman,' she muttered.

'What?' I said.

'Nothing,' she replied, guiding Nina up the path to the road.

We made our way back to my bungalow. Nina could only go very slowly, and it took at least twenty minutes. The kids were light, but they were awkward to carry for that length of time. I kicked the door when we arrived 'Freya,' I called.

We put them all on the sofa in the living room and I quickly researched starvation on the internet, I had a vague idea that it would be bad to just start feeding them normal food, Wikipedia as usual came up trumps, recommending a glucose syrup solution to avoid something called 'refeeding syndrome'. I mixed up some sugar and water whilst Freya made some peppermint tea and Nina sat broken, leaning against the sofa and staring into the fireplace.

'Where are Mark and Alex?' I asked.

'They decided to get started in their garden' she said, 'digging out some vegetable beds.' She lowered her voice slightly, 'Who are they?' I had no trouble understanding who she was referring to. I explained how I knew Nina. I felt odd; six months ago, I had been determined to conserve resources, now I was quite happy to take in a mother and two small children who couldn't contribute at all.

Over the next couple of hours, I circled round the estate, calling in at the other two houses that had shown lights the previous night. The inhabitants were both also returnees, Robert and Sheila were in better shape than Nina had been; they had made their way to their daughter who lived in St Albans. They had stayed there for the winter but decided to return a month ago when the soldiers had arrived to turn it into a settlement camp. Their daughter and her family had come with them and they were all doing ok on the food they had left hidden in their house. Robert had started growing the new season's vegetables in his greenhouse and although they agreed to regularly meet up and collaborate, they decided to stay in their house at the far end of the estate.

The final returnees were Amin and Rabia and their son Adam. They'd had a tough time when the Londoners had arrived, and had been hounded out of their home. They had moved in with friends on the other side of the railway in South Oxhey. Rabia was very enthusiastic about the friendliness of the community there 'They have allotments where they grow food, it is a communal project, everyone helps out,' she said. 'They cook food in the church and then take it round to all the older people.'

'It sounds nice,' I said, 'why did you leave?'

'The virus returned, people were getting sick again,' she replied sombrely, 'we just couldn't risk Adam.'

This was important news; none of us had known that there was a second wave of the virus. We went online and did some research. It turned out that the virus had mutated again when the weather had warmed up. People who had avoided it first time round were catching it this time, however it seemed only to be spreading in areas where there was still movement between populations, in the cities and larger towns.

I did a quick search to see if there was anything about the Chiltern Camp online, but apart from a single touristy page with the slogan 'Homes and Jobs for All' written in a large ornate font across the top, with platitudes and promises beneath, the internet came up blank. As I was about to close down the page Mark stopped me 'Click there,' he said. He pointed to a small hyperlink in the top right-hand corner.

'COUNCIL MEMBERS'.

The link took us to a simple login page. 'I recognise this,' said Mark, 'Hold on.' He left the room and I heard the front door open and close.

He came back waving a post-it note and looking more animated than usual 'I found it!' he said, 'I wasn't sure if I had given it to Ruth.' he passed the post-it note to me and I saw that it was a username and password.

'Is this the login?' I asked.

'Yes,' replied Mark, 'From Mr McAteer, it's what we used to get into the system in the first place.'

I typed it in and pressed enter. A new page loaded with multiple hyperlinks. We were inside their network. I looked up at Mark, then stood up and moved out of the way. 'Can you find them?' I asked.

'I can try,' he said.

18

Researching

After about ten minutes, the others drifted away. The system we had logged into was huge and difficult to navigate. Often clicking on a link would open new windows with searchable databases, but the search terms weren't obvious, Mark had to guess a lot of the time.

Our examination of the network uncovered some of the things that had been puzzling me about the Chiltern camp. Apart from the articles I had read online, I hadn't any real idea of how the government in the UK was operating. At national level, there were no political parties, but I had assumed that at local level things would be their normal inefficient self. But in Wendover it had seemed very much as if a small cabal of rich residents were in charge, and not any sort of elected representatives. In my limited experience, pre-outbreak councils were run by members of different parties, and it was the constant bickering between different councillors as they fought to get re-elected that made them so inefficient. However, the Chiltern parish council had seemed well run and organised; and in all the time I had been there, no one had ever mentioned politics or parties.

The databases revealed that the camps were all outside the M25 and were well connected, with constant transfers of resources between them. New camps were being added all the time; towns and villages that had survived the virus with some sort of structure in place. Places like Wendover, where everything still operated as normal. As long as they could produce resources to help support the new government, the government in turn supported whoever was in charge when the town was absorbed into the new system.

I found it odd that everyone seemed to buy into it, into the local currencies and allocated jobs, the use of refugee children to build a compliant workforce, but maybe they were just grateful for the appearance of normal life and didn't care who was in charge. Grieving for loved ones and shell-shocked from all the changes, they were probably happy to have someone tell them what to do. I know I had appreciated it; had been willing to be sucked in. If it hadn't been for what happened to Frank, I might never have looked much closer at the system.

The way they had caught us though…had they been searching for us? Or had they just been watching the roads, looking for people escaping the city? They certainly couldn't afford competition from alternative groups, People were in shock from the outbreak, but they must soon realise that democracy had disappeared.

I waited patiently until Mark clicked on a link labelled 'Transfers'. My eyes skimmed down the list of jobs and names and my gaze snagged on 'science teacher'. I recognised the name… Mr Webster.

'Stop' I said, 'go back'

Mark scrolled back and I read across to the destination. Glynneath, Wales. 'Click there' I said, breathlessly.

Mark clicked on the destination and a new page opened; it was a coal mine. He had found the transfer lists.

He looked at my aghast face, 'what is it?' he asked urgently.

'That was the old science teacher,' I said, 'he criticised the way things were run.'

Mark looked back at the screen. 'It looked like he paid a heavy price.' he said grimly.

He scrolled down the page, there were a lot of names; people placed in factories, spread out amongst farms and working in warehouses. I thought back to Stephen and his odd behaviour; caring for the kids, but compliant with a system that maltreated them. Maybe this explained it…if you spoke out against the system or caused any disruption, it would be easy to lose your assigned job and house, and if you couldn't pay for food… I suppose you would have to accept being transferred to work down a coalmine, especially if you had a family to feed.

Mark stopped scrolling and looked at me, we still hadn't found the others, and it seemed more urgent than ever.

'Maybe we should be more logical about this,' I said, 'let's map it out and see if we can see if there is an underlying structure.'

I picked up a pen and an A4 pad of lined paper. Mark went back to the initial page and I wrote down all the hyperlinks, each one on a separate page. Then we slowly went through. It took ages, but after a while, a pattern emerged. Each hyperlink was for an aspect of the camp, housing, jobs, food, sanitation etc. Each then linked to each of the separate camps but also to central services, then there would be links between sections so clicking on jobs there would be a link to sanitation and the dates of rubbish collections in each of the camps and the personnel involved. By writing it all down, we identified that some personnel worked at several different camps. The link for security seemed promising, but it wasn't until we accessed the information from a security job on the correct date, which linked to a set of new registrations at one of the hostels, did we find them. Clicking on the registrations the names came up; Ruth Sanders, Kai Perth, Eddie Leathers, Drew Taylor Alisha Gill, Jasmine Gill. We had found them; but they weren't in the Chiltern Camp, they were up at Potters Bar. And they weren't registered in the school.

'Great!' I said, 'But where are Jack and Liam?'

'Liam is younger than the others, maybe he was sent somewhere else,' said Mark.

I remembered Frank, and Ruth's friend; Michael. They had both been unable to work, Frank had been too old, Michael had been injured. And they had both died. The thought passed through my mind; Liam was young, and small, and after our escape he would be labelled as trouble. Would they bother to keep him for another three years until he was old enough to be allocated a job?

I shrugged off the awful thought and left Mark to find out as much as possible whilst I went to tell the others the good news. We had found them, now we just had to put together a rescue plan.

Leila and Taz were in their bungalow, rearranging the furniture to suit them. They were ecstatic when they heard we had found Ruth and the others, but I needed to bring them down to earth.

'Guys, what did you do for food before you joined the camp?' I asked.

'We scavenged,' said Leila.

'We were good at it,' said Taz, 'we could find food stashes people had left behind and no one else had found.'

'We lived in Hackney,' added Leila, 'we tried to stay away from the different gangs but eventually one expanded out to where we were living so we had to move.'

'We had heard about the settlement camp from a friend and we went online and applied,' said Taz.

'Why do you think they accepted you?' I asked; according to Ruth, they only took people with useful skills, as kids I would have expected the camp to turn them down.

'They accepted everyone, but I think the people they didn't want were told the wrong pickup point, several of our friends made the journey but returned having missed the pick-up.'

'But why did they take you two in?' I asked again.

The two girls were silent, then Taz spoke tentatively 'Maybe it's because we can sew; we designed all our outfits for our dance shows before the outbreak.'

'Yes,' agreed Laila, 'we put a lot about our ambitions to be dancers in the entry essay, but we also mentioned how we design and sew all our outfits, we even uploaded a couple of pictures of us in our outfits.'

I pondered what they had said, and then looked at them, there were enough clothes left in shops and warehouse across the country to last for at least ten years, so that wasn't it. But both girls were pretty to look at, their dancing background had made them fit and strong and in a few years' time the boys would be all over them. I shook my head, but the thought wouldn't go away; they had been accepted for their looks, as girlfriend material for the Wendover boys.

The scale of the social engineering stunned me. If it was true, then the new government had gone way beyond its remit. I shook off my thoughts, 'so you're good at finding food,' I said, 'would you like to take charge of that here? I have some stocks but we are going to need more.'

'Sure,' said Taz.

'I've checked most of the houses here in Carpenders Park, and there seems to be a lot of people still in South Oxhey, but you could walk over the hill to Bushey. I've not been over there at all. Or perhaps go south across the fields to hatch end.'

'Don't worry,' said Leila, 'we'll rustle up some supplies.'

'I have a map...' I said. I was nervous about sending them off into unknown areas; they seemed so young.

'Thanks but I'm dyslexic,' said Taz.

'We don't really need a map,' said Leila.

They must have read the doubt in my face. 'Don't worry, we did this for six months after our mums left, we'll be fine,' said Taz.

I remember her muttered comment to Nina, it sounded like Taz and Leila had been on their own for a while. I felt a pang of sadness for all the kids who were now alone.

'Can I see your garden?' I asked, changing tack. I wanted to remind myself of what it looked like and what we could easily grow.

We walked around together mapping out which beds could go where. We peered over the top of the fence on the right side, it was flimsy and would be quite easy to take down so we could combine the two gardens. I was glad I had bought so many seeds; it looked like we would be able to cultivate enough food for all of us and more.

I walked across the road to Alex next. He was in the garden, digging away. I gave him the news and he gave me a big hug, 'sorry Miss, I'm just so happy,' he said, 'it will be great to see Drew and the others again, plus they can help with the work.' He picked up the spade again and set to with a will, whistling while I wandered around. The gardens on either side had large raised patio areas and mature shrubs. It would be hard laborious work to dig out the shrubs or lift the patio. When I had looked at Leila and Taz's garden I'd had a vision of a large combined strip of gardens, stretching all along behind the bungalows, farmed all together rather like the allotments at Wendover had been. However, on this side, it looked like it would be too much work to do that. The gardens would have to stay as individual units.

I stared over the fence at the sun shining down on the patios. I looked at the overgrown lawn with the swings and slide in the middle. Maybe it would work for Nina and her two children. She should hopefully be up to some light container gardening soon. The patios were south facing and would suit the potato plants. They wouldn't require much work, especially if we moved the irrigation system from my garden.

I walked back to my bungalow making plans but as I entered Mark called out 'I have bad news,' he said, 'they're being transferred to a salmon fishery in Scotland.' I walked into the kitchen and sat in the chair beside him.

'That sounds a bit drastic, even for David' I said.

'That man is vicious.' he replied, 'he shows a pleasant face to all the camp residents, but he was always nasty to the refugees, especially the girls.'

'I saw,' I said, 'but why? What does he have against them?'

'I don't know,' replied Mark, 'But they couldn't run away if they were stuck up in the wilds of Scotland.'

'Who's decision would it have been, to send them up there?' I asked.

'If it was David that raised the alarm, then he would have been in charge of what happened to them.'

'Is there any way of checking where he is?' I asked.

Mark clicked through some links and reached the schedule for the Chiltern Camp parish council desk. 'The office is open as normal so he must be at the Chiltern camp.' he said, as I sighed in relief.

'When are they due to leave?' I asked.

Mark clicked on a link labelled Great Northern 'See, it's the train timetable.' There were very few trains listed, one every couple of days. He clicked on Wednesday and a new window opened 'and here is the passenger list.' the list was small, only about twenty passengers. All six of them were listed.

'That's only three days away!' I said in dismay.

He clicked back a couple of times and then opened a new link to a salmon farm. He clicked on a personnel list, at the bottom were the six familiar names with the word 'pending' beside them.

I sat back, stunned for a second, we only had a couple of days and then they would be gone. There was no way we would be able to get up to Scotland to rescue them. We needed a plan. I pulled out a road atlas from my bookshelf, if we were going to rescue them, we needed to see exactly where we were going.

'Have you found Liam or Jack?' I asked.

'No,' said Mark, still intent on the computer.

I found the page for Potters Bar; it was a small town, nearly circular, just off the M25. The south side by the motorway was probably well protected but on the north side there was a large green golf course stretching alongside the railway line.

'Mark, where exactly is the hostel?' I asked. There was a pause and a couple of clicks.

'Ash Park community centre on Mutton Road,' he pulled up google maps and I watched as he zoomed into Potters Bar.

'There,' I pointed at the screen, 'it's not bad, next to a primary school and surrounded by playing fields. Those trees along the edge look like they would provide some cover.'

He zoomed out a bit, 'Looks like warehouses to the north, and …what this?'

'The railway,' I replied, and the golf course.'

He zoomed in to Street-View and we saw a big stone building with huge bay windows and a large strong looking door. 'Hmm,' I muttered, 'Not promising.'

'Do you think they're being held there all the time?' It was Freya who had silently drifted back in from Matty's room without us noticing.

We looked at each other, there was no way to know except by actually being there and watching. Google maps was all very well but it was out of date and wouldn't show the new fences and security measures.

'I could go,' said Freya, 'sneak in via the golf course, across the streets,' she indicated the streets she meant on the screen, 'and then climb a tree. No one would see me.'

I looked at her, it was true, she moved quietly, and I had seen the way she had scaled the fence at the overpass. She was athletic and unobtrusive. And as a girl the soldiers would probably go easy on her, if Mark went it would be a different story, and I wasn't sure if I was up to scaling trees. I nodded slowly.

'No way,' said Mark, 'you must be insane,' he looked at us both.

'Why?' said Freya, 'we know the guards probably aren't that observant.'

'But…' said Mark.

We both knew what he wanted to say, but it seemed silly, yes, he was big and strong and used to looking after the others, but Freya was no less capable.

'I have a good road bike stashed, it's fast and light, you could be there in just over an hour.'

Freya nodded.

'Dawn is about half five,' I said, 'early morning is a good time, most people are asleep, and the soldiers seem less alert.'

'But what about meeting people on the way there,' said Mark, 'we have no idea how safe it is or if the route is open along the roads.'

'Okay…' I said, 'How about you go with her and…' I looked at the atlas 'wait here,' I indicated a road to the north of the town, 'there's a path marked across this field that goes down to the golf course.'

Mark zoomed out on google maps and scrolled the image northward. Then he zoomed in to Street View again. It looked good, a nice open road, and a path that started at a gate beside a large complex of buildings.

'You just need a bike,' I said.

'I think there's a men's bike in the shed at our place,' said Mark, 'I'll check it out tonight.'

I left Mark and Freya to plan their route and sort out supplies, and went in to check on Nina and the children.

'They keep falling asleep,' she said in a whisper, I looked over at William and Rachel, they looked peaceful, but I knew that what they needed was food.

'How much of the glucose syrup did they drink?' I asked.

'Not much, a couple of sips,' she replied.

I opened my phone and sat beside her doing more research. 'Okay,' I said. 'We need to get them to drink about 100ml every two hours.'

I went back up into the loft and found my stash of medicines. The surrounding houses had yielded a lot of different pills and liquids, and I had organised them into airtight food containers in a box in the eaves. I rooted around until I found a bottle of Calpol. Inside the box was a syringe. I took it back down and filled it with the glucose syrup. 'Pick up William' I said, 'hold him upright so he swallows.'

Nina picked him up and took the syringe, squirting the liquid quickly into his mouth. Half dribbled out, but he swallowed. She smiled in relief, 'thanks.'

I sat beside her whilst she fed William and then Rachel, scrolling though articles on my phone. Most info agreed that we would need to switch to something with protein in soon. Special formula milks were used in hospitals, but maybe just normal baby formula would work, I would get Leila and Taz to look out for some.

Next I went to check on Matty. He was still sleeping but tossing and turning and when I checked his forehead, he was very hot. It looked like he had an infection. I didn't have any antibiotics, but I had a lot of paracetamol and aspirin to bring the temperature down if it got dangerously high. The only problem was how would I administer it? I walked back to Mark and Freya.

'Matty has a temperature,' I said, 'I'll monitor it and if it reaches 40 degrees, I'll give him some paracetamol.' I looked at the gear they were collecting. 'What's with the towel?' I asked.

'It's an easy way to hide,' replied Freya, 'people don't check under a grubby towel in a hedge.'

'In fact they positively look away from something they don't like seeing.' said Mark, 'A towel with a few dodgy stains and you're invisible.'

The towel they had on the table looked fresh and new, but I had no doubt that by the time they had arrived they would have found a way to mess it up thoroughly.

'What time will you leave?' I asked.

'Just after 4am,' said Mark.

I looked at the clock; it was getting on to 6pm, time for some dinner, my evening walk around the estate, and then an early night.

Just as I was thinking of making dinner, Leila and Taz popped in. 'Can you guys cook?' I asked.

'Move over,' said Taz, looking through the cupboards. I sat at the table and watched the magic in action. They were just like Frank had been; adding spices and odd ingredients, they sent me out to get some garlic and an onion which they chopped up with speed and panache, they fried them then added the tomato paste and the spices. The resulting pasta meal was an explosion of flavours. I promised myself yet again that I would learn how to cook.

Nina woke me just before 4am. Freya was almost ready and very soon Mark was knocking at the door.

Before I was really aware, they were ready and standing in the open doorway. 'I'll expect you to be back tonight, but will wait till tomorrow to come looking for you if you're not,' I said. 'Be careful.' I anxiously watched them go; it okay when it was me having the adventures, sending someone else off into danger was much harder.

19

Finding

Although it was very early, I didn't feel like going back to sleep so I helped Nina with the 4am feed. The children seemed to be a bit livelier, squirming against the syringe and generally moving around more. Nina had taken out some of the toys that Taz had packed and William was holding a boat. For some reason that snagged in my mind and reminded me of Liam.

'I wonder what has happened to Liam,' I said.

'Who?' asked Nina.

'Liam was the youngest kid who came with us; we were resting under the M25 when the soldiers started chasing us. Freya said he went into the water, aiming for a boat on the other side of the canal.'

'Did he make it?' she asked.

I thought back to what Freya had said, 'I don't think anyone saw,' I said, 'we just assumed he was taken, but he might not have been.'

'So where is he now?' she asked.

I frowned; we had left the camp on Saturday, I had arrived home in the late afternoon, yesterday we had spent settling in. That meant if Liam hadn't been captured then he would have been alone for almost two whole days. If he had escaped, he would be wet and cold. He hadn't turned up yesterday so he could be anywhere. Hiding in the boat we had seen, or somewhere along the canal or in the surrounding countryside. He was young but sensible; he hadn't been particularly close friends with anyone in the group, so he had probably arrived at the camp alone, which meant he was used to getting by on his own. What would he have done? If he had made it to the boat and hidden, and then come out much later to find us all gone, would he have stayed at the boat, hoping someone would come and find him, or would he have made a dash along the canal hoping the soldiers wouldn't be around? And he would be cold and wet, last night the temperature had been in the single digits.

How likely would it be that the soldiers hadn't found him? I didn't think they had followed us from Wendover; they had come down the sliproad from the M25, rather than along the towpath. I walked into the kitchen and switched on the computer, google maps showed the time to drive between Potters Bar and the canal as 11 minutes. That worked; it seemed probable that the soldiers had come from Potters Bar, which is why they had deposited the other kids there.

So they must have been alerted by someone. And the only person who knew we had left had been David. How had he got free? I thought back to the encounter in the kitchen; he had been very loud, it was quite probable that Irina had come over to check on me, she was nosy that way. And then they would have raised the alarm.

Would they have been able to track us using CCTV? I hadn't seen any cameras along the towpath, but maybe there had been some, where we had crossed the road at Halton, or in Tring. Or maybe there were cameras under the motorway.

Would they have been able to see Liam slip into a boat? The only way to find out would be to go back and check.

I debated taking Alex with me, but he was still sleeping. Google maps said it would take 37 minutes to cycle there if I went through the park in Watford. I could be there and back before the rest of the kids woke up. And at least I would know, remove some of the guilt I felt for not realising earlier that he might still be there.

I wrote a brief note explaining where I was going, then I packed up a rucksack with some food and water, a map of Watford and my usual bits and pieces. I grabbed my other bike, put a pair of spare trainers and a change of clothes in the paniers, and then cycled out of the driveway.

It was still dark with a faint lightening of the sky to the east. I was heading north but some of the streetlights were still on. There were two hilly bits and by the time I reached the park, the muscles that had just recovered from the excursion two days past were complaining again. The hills were much harder than riding alongside a flat canal and I ended up walking for a bit. Then I was into the park and coasting along. After about forty minutes I stopped and checked the map; I was probably less than ten minutes away.

I cycled on slowly, looking for escape routes and places to hide. There was a lock, and a stretch full of narrowboats, and then I came to a low bridge where the path split. I followed the upper path into a village; if we were chased, we could lose them here. I went back down to the towpath and took a deep breath. The sky was lightening, and the birds were kicking up a racket. I knew I was close. I rode flat out, aiming to get there as quickly as possible. I passed the lock I had run over to escape, I zoomed past and it was only when it was behind me that I realised there was a boat there, trapped behind the gates. I skidded to a stop and ran back. Then I stopped. I had no idea if this was the same boat. I looked up at the path ahead, then at my watch, if I had been seen I had about fifteen minutes before the soldiers arrived.

The boat was an attractive deep blue colour with decorative yellow borders. The front of the boat was trapped by the sides of the canal and the gate, with only a couple of inches of movement. The back of the boat was drifting unmoored, floating from side to side in the wider stretch of water. I walked up onto the lock gates and looked down. There didn't seem to be an opening at the front of the boat, just a triangular wooden window and a canvas covering. I sat down on the edge of the lock gate and put my feet on the small triangle of deck. Hanging on to the rail behind me I leaned forward and knocked on the windows.

I waited and knocked harder, then harder still, but there was no response. Either he wasn't here, or he was hiding. The deck was fairly steady so without thinking too much, I put my weight on my feet and stepped onto the front of the boat. It dipped and I wobbled sideways, snatching at the top of the canvas. As I grabbed, several poppers at the edge of the canvas popped open; it was some sort of removable covering. Steadying myself with my left hand on the top and swaying slightly as the boat jiggled under me, I snapped open the remaining poppers and rolled back the fabric. There was a small space inside, behind the triangular windows and below the level of the sides. Hanging on to the canvas I swung my leg around the edge of the window and stepped down into the well of the boat.

At the back of the tiny well was a door into the main part of the boat. It was inset with two windows and I knocked hard as I peered inside. It was still too dark to see much so I pulled a torch out of my rucksack and shone it round inside. As the light moved across the room, I could see a bed, and a flash of movement. I knocked again, 'Liam?' I called. I tried the door handle, but it was locked. 'Liam?' I called again, 'it's Zoe, are you in there?'

I waited but there was no response. I looked at my watch, time was moving on. 'Liam, it's Zoe, some of us made it home, Mark and Freya have gone looking for the others and I came looking for you.' I had a sudden idea and screwing my eyes tightly closed I shone the torch against my face. I waited. 'See,' I said, 'it's me.' there was still no response. I waited a little longer. I was sure I had seen movement. But maybe I was mistaken. I pressed my face up against the door. In the silence the cough was clear, there was someone in there! I shone the torch in through the window 'Liam,' I called, 'Liam please come out, there isn't anyone here but me.' I waited hopefully but heard nothing more. I looked at my watch again. I had time, I could wait. I slid down into the well and sat with my back to the door. Then I began to talk, I spoke about how I had escaped, falling in the canal, running along the train tracks and through the tunnel, sleeping in the shopping centre, finding Alex at the station and then Mark and Freya and Matty at the house. I talked about Matty's injuries and about Alex finding Taz and Leila. I looked at my watch again. I was running out of time; I would have to leave. I was sure there was someone inside, but maybe it wasn't Liam, maybe it was someone else.

I stood up and eyed the front of the boat. I would have to swing myself back out onto the front, stepping up onto the edge of the boat to do so. I scrambled up, grabbed the lock gate rail and stepped up. I looked at my watch; it had been over ten minutes. I stared down at the boat and then walked down to the tow path. I picked up my bike and looked around, not knowing what to do next. Then from behind me I heard a faint noise. 'Zoe...'

I turned around; standing in the well at the front of the boat was Liam. We stared at each other and then I dropped my bike and bounded back onto the lock gate as he stepped up onto the front of the boat. I reached out to steady him and pulled him off the boat and into a hug. He was cold and still damp and looked very, very tired. 'Let's get away from here as quickly as possible,' I said.

I wheeled the bike along the path as he walked beside me, stumbling and silent. 'What happened?' I asked, 'Have you been here since Saturday?'

'I hid in the boat,' said Liam, 'and then when everyone was gone, I untied it, but I couldn't get past...' he trailed of exhaustedly and I decided that questions could wait.

I took us up into the village and we went into the first house we found; it was a big white house overlooking the canal with small windows but nice enough inside. I took out the clothes and trainers. 'They're size five,' I said, 'is that ok?'

'Yeah, close enough.' Liam took the clothes into the front room while I poked around in the kitchen. I tried the electricity and found it was on, so I took the bottle of water from my rucksack and boiled the kettle. A hot drink would do him the world of good. There hadn't been any sign of soldiers, but I wanted to be sure.

'When you've dressed, I put food and a hot drink on the table, eat quickly and we'll get going,' I said, as I climbed the stairs. The room at the back had a window overlooking the canal and I scanned the towpath as I waited. Soon enough

Liam was ready. My old tracksuit bottoms and fleece were a bit big for him, but at least he would be warm.

'Are you up to cycling back?' I asked, he nodded, 'then we need to find you a bike.' I hadn't planned this very well; I could have found the bike on my first trip through the village. We went back out onto the road and began methodically searching. We were in a small estate of new-build houses with tiny gardens and block parking at the rear. Fortunately, someone had methodically smashed in the wooden fencing, giving access to all the houses. I made him sit and eat the refresher bar from my survival kit as I searched; he looked like he needed the energy.

I found a lot of children's bikes; tiny princess bikes with training wheels and small bikes with reflectors and bright colouring for younger kids, but eventually found one that Liam could use. It was small but functional. I took it back to him and found him staring into the distance. 'Come on, let's get you back,' I said.

The journey back was quicker, and we were up by South Oxhey in less than thirty minutes. 'Nearly there,' I said quietly, but Liam just nodded in reply. We pulled up outside my bungalow and I left the bikes at the side. I opened the door and called out quietly 'it's just me, and I found Liam.'

Nina came out into the hallway, 'that was quick,' she said.

'And easy,' I said, 'I should have gone yesterday.'

'But you were busy, you were helping all these children, and you found me and William and Rachel, you did the best you could,' she said, as we moved into the kitchen.

I looked at Liam, 'are you injured?' I asked, 'You're very quiet.'

'No,' he replied, 'Just tired, I didn't sleep much on the boat.' He stood patiently as I looked at him abstractly. There wasn't room in my place, but I could put him with Leila and Taz for now, and we could work something out later, maybe secure another bungalow.

'Are you hungry?' I asked.

'No I'm fine,' he said, the exhaustion showing.

'Ok, this is my house, I'm going to take you to Taz and Leila, it's a little early, but hopefully they won't mind.'

We walked over silently, and I rang the doorbell. I heard a quick movement inside and then Leila was at the door, 'Liam!' she pushed past me and gave him a hug then looked at me concerned when he just stood there, unresponsive.

'He's very tired, and perhaps coming down with something, can he sleep at yours?' I asked.

'Of course,' she replied as she pulled him in.

We had regained another member of our little group. Now we just had to wait for Mark and Freya to come back to see if we could rescue the others.

20

Planning

I couldn't settle to anything, just drifted from task to task waiting for Mark and Freya to get back. Vik hadn't messaged and the worry was starting all over again. I checked on Matty who didn't seem to be any worse. Mark had changed his dressing and clothes and taken him to the bathroom the night before, but he hadn't really woken up properly. He hadn't eaten anything only drunk some water. I was worried about dehydration. I made a large flask of peppermint tea and periodically woke him up to make him drink some. It seemed to me that he was slightly better, and I was encouraged when he asked for Mark so he could use the loo. I went off to get Alex instead who then stayed for breakfast. He was surprised and slightly upset to hear about Liam, I think that, like me, he felt guilty that we had just left him there. He wanted to go see him immediately, but I held him back explaining that Liam needed rest more than anything else. I did some desultory gardening, and then walked down to Robert and Sheila, just for a chat really.

Robert was in his greenhouse, pricking out the seedlings from trays into individual pots. Like me, he had a lot of old seed packets and had more than enough to grow the food he needed.

'I'm going to need to save the seed from the veg this year,' I said, 'I just wish I didn't have so many F1 varieties.'

'It will add variety,' said Robert cheerfully, 'we won't quite know what we will get when we plant the seeds.'

I smiled, 'I wonder if the garden centre has spare seeds,' I said, 'open pollinated varieties. I wish I could make contact with the people there, I'm sure we could help each other.'

'You mean Ben?' asked Robert.

'Do you know them?' I asked in surprise.

'I was there when they first arrived,' he replied, 'Ben worked in the store, he lived in Wembley but when people started falling ill, he moved up here. He brought his sister and her family with him, I think. The owners were leaving to stay with friends in the country, so they gave the keys to him in return for him keeping the plants alive while the place was shut.'

'Do you see them at all?' I asked, I was curious to know what they were like.

'Not since that first day when they moved in,' he said.

'Would you go with me to visit them?' I asked, 'I left my wheelbarrow with all my perishable food at their front gate when I left.'

'Sure,' said Robert, 'we could go this afternoon, if that suits you?'

'That would be great,' I said, 'I'd quite like my wheelbarrow back.'

For lunch, Nina cooked a spicy Mexican dish with beans and rice. William and Rachel seemed to be recovering nicely so I put my mind to obtaining baby formula. It wasn't something Frank or I had collected so we discussed where we were likely to find some.

'How about the pharmacy?' said Alex, 'Did you check it out already?'

'Yes but there were a lot of medicines and we had no idea what most of them were for, we only took things we recognised.'

'Ok well, let's go back there and have a look.'

I wasn't due to meet Robert until two o'clock, so Nina and I nipped down to the pharmacy whilst Alex watched the kids. We stepped over the shattered glass frontage and into the shop. The shelves were stripped bare, just a couple of bottles of sunscreen and hair products lying around. I had been inside several times over the past nine months but this time my eye zoned in on kids' products. I moved into the back area where the medicines were stocked.

'Perhaps it would be easier if we tidied up,' said Nina, 'pass me everything back there, and I'll stack it on the counter so we can see what we have.'

'There's still quite a lot here,' I said, as I began passing it though the hatch to her.

Eventually the shelves were all empty, and I turned my attention to the cardboard boxes on the floor. Most had been opened and contained small white boxes of medicines. I passed those through also. Behind them, right in the back corner under the bottom shelf, tucked away was a couple of sealed boxes. I pulled out my tiny knife and slit the tape on top of the first; more white boxes of pills, then I opened the second. Inside were large cans.

'I've found something called Aptomil,' I said, is that any good?'

Nina gave a shriek and bounded round the door, snatching the can out of my hand. 'This is perfect, it's infant formula, but that should work fine.'

I brought the boxes round to the front and stared at the mass of pills, jars, and bottles. 'What we really need is a catalogue, listing what all these are,' I said, remembering the book my dad had used, before the internet became the go-to source of knowledge. 'Then we could arrange these over the shelves and have the book on the counter and people could just select what they need.' I looked around, that was for the future, for now Nina was eager to get back to her children and it was coming up to two o'clock, I had an appointment to keep.

Robert came to my house and I re-introduced him to Nina, William, and Rachel, he was shocked at the state they were in and apologetic that he hadn't been to check on her. I took him round to Leila and Taz, partly so I could ask after Liam, and then we popped in on Alex who was making great strides in the garden. The new beds were taking shape and would be ready for planting soon.

'This is great,' said Robert to Alex, 'come up and see me at my place and I'll get you started with some seedlings.'

We then walked up the road to the garden centre where Robert rang the bell on the gate, we waited, looking at the empty beds surrounding the car park...all that arable soil and nothing planted, it was such a waste.

'Do they know you are coming?' I asked.

'No, I just assumed they would be here' he replied.

'They probably are,' I said, 'but I think they are still hiding.'

I wondered how long they would stay locked up in the garden centre alone, and if they would be surprised to see how well we were getting on, working together.

I turned to leave 'we'll find another way to get in touch,' I said, as we walked back down the road.

We parted in front of my house and I walked in yawning. I was tired after my early start to the day and all I really felt like doing was sleeping. I checked in on Matty and Nina and then succumbed to temptation and went for a nap.

I was woken by the doorbell. It was dark in my room; I must have slept for hours. I dragged myself out of bed, as I heard voices at the door. Naps always made me drowsy. It was Freya and Mark, back from their stakeout, and standing between them was Jack.

'I'm starving,' he said with a smile, 'is dinner ready?'

Nina had let them in and now she backed away into the living room so I could get closer.

'Sorry,' I said, 'I fell asleep...but I have a surprise for you guys also.' I grabbed my jacket and indicated they should go out. We walked over to Leila and Taz and rang the bell. I heard a muffled shout from inside the house and then the door opened. It was Liam, looking much refreshed.

'Liam!' said Freya and Mark together, moving in to hug him simultaneously. There was a bit of a crush on the doorstep.

'How did you get back?' asked Mark.

'Did you escape the soldiers?' asked Freya.

'Is there any food?' asked Jack.

Liam answered the last question first. 'Taz is cooking, she went over to your place first,' he said, looking at me 'and when she saw you were asleep, she started on dinner.'

'But how did you get here?' said Mark again.

'Let's go inside,' I said, 'we're letting all the warm air out'

We trooped into the kitchen where, yet again, Leila and Taz were producing delicious smells. They had magicked up a lentil and chickpea curry with rice and homemade flatbread. They were delighted to see Jack but after the initial round of hugs went back to the cooking.

'I wasn't worried,' said Taz, 'I knew you were ok.'

'No-one would ever catch Jack,' said Leila to me.

'I'm sure you have some good stories though,' said Taz.

'Shall we get Alex first?' asked Leila, lifting the pot of curry off the stove and onto a trivet on the table 'so we can eat?'

I went out to let the kids have their own private reunion. Alex was hungry as usual and I sent him over and went back to check on Nina and Matty and the children. Matty was still sleeping and I was beginning to worry. Surely he should be awake by now. But I believed in the curative powers of sleep, so I let him be. Nina was fine, she had correctly assumed Jack was another of the kids that had escaped with me and was busy giving the children their first feed of milk.

'Taz and Leila made curry, so I'll bring you back some later,' I said.

'No problem,' she replied, lifting William on to her lap, 'this is going to take some time.'

I washed my face and tried to feel more awake. Then I walked back over to hear what Mark and Freya had found out.

Taz answered the door this time.

'We wondered where you had got to; Freya and Mark were just about to start,' she said.

I went in, grabbed some food and sat down.

'Ok,' said Mark, 'the ride there was uneventful, but when we got to the road, we found that the buildings next to the path we had chosen were being used as a military base. The fence had been extended north all the way to the road.'

'The council members like their game of golf apparently,' said Jack.

'We rode back a way and stashed the bikes in a field, then we walked back looking for a way to get through,' said Freya. 'We managed to avoid the patrols but the only place we could get over the fence was right by the base. There was a gate there which was just about climbable.'

'For Freya,' said Mark, 'I couldn't get over, so I crawled into a hedge in the field on the other side of the road, covered myself with the towel and waited.'

'Once inside the fence it was easy, there were only a few early morning joggers,' said Freya, 'I made my way across the train tracks and down to the hostel, looking for a good tree to climb when suddenly a load of twigs fell in my face. I looked up and there was Jack, right in the middle of the very tree I would have picked.'

'So how did you end up there, Jack?' I asked, 'had you escaped already?'

'Sort of, only I was never really caught; I climbed up onto the motorway, there was a truck up there, so I jumped in and hid behind some boxes. I was hoping to get out before the soldiers left but didn't get a chance. When the others were caught, they were put into the same truck with two guards. Ruth saw me but not the others, their hands were zip-tied otherwise I would have tried helping them get away.'

'Did they look ok?' I asked, 'Did anyone get hurt?'

'No, they were all fine,' he said, 'Jasmine and Alisha were wet through, but the soldiers gave them a blanket.'

I nodded in relief, the two girls had seemed the least able to take care of themselves, and I had been worried that they would be left cold and wet.

'When we reached the town, the truck got waved through the gate without any checks and they were really slapdash at the hostel, just pushed them out and escorted them inside, leaving the truck unguarded. It was easy for me to slide out. I was trying to work out a way to get them free when I saw Freya stumbling about below me.'

'But where did you sleep?' I asked.

'Oh, there are plenty of empty houses; it doesn't seem like a normal settlement camp, more like a place for council members and army families.'

'Once I found Jack I wanted to leave immediately, but he said there would be too many people on the golf course to cross safely,' said Freya.

'So we went for a look around town,' said Jack. 'Did you know there was a hydroponics shop there?'

'Is there?' I was excited; more irrigation kit would be so useful.

'Yeah, and it wasn't guarded at all,' said Jack.

'Aren't they using it then?' I asked.

'Like I said, they're pretty slapdash, although there was a sign on the door saying, 'council property' the front shutters were open, and the door wasn't locked,' replied Jack.

'Oh, I brought you a present,' said Freya, she reached into her backpack which was under the table and pulled out a blue and green rectangular box about ten inches long.

'Oh, this is great!' I said, immediately recognising it, 'I have one of these, it's an Autopot.' the rest of the kids looked blankly back at me. 'It has a float inside that opens and closes a valve that controls the flow of water…it's an automatic watering system,' I said, excitedly.

'I knew you'd like it,' said Freya.

'Did they have a lot of them?' I asked.

'Yes, a shelf full, a couple of different types.'

'But that won't help us get Ruth and the others back,' interjected Mark. 'We need to know if we can get them out, Jack refused to answer any questions before we got back,' he said, a shade disgruntledly.

'So were they in the hostel?' I asked.

'Yes,' said Freya, 'in a bedroom at the back, on the first floor, we were very lucky, we could see right into their room.'

'I watched them for the rest of Saturday and on and off on Sunday,' said Jack, 'by the time I had worked out where they were, they were free of the zip ties but locked in. They were let out of the room for meals but not at any other time.'

'What about bathroom visits?' I asked, 'how did they arrange that?'

'Their room had a bathroom attached,' said Freya, 'but it didn't have a window.'

'How big were the windows in the bedroom?' asked Mark. 'Could we get in that way?

'They were tall windows where you pull the whole window up and down to open and close it, a pair of them, starting low down, about a foot off the floor,' said Freya, using her hands to mime pushing something up and down.

I nodded in recognition 'sash windows, I know what you mean.'

'They didn't open,' said Jack, 'I saw Kai and Eddie trying to force them, several times.'

'They had window seats,' said Freya, 'Ruth spent a lot of time sitting in one.

'What about a back door?' asked Alex 'was there a way to get in?'

'There was a door into the kitchen, but they didn't go there, they used the other room at the back for meals.' said Jack.

'Was the door locked?' asked Taz.

'Yeah, I tried it Saturday night; I was hoping to break them out.'

'Someone opened the door whilst we were watching, Monday morning,' said Freya, 'they unlocked it, got something from the shed and then went back in and relocked it. Then they hung the key on a hook by the door, you could see them putting it back through the kitchen window.'

'Is there any way we could get the key?' I asked.

'Well normally I would use a fishing rod' said Jack, 'but that's if the keys are by the front door and we can get through the letterbox. Back doors are harder.'

'So who had keys to the front?' I asked 'or were there always people inside to let visitors in?'

'It's hard to say,' said Jack, 'I'm pretty sure they left one guard behind when the staff went home in the evenings.'

'Staff?' I queried.

'Yeah, they had other people staying in the hostel, people who weren't locked in their rooms,' said Jack, 'they were in the rooms upstairs at the front and used the front rooms downstairs during the day.'

'Did you find out who they were?' asked Mark.

'No, well I couldn't exactly ask anyone,' he said.

'Some new guests arrived on the Monday,' said Freya, 'early, just after I had found Jack. I went to look round the front and saw them with their suitcases being greeted at the front door.'

There was a silence as we thought about that.

'So it's not a prison?' I asked.

'No,' replied Freya, 'I think it's just a hostel for visitors to the town. They're just locking Ruth and the others in to keep them from escaping before they transfer them up North.'

It didn't sound promising; I couldn't think of a single idea that didn't have serious problems. If we could get a ladder, we might be able to break the window to the room, but it would be noisy and dangerous. That type of window usually had thick glass in, which would break into shards and rain down on whoever was holding the ladder. I could perhaps pretend to be a new council clerk and knock on the backdoor and swipe the key somehow, but they would expect me at the front door not the back, and they would lock the door after I had left. The fishing rod idea sounded good, but we needed a hole for access.

'Was there a cat flap?' I asked hopefully.

'No,' said Freya. 'Remember it was a community centre before the outbreak.'

'Could one of us get captured and swipe the keys as we go in?' asked Alex.

'Not if your hands are zip-tied,' said Mark.

'How about if we start a fire,' said Taz.

'That might work,' I said slowly, 'a fire at night, if they evacuated the building, with only maybe one guard, in the confusion we might be able to grab them and get away.'

'It would draw a lot of attention,' said Mark.

'Well maybe we don't need an actual fire,' I said, 'maybe we could pretend a fire to get the guard to let me in, and then I could incapacitate the guard somehow. Get them to let me in and then drug them like in the movies.'

'How?' asked Alex.

I went to the computer and opened google. After a quick search, I saw something familiar - Chloroform. It was in all the old detective stories so should have been quite easy to make. Some further research revealed that all I needed was some acetone and bleach. But then I looked at the side effects;

it looked like pretty horrible stuff, vomiting, liver damage, even heart failure. I suddenly had second thoughts.

'No I don't think this will work' I said, 'let's go back to the fire idea.'

'Was there a fire station in the town?' Alex asked Jack.

'We didn't see one,' he replied.

I googled Potters Bar fire station and quickly came up with a picture of the station, 'yes they do,' I said.

But would they have firefighters?' asked Leila, 'I haven't seen any in the past nine months and there weren't any in the Chiltern Camp.'

This was news to me 'what did they do if there was an emergency?' I asked.

'They called in the army for any emergencies,' said Taz.

'And we definitely don't want that to happen,' said Leila.

'Yeah but if we rescue the others that will trigger a search anyway,' said Jack.

'Not if we get them out without them noticing,' said Mark.

'Well they'll notice if they all run off during a fire,' responded Jack.

There was a pause then Liam spoke for the first time, 'Could we use the chaos to get someone in, rather than get people out?' he said.

'What do you mean?' I asked.

'Well, if someone slips inside, they could hide and wait until everything calmed down and then use the backdoor key to unlock the door.'

'We would still need the key to the room,' said Mark.

'And need to avoid the guard,' said Jack.

'So where would the key to the room be?' I asked, 'Would the guard have it?'

'I don't know,' said Jack, 'there isn't a window into the hallway.'

'But was it a staff member or the guard who let them out for meals?' I asked.

'The guard I think,' said Jack, 'he would leave the kitchen and then they would arrive in the downstairs room a couple of minutes later.'

'And did the guard take a key with them?'

'No…. I don't think so,' said Jack.

'I didn't see them take a key either,' said Freya.

'So maybe the key is upstairs by the door,' I said, 'if they hang the backdoor key by the backdoor, it would make sense that they hang the key to the locked room, by the locked room.'

'It's a bit of a gamble,' said Mark.

'But there would be no harm in trying,' said Alex, 'what's the worst that could happen?'

'The worst would be that the fire alarm goes off, the army arrive, they realise there is no fire, get suspicious and take them somewhere more secure,' said Mark.

'If we just need someone to get inside, I could pretend to be a new guest,' I said, 'could you add my name to the hostel list using the computer?' I asked Mark.

'Probably,' he said slowly.

'So I could get in, then at night I could get the key and unlock the room.'

'But what about the guard?' said Taz.

'The guard mostly stayed in the kitchen,' said Jack, 'The house is not that big, so he just stayed in the one room.'

'Did he take toilet breaks?' I asked, 'Could we lock him in the toilet?'

'I don't know,' said Jack,' 'he left the kitchen twice whilst I was watching but I don't know where he went…and remember, I didn't stay and watch the whole night.'

We looked at each other; it seemed we had the beginnings of a plan.

Mark booked me in under a false name at the hostel, arriving in the evening. I didn't want to be waiting around too long and increasing the risk I would be found out. Freya said the new arrivals had been checked at the hostel gates, so Mark searched through the intranet to find the gate security lists and add my new name there also.

Getting into the camp would be difficult. Freya had gotten over the fence, but she was a good climber and tall which helped. Mark hadn't managed it even though he was the same height as Freya. I was several inches shorter than them both and I doubted I would have any chance getting over, even with help. In the end we decided to take a number of tools and see if we could get through the fence somewhere else. Then a couple of us would make our way to the residential area to the north of the hostel, find a suitcase and then I would make my way to the hostel gates and hope to be let in without any trouble.

The biggest problem would be getting away quickly enough so weren't caught if the alarm was raised before morning. Alex was in favour of taking a car, mostly because he knew how to drive, but cars on the road were so rare now that they would always attract attention. We settled on taking bikes. The trailer Mark and Freya had used to carry Matty was still parked around the corner and we picked up six of the lightest bikes I had found last summer and stacked them inside, using bungee cords to keep them fixed in place. It weighed about the same as Matty had according to Freya as she and Mark practised pulling it.

There was some debate about who would be going. I needed to go of course, and Jack knew where the empty houses were. Mark seemed an obvious choice as he could pull the trailer. Freya wanted to come, and it seemed sensible to have her along just in case. She had been inside the town and could help guide the other kids out. Leila and Taz wanted to come of course, and Alex, but it seemed silly to put them at risk when they had just got to safety. The kids looked set to debate it for a while yet, but I had been up since 4am and was shattered. I put a good portion of food in a plastic container and left them arguing over who was staying behind.

Nina was just about finished feeding the kids when I arrived and was ready for dinner. I asked her to wake me at 4am and went to bed. By this time tomorrow we would have everyone back safely or I would be locked up and heading out to spend the rest of my life working in a chicken factory or down a coal mine.

21

Freeing

The morning was cold but clear with ample moonlight to see by. I was going to have to cycle for about an hour and a half, so I put on some leggings and a t-shirt, with a fleece top to keep warm. In my rucksack, I packed some normal clothes; jeans and a jumper similar to the ones I had worn in the Chiltern Camp. I also packed the pliers I had used to undo the chain link fence of the garden centre, all that time ago. I picked up my heavy secateurs and added them; Mark and Freya had mentioned hedges and it would be much less obtrusive to cut a hole in a hedge than in a fence.

I wandered round the house picking things up and putting them down, trying to figure out what else I could take. A candle? Blue tack? Glue? Maybe we could glue the toilet door closed, then I saw the door stop; that would work even better. I picked it up and added it to my bag. There was a light knock at the door, I opened it; Mark, Freya, and Jack were standing on the doorstep kitted out and ready to go.

'Morning,' I said quietly, 'Sorry Jack, I forgot to check; did you find somewhere to sleep?'

'Mark and Alex gave me the living room at their place,' he said, 'but I quite like the house beside theirs, if it's available?'

'We'll see about making it habitable when we get back,' I said.

Freya passed me back my bike. She had found another, slightly larger, and more suited to her longer legs. Jack was on a bike I didn't recognise.

'Jack,' I asked, 'how did you get to my place? Did you cycle?'

'Yes,' said Mark, 'It was too cold to just lie in the hedge for long, when Freya didn't return immediately, I assumed she would be a while and started scouting around. I found that bike in a hamlet that we passed through getting there. When Jack came over the fence, I nipped back and got it.'

Jack nodded, 'it's a great bike, carbon fibre, super light.'

I looked around, 'Is there anything we've forgotten?' I asked; it was Tuesday, tomorrow the others would be leaving on the train, so we only had one chance at this.

'Stop worrying,' said Mark, looking just as concerned, 'remember, once we get Ruth out, she can help in the escape.'

We got on our bikes in the dark, the silence total; the birds weren't even up yet. I let Mark and Freya go ahead of me, they knew the route and I just needed to concentrate on keeping going the whole distance. This was my third day doing a long cycle ride; my legs were already complaining, and we were barely out of the door.

I followed them through the streets. The roads were empty apart from a solitary fox, which darted into a garden and disappeared. We cycled along, going under the M1 and crossing the A41, following a minor road that bypassed all the local towns. After about 50 minutes, we reached a large roundabout and Mark and Freya turned onto the A1.

'Hey!' I said, as I increased my speed to pedal alongside, 'are we really going up the motorway?'

'It's easier and quicker and the only other route is through a town,' said Mark.

I could see his point, the road was wide and flat and had a fairly good surface, we were making good progress with little effort; it just felt weird to be cycling on such a road. Fifteen minutes later we were at the M25. we turned off and headed down a tree lined road until we came to a fork. Mark veered right with confidence and then cycled over a little humpbacked bridge under which I could hear a stream gurgling. The road led to a small hamlet, which although overgrown, was very pretty in the faint pre-dawn light, with picturesque bungalows on large plots. We cycled through the hamlet and up over a bridge across a railway. On the other side the road was bound to the south by a chain link fence; the northernmost perimeter of the town.

I was exhausted by the time we stopped. We sat hidden in a field that bounded the road, sipping water and recovering. Dawn was not far away but it was dark enough that we could see the torches of the patrols as they walked towards us on their circuit around the perimeter.

'That's odd,' I said.

'What's odd,' asked Freya.

'The guards are on the outside of the fence here,' I replied.

'And?' said Jack.

'They were on the inside at the Chiltern Camp.'

We sat, puzzling over the anomaly, until seeing the clouds above start to turn pink, and the sky lighten, we collectively stood up. Leaving the bikes under the hedge and the trailer disguised as best we could, we crossed the road to take a look at the fence. Along this part of the road there was a hedge and behind it they had erected the chain link fence. I took out my secateurs and, making a couple of quick cuts, soon had a hole big enough to crawl through.

There was enough space on the other side to crouch, hidden from sight, and I used the pliers to untwist the wire near the ground.

'We only need a small hole,' said Mark, 'so it escapes the notice of the patrols.'

We were soon inside and set off across the field to the golf course. The four of us were much more conspicuous than Freya must have been the day before, but we still were able to walk all the way to the hostel unchallenged. Freya and Jack pointed out the sash windows and I could see the layout much better now I was there on the ground. Eventually we retreated to a house that Jack assured us was empty and started searching for an appropriate suitcase.

'Something small,' I said, 'like hand luggage for a plane trip and with wheels'

Eventually we found a couple of suitcases in the loft; I picked the nicest and placed my backpack inside, covering it with a selection of clothes from the closet... I left the secateurs and pliers with Mark. If they searched my luggage, those would be too difficult to explain. Finally I changed into the jeans and jumper I had brought. Now we just had to wait until evening.

Jack found a pack of cards and we played a couple of different games. Mark went out around midmorning just to familiarise himself with the town. On his return, he sank down at the kitchen table we were sitting round and announced that our plan was doomed.

'I just saw about twenty soldiers walking along the main street,' he said, 'they're preparing for something at the theatre.'

'What?' asked Freya.

'I don't know, but there were a lot of soldiers and people running around looking busy.'

'We need to know,' I said.

'I'll go,' said Freya, 'I can ask someone and then disappear.'

'I'll go as well,' said Jack, 'I bet I can find out more than you.'

I looked at them both. 'Ok, but don't get caught,' I said, 'that would definitely ruin everything.'

They left quickly. I didn't blame them; the house we were hiding in was cold and boring, we couldn't risk turning on the TV and the rooms seemed to have been cleared out of any reading matter.

Mark had packed sandwiches for lunch, so we ate and then I taught him how to play rummy. I was just about to put down three aces when Freya came back.

'So?' asked Mark.

'It's a celebration of the start of spring; apparently they celebrated the equinox in the autumn and had a harvest festival which went down very well, so they decided to do a spring one as well. A lot of people are coming from the different settlements, and the government will be giving speeches and handing out community awards to people.'

'Don't' they have anything better to do?' said Mark.

'Maybe not…' I said, 'the government don't seem to be holding elections or anything, so they probably have to do something to engage with the community and keep the settlements happy.'

Freya chose a couple of sandwiches for lunch and I had just introduced her to the rules of rummy when Jack arrived.

'Spring equinox,' he said.

'We know,' said Freya.

'But did you know that the new prime minister is coming this afternoon? That is why there is so much extra security,' he replied.

'I didn't know there was a new prime minister at all,' I said.

'Well the new one wasn't elected by the public, just by the remaining members of parliament,' he said, 'who actually no longer meet at parliament but at somewhere called Chequers not far from the Chiltern Camp.'

I nodded, I had heard of Chequers, but hadn't known exactly where it was. 'Did you find out anything else?' I asked.

'They're going to officially launch the new Peoples' Charter at the ceremony, apparently it sets out the rights and responsibilities of the British people, post outbreak.'

'Oh?' I said.

'Yeah apparently we have the right to a state assigned job,' he said.

Mark gave a short bark of laughter. 'Yeah, right, state sanctioned slavery, in other words. Do you know when all this takes place?' he asked.

'Starts at 5pm, finishes around sundown, then they all go into the theatre for drinks and food.'

'This is actually a good thing,' I said, 'there'll be less focus on me when I check in and if there is a lot of celebrating then maybe it will be easier to slip away.'

'And there will be a lot of strangers in town,' said Freya, 'and a lot of movement after dark.'

'There's also a full moon tonight,' said Jack, 'a super-moon, so that should help too.' He sat down at the table 'what are you playing?' he asked.

'Rummy,' I replied.

'Oh I know this one,' he said.

'Of course you do,' muttered Freya, as she re-dealt the cards.

At four we ate a snack and then got ready, I wanted to arrive at five to coincide with the start of the event so at ten minutes to, I picked up the suitcase and left the house. I wheeled the suitcase up to the front gates in as confident a manner as I could manage and smiled at the guard.

'Hi,' I said.

'Name?' was the curt reply; it looked like the guard wasn't particularly happy to be on duty, but Jack said the gate guard left at seven-thirty, so I wasn't worried about his unfriendly attitude.

'Zara Ball,' I answered. We had kept the fake name simple, so I could remember it.

He ticked his clipboard and, without saying anything, buzzed the gate open. 'Thanks' I said, as I stepped through the gap and walked across the tiny car park to the supersized door; the house was a regular size but had delusions of grandeur. Everything seemed magnified, huge door, massive bay windows, big stone doorstep. I rang the doorbell and then stepped back, rubbing my hands nervously on my jeans. After a good long pause, I could hear the door being unlocked and then it swung open revealing a young woman in her early twenties.

'Hi,' she said, 'can I help you?'

'My names Zara Ball,' I said, 'I'm staying here for the next few nights...' I could feel my palms go clammy and hoped my nervousness wasn't too obvious.

'Oh yes, we were expecting you earlier when the train came in,' she said.

'Um, I had a late lunch with an old friend from Uni,' I smiled, 'it ran over, you know how it is...'

She laughed, 'yes indeed, this is the day to meet people, I'm Tanya, come in and I'll take you to your room, then I'll show you around.'

I was in.

She turned back into the house and I stepped over the threshold into a high-ceilinged hallway, closing the door behind me. To the left was a wooden staircase and she headed towards the stairs and began to climb them.

'The front door unlatches from the inside if you want to go out this evening,' she said over her shoulder, 'the gate entry code is 2024.'

I nodded as I followed her up. This was great; we had our way out.

'I leave at 11pm so you need to be back by then so I can let you in, otherwise you'll be locked out for the night.'

'Okay,' I said, as I lifted my suitcase up onto a spacious landing area.

There were two tall closed doors to the left, but she turned right and walked down a short hallway to the front of the house. There was a large window at the end of the corridor and either side were two rooms, both of which were open. We walked through the left doorway into a large room with a huge bay window. The room had been subdivided into four tiny cubicles to the left and a small seating area in the bay window. The cubicles were open at the front, with just a narrow single bed and bedside table inside. At the end of the room there was a shared bathroom. 'Are there many people staying here tonight?' I asked.

'Yes, we're fully booked, people from all over the country,' she said, 'they're all at the equinox celebrations right now, 'I'm surprised you aren't there,' she added.

I couldn't think of anything to say so just smiled blandly.

She indicated to the cubicle beside the door. 'This one is yours.' I left my suitcase at the side of the bed and followed her downstairs again; walking back towards the front of the house and two doors that I had missed seeing earlier.

'This is the lounge,' she said, opening the door to a spacious front room on the right. She turned and crossed the hallway, 'and here is the reading room.' The room had desks scattered around and looked a bit like a library. 'We get a lot of people staying here for work,' she added. We walked along the hall past a small doorway under the stairs labelled 'TOILET', to the back of the house. She opened the door to the right, 'This is the dining room, dinner is at six-thirty, we're having a chicken casserole tonight,' she said, as she stepped into a dark, wood panelled room with a table large enough to seat twelve. She turned and walked back out into the hallway, and towards the closed door opposite.

'This is the kitchen,' she said, 'it's staff only, I'm afraid, but I just need to introduce you to someone.' She knocked twice and opened it. The kitchen was enormous, with steel work surfaces and sinks. There was a pot bubbling on the stove and, at a large blocky oak table, sat a man in black jeans and a black polo shirt. He looked up and smiled as we walked in.

'Peter, this is Zara, our last guest for tonight' said Tanya.

'Hallo,' he said, standing up and shaking hands, 'I hope you have a lovely stay.'

'Thanks,' I said. If this was the guard then I was rather glad that my plan didn't involve trying to overpower him with chloroform; he was at least six foot tall and looked both incredibly intimidating, but strangely, also rather friendly and open. Not what I had been expecting.

'Do you work here?' I asked.

'Sort of,' he replied, 'I'm staying here a couple of nights this week, but mostly I'm up at the military base. This is a temporary placement.'

'Peter is extra security for us,' said Tanya, smiling up at him.

'Yes,' said Peter, 'did you see two closed doors upstairs?'

I nodded.

'Please don't try and go into them.' I looked at him enquiringly expecting him to go on, but he remained silent, looking at me, as if expecting an answer.

'Okay,' I said. I felt a bit confused; I got the feeling that this was no ordinary soldier, but he couldn't be here for Ruth and the others, they were hardly that much of a threat.

'I'll ring a bell when dinner is ready,' said Tanya turning to the stove.

'Thank you,' I said, 'it smells delicious.'

I made my way back upstairs and sat on the bed. The guard was not what I had expected, and I didn't think he would remain trapped behind the flimsy door of the toilet for very long, even if I could get him there. However, there was good news; once I got them out of their room, it would be easy for us to get out of the house using the front door and gate code. I looked through the suitcase at the clothes we had packed; someone had added some pyjamas, so I took them out and placed them on the bed. The open plan nature of the room would make it much harder to sneak out in the middle of the night, but hopefully the other guests would be heavy sleepers.

I stood quietly and padded out of the room to the back of the hallway. It looked like the house had undergone considerable reconfiguration over the years. All the rooms seemed to have their own en-suite and there was no family bathroom. The two locked doors faced each other, either side of the hallway, with a blank wall between. Probably the original bathroom had been behind that wall, but it had been split into two to serve the rooms either side and the original door removed. I stood looking at the door on the left. According to Jack and Freya, just behind this door were Ruth and the others. I stood closer and listened intently; through the thick wood, I could just about hear the murmur of voices. I searched quickly for the key. The light was dim but it was undeniable, the key wasn't hanging next to the door. I would have to wait to see how Peter let them out. In the meantime I knocked very quietly, barely grazing my knuckles against the wood. Nothing. I knocked again slightly louder, and this time there was a hush from within. I heard the patter of feet and then silence.

'Ruth?' I hissed as quietly as I could.

Silence, I bent down to the keyhole, 'Ruth it's Zoe,' I said.

'Zoe?' It was Ruth's voice; I could hear the exclamations from the others inside, before they were hushed by someone.

'Ruth, are you all ok?' I said

'Yes we're fine,' she said, 'what's the plan?'

'I'm going to try and get you out,' I said, 'just before dawn when it starts to get light, be ready.'

From below, I heard the sound of a door opening. I zipped back to my room and was sitting back on the bed in an instant; listening to footsteps pacing along the hallway and around the rooms. I heard a stair creak loudly as the footsteps moved closer. The creaking would give us away when we left, if we weren't careful. The steps stopped at the top and then retreated away, stair creaking again, as whoever it was moved back down. A couple of seconds later the kitchen door opened and then closed. Had Peter heard me and come up to check? Impossible through a closed door and over normal kitchen sounds... maybe he was just doing rounds of the house. I sat there thinking. Who was in the other room that warranted such vigilance?

After a minute or two I took out my phone, but just like at the Chiltern Camp, there was no signal. I sat there mulling over the plan. I was soon bored; it would be at least an hour until dinner. I debated going back to talk to Ruth, but what more was there to say? I looked around the room, got up and walked over to the bay window. The original wooden frames were still intact and I pushed open a window. In the still evening air I could hear faint noises from the festivities down the road. Music drifted in and I debated going out; Tanya obviously expected me to be at the festival. Then I reconsidered; there might be people from the Chiltern camp who would recognise me...it was just too risky. Instead, I went downstairs and knocked twice on the kitchen door, much as Tanya had, but I waited, rather than going straight in and after a couple of seconds, the door opened. It was Peter, with an enquiring look on his face.

'Hi,' I said, 'I don't suppose I can sit in here with you?' I asked, 'Only it's rather cold in the other rooms.' it was true; there was a definite chill in the house.

'Oh,' said Tanya, as Peter opened the door wider, 'as the other guests are all out, it didn't seem worth lighting the fire in the lounge,' she looked at Peter who nodded, 'come in and have a seat.'

I pulled out a chair, ninety degrees to Peter and facing Tanya who was stirring the casserole and adding some extra spices. I wasn't quite sure how to start, asking Peter straight out how often he patrolled the house and where the keys were, might not be the best idea if I was to avoid raising suspicion. 'It's a lovely house,' I said, picking a neutral topic.

'Yes,' said Tanya, 'I used to work here when it was a community centre, all yelling kids, fighting and graffiti.'

'Did they do activities here?' I asked.

'Oh yes, they did art, and music, and that Duke of Edinburgh award, with the camping,' she said.

'Oh I used to do that,' I said, 'I ran it, I mean...at the school I worked at...' it came out unintentionally.

'Were you a teacher?' asked Peter.

'Yes,' I said, 'I taught science in secondary school, but I really liked taking the kids out camping,' I hurriedly added, trying to head off any questions about what I did now. I hadn't prepared a backstory at all. If they asked me what I was doing in Potters Bar, I wouldn't have a clue how to answer. 'Some of them were so bad at navigation, they would get hopelessly lost.'

I segued into a series of stories of the calamities we had faced over the years until, before I knew it, it was six-thirty. I had gotten lucky; Tanya was an easy conversationalist and Peter had seemed content to let me chatter away, and he hadn't left the kitchen at all during the time I was there, so hopefully he didn't patrol regularly.

Tanya ladled some of the casserole out of the pot into a large serving dish and placed it on a trolley that contained plates and cutlery. She added a dish of potatoes and boiled Brussel sprouts before wheeling it through to the dining room, indicating for me to follow. Once inside she indicated the dishes and said, 'Please help yourself.'

'Is it just me?' I asked in surprise.

'For the first sitting,' she said.

I put a confused look on my face and seeing it, she continued. 'Our other special guests eat after the regular scheduled visitors.'

I wondered whether to ask more, but decided to stay quiet and not push my luck. I seemed to have passed as a regular guest, despite not knowing anything about what was going on. I wasn't going to risk drawing attention by asking questions. Instead, I tucked into the food, which tasted as good as it smelled. After dinner, I went up to my room but hovered near the door.

I didn't have long to wait before I heard footsteps again; coming up the stairs was Peter. I ducked hurriedly out of sight as he came into view. I heard him step towards the locked doors and peered around, just in time to see him take a key off the top of the doorframe and open the door to the room with the kids in. I waited to see if he would replace the key in the same place, but he just pulled the door closed and left it unlocked, pocketing the key as Ruth and the others bounded down the stairs. They were obviously hungry.

I slipped down to the reading room, found some paper and wrote a quick note, explaining that Freya, Mark and Jack were in town and we would be escaping out the front door just before dawn. As an afterthought, I included the gate code 2024, just in case. I then nipped back up to their room and slowly turned the doorknob and opened the door, hoping it wouldn't creak as much as the rest of the house. It opened without a sound, and inside I saw four bunkbeds, two against each wall. I left the note on one of the pillows and moved towards the sash window.

I waved hopefully, searching for Jack or Freya, and saw a tree branch shake. I searched the leaves but it took me a while to realise that the white patch against the bark of the trunk was Jack's face. I took out a whiteboard pen from my pocket, thought briefly, then wrote as large as possible, on the windows:

FRONT GATE
CODE 2024

His head nodded vigorously, he had understood. I wiped the windows clean with my sleeve and crept back out of the room.

Twenty minutes later, I heard them coming back up the steps. I stood with one eye round the edge of the doorframe, trying to see whether it was Peter coming up first or one of the kids. It was Ruth. She looked at me and opened her left hand to reveal a slip of paper. As she turned the corner, she let it slip so it fell to the side of the top step. I ducked back as Peter reached the top of the stairs and then watched as he locked them back in their room and placed the key back on top of the doorframe.

Once he had disappeared back into the kitchen I darted to the stairs and retrieved the paper. It was bulkier than I had realised, I unfolded the layers of paper and inside found a small key. I hefted it in my left hand and straightened out the paper. The message was short: 'rucksacks in cupboard in reading room.'

I smiled, I didn't know how she had done it, but now I had to do my part. I walked down to the reading room and started searching for a cupboard big enough for six rucksacks. The room had bookshelves around three sides but no cupboards. I was stumped for a second, then I saw that the bay window had large wood panelled box seats. I examined them more closely and saw the small keyhole in the front, near the top. Using the key, I unlocked it and pulled slightly. The whole of the front section fell open, and I only just managed to catch it before it hit the floor. Behind the panel were the rucksacks.

The sun had set now and the stars were starting to appear outside. I pressed my face against the windows and cupped my hands around my eyes to block out the light from the room, outside I saw the gate guard sitting in his sentry box. Surely it was seven-thirty by now, I looked at my watch, seven-twenty-eight. As I looked, the gate guard started to stir. I waited, watching intently until I was disturbed by the sound of the kitchen door opening. Hurriedly I pushed the panel back into place and locked it. I jumped up so I was standing by the nearest bookshelf when Peter appeared in the doorway.

'Hi,' I said nervously.

'Hi,' said Peter, 'looking for something to read?'

I nodded, 'are you making your rounds?' I asked, pulling a random book from the shelf.

He nodded, 'Have a good night.'

I watched as he walked up the stairs, absently thumbing through the book I had picked as I waited for him to return to the kitchen.

Once the house was quiet again, I peered out of the window to see the gate guard was gone. I opened the cupboard and removed three of the rucksacks, then crept to the front door; a rucksack on each shoulder and holding one in my hand. Tanya hadn't lied, there was a simple Yale lock on the door; turning it would let me out. What she hadn't said was that I could leave the door on the latch so it didn't lock back again. I opened the door and moved towards the gate. I keyed in the code and looked around for the others, it was good timing; coming along the road was Freya.

'Hey, how's it going?' she said quietly,

'They're all ok, locked in the back room and the key is outside like we hoped.' I said.

'What's the plan?' she asked

'Wait until just before dawn, when everyone is asleep, and make a run for it.' I handed her the rucksacks, 'Can you take these and stash them back with the bikes? I'll go get the other three.'

I ran quickly back inside, grabbed the other three bags, and then ran out again, checking the latch was off, I didn't want to lock myself out and have to disturb Tanya or Peter. Outside Freya had been joined by Mark and he looked agitated.

'David's here' he said.

'What? Why? Are you sure?' I asked, alarmed.

'I saw him at the government presentations. All the different settlements were represented. David was there with some of the Chiltern camp councillors.' Mark paced angrily, and I watched him worriedly. He hated the Chiltern councillors and had a look on his face that boded trouble.

'Maybe you guys should hide up for now,' I said, 'take turns to watch the gate in case we have to leave early. Or wait further out by the golf course.'

Freya nodded looking at Mark, 'Ok, don't worry, we'll sort something out.'

I hovered a second, then ran back inside. There wasn't anything I could do about David except stay out of sight as much as possible. I walked quietly up my room, avoiding the creaking stair and lay down to wait.

The other guests trickled back in over the evening; they had obviously been celebrating and were very noisy. I put the pyjamas on over my clothes and lay in bed pretending to be asleep. I had been up since 4am and the bed was surprisingly comfortable, if I had been a real guest at the hostel, I would have been very put out by all the disturbances, but as it was, the noise kept me from drifting off. Eventually the other guests settled down and by 1am the room was full and everyone was gently snoring.

It got harder and harder to keep my eyes open. In desperation I set the alarm for 4am and put my phone on vibrate. I clenched my hand around the phone and stuffed it under the pillow, before drifting off to sleep. I woke abruptly; three hours later, confused for a second, before I felt the phone vibrate again and quickly switched it off. It had sounded loud in the darkness, but a snore rose from the next cubicle and I relaxed a fraction. I slid out of bed and crept forwards, trying not to let the floorboards creak. I glided to the door, cautiously placing each foot down and slowly transferring my weight. Even with all the care I took, the boards still groaned twice. Each time I froze but the snores continued and I made it to the hallway, the bright moonlight slashing sideways through the window, painting the wall a burnished silver, and shining in my eyes.

I stood at the window staring up at the full moon. Down below I could see the closed gate and yes, there was a shadowy figure couched by the gatehouse. I waved a couple of times until the figure stood and waved back.

I turned; the darkness in front of me was in sharp contrast to the brightness before and I stretched out my fingers to find the banister ahead. I crept down the hallway towards the locked door, it seemed a long distance, but suddenly my fingers were at the end of the bannister, the open stairway to my left. I inched forwards, until my fingers touched the wall. Back there in the shadows I could hardly see. My fingers scrapped over the doorframe and I turned to the left and reached up, fingertips scrabbling for the top of door. I strained upwards, standing on tiptoes, but was still a fraction too short. I stood back from the door, frustrated; I would need to find something to stand on to reach above the taller-than-normal doors. Then, right behind me, there was a muffled laugh and a hand reached over my head and took the key down from its position. I spun round so fast I almost fell over. Standing in the shadows, camouflaged in his black clothing, was Peter. How long he had been there I didn't know, he had been utterly silent, waiting for me.

He handed me the key, which I took automatically. 'What…' I began.

'I don't believe in holding kids prisoner,' he said quietly, 'especially ones that don't seem to have done anything wrong.'

'But…' I said, speechless.

'I'm not here to guard them,' he said, 'I'm here to look after some people who actually should be locked up, in a proper jail, with the key thrown away,' he indicated the door behind him and looked grim.

'How did you know?' I asked, managing to get out a real sentence.

'I saw you earlier, in the doorway,' he replied, 'and you said you were a science teacher…you're the one who helped them escape Wendover,' he said.

'I…'

'It's ok, I actually don't agree with the current system of forced labour.'

'Then why are you working for them?' I asked.

'It's my job,' he said, 'and most of what I do is necessary to keep the county functioning with some sort of semblance of order.' He reached into a back pocket and pulled out a card. 'However, I admire what you're doing, if you ever run into trouble you can't handle, get in touch and I'll help if I can.' I took the card from him but it was too dark to read it. I put it in my pocket and unlocked the door.

Ruth was standing just inside with the others, all ready to go. I stepped forward and looked around, the room was dark, and I couldn't see much, but they all seemed to be there. Drew, Kai, Eddie, Alisha and Jasmine. I turned around to thank Peter, but he was gone. I ushered everyone forwards and whispered, 'mind the squeaky step' as they streamed past. Drew was in front and he had reached the front door and unlatched in seconds. In no time at all everyone was out and free. I looked around one final time, Peter wasn't anywhere to be seen. I stepped out and saw Jack in the courtyard, gate open, silently hi-fiving the others.

'Let's go,' I whispered, urging everyone forwards. As I turned back for one last look at the house, something drew my eyes up to the large window on the first floor. There, standing at the window, was a figure. The silhouette looked familiar; moonlight outlined the face and beard. The figure stepped forwards and raised a hand to the glass…it was David. We had been discovered.

'Move!' I said urgently, and then we were running into the night.

22

Conflict

Behind us came a strident shout. A familiar voice rang out.

'Stop!, stop right there.' It was David. I turned to look and saw him at the gate.

We ran. Down the road and back up through the residential streets. The kids were fast and I had been training for months. I turned to look back at every junction. He wasn't gaining at all, in fact we seemed to be lengthening the gap. At the railway line, Mark and Freya were waiting; they looked up in alarm as they saw us approach in full flight.

'What went wrong?' said Mark, as he helped Jasmine over the fence and onto the tracks.

'It's David.' I gasped out, as I scrambled over. Ruth looked up sharply, 'Are you sure?' she said.

'Yes,' I replied, breath heaving, checking that everyone had made it across the railway. I began to climb the fence on the other side. 'He must have been staying at the hostel.'

We gathered on the golf course and looked back; no David. I doubted he would climb the fences as we had done, but he would find a way to get across. We turned and began running again, over the greens and through the trees, falling into sand bunkers in the dark. Finally we reached the fields at the edge of the town. There was another shout behind us; David had found a way onto the golf course.

In the bright moonlight we raced across the field. By the time we had found the hole in the fence I could hear David yelling at the soldiers on guard at the base, and there were noises coming from the barracks. Mark quickly released the bungee cords and passed out the bikes and rucksacks. We were on and cycling away in less than a minute, but behind us we could hear the squeal of a large gate opening and the roar of motor bikes throttling up.

We raced back over the railway line and through the hamlet, cycling along the road with the sound of the motorbikes getting louder. The headlights shone on our backs, casting long shadows in front of us. My feet pumped the pedals as we flowed over the humpbacked bridge where Mark, instead of turning left, kept going, leading us through a narrow path until we reached the main road. In front of us, the moonlight revealed a narrow footpath between white tipped fence posts.

We sped across the road onto the path, leaning in as it veered sharply left. A bridge appeared beside us and the kids in front screeched to a stop and turned a hundred and eighty degrees, cycling up a footbridge ramp and then across the motorway. The other side ended in darkness, steps leading downwards. I ran down carrying my bike, adrenaline giving me speed and strength.

'There's a large wood just up ahead,' Mark called, 'stick together and don't get left behind.'

I could hear the bikes roaring over the footbridge and then come to a rumbling halt, working out how to get down. We had managed to cycle to the edge of the trees before we heard the bike engines throttle up again. Mark was at the front twisting and turning along the paths beneath the bare trees. The others were stringing out, further and further apart, I was near the back, tiring quickly. Turning to look, I saw that only Alisha and Jasmine were behind me, but they were barely in sight and being left further behind every second. The motorbikes weren't visible yet but light from the headlights of the lead motorbike shone through the trees. I turned forwards just in time to see the rider in front of me trail the others into a narrow passage. I followed them through and down to a carved out streambed. A chain link fence crossed our path and the others were pushing their bikes through the gap where the streambed passed under the fence, one by one assembling on the other side. There was no way the motorbikes could follow us. I waited, desperate to get through to safety. Hurry, hurry... one of the bikes was stuck. I turned as I heard a sharp cry behind me. Where were Jasmine and Alisha?

I scrambled back up through the passage and up out onto the trail. Jasmine was on the ground, tangled with her bike, Alisha standing beside her. I could hear the lead motorbike getting closer. I looked up at the headlights dancing on the vegetation in front of me and then back at the passage to safety. Then I looked across at the girls. We were so close.

A slash of light cut my face as the motorbikes bounced into view. Survival; it was all I had thought about for nine months. But as I looked at Alisha and Jasmine there was no hesitation any more. I leaped across the trail, grabbed them both, and dived into the bushes on the other side.

I heard the bikes screech to a halt. We scrambled upright and raced through the trees together. I heard crashing behind me as the soldiers entered behind us, and we ran, weaving between the trunks and ducking low branches. Then I heard a voice. It was unmistakably David.

I froze and pulled Jasmine and Alisha close. The chasers had stopped also, and the woods were silent. I was scratched all over from the vegetation and sweat was dripping down my face, cuts stinging from the salt, but I didn't move, focussing only on the murmuring of voices and the small bodies shaking silently by my side. The moonlight dappled the trees as I heard David's voice rise and fall. Had they found the fence? Or were they just coordinating the search? The woods weren't big, we would be found quickly if we continued to run. We needed to hide. My eyes swept the woods. There; a thicket of brambles. I tugged the girls towards it, crouching to the ground to crawl beneath the arching stems, but the shadow beneath was an illusion; the undergrowth was impenetrable.

We didn't stand a chance. We couldn't go forwards and we couldn't go back. My eyes skittered over the moonlit bracken... what was it Freya had said? People never look up? My gaze locked on a knobbly tree trunk and followed it up into the sky. The branches were silhouetted against the moon, bare of leaves, and at the top of the trunk there were several horizontally branches, forming a space that we could perch in. In our dark clothing, we would blend right in. invisible in the dark.

I crouched down to Alisha and Jasmine's level and put my mouth to their ears, 'Can you climb that tree?' I whispered.

The two girls looked at me uncertainly, then up at the tree, they looked at each other and then slowly nodded. The three of us stood by the tree looking at it hesitantly, should I let them go first so I could catch them if they fell... or go up first and help pull them up?

I stepped up to the tree and put my foot on its side above one of the knobbly bits of bark. I pushed upwards and grabbed the trunk. Digging my fingers into the gaps in the bark, I pulled myself up, scrabbling with my feet to find footholds. Some of my climbing experience came back to me and I began clamping my hands tight, so I was secure, and then reaching up with my feet to find new footholds, pushing myself higher with my legs. My arms grew tired and I found a couple of good footholds and paused, breathing hard. I looked up, the first branch was just above me, I stretched up but couldn't quite reach it. Steadying myself on my left foothold, I brought my right foot up. Heart in my mouth, I pushed against the trunk and jumped up to grab the branch scrabbling for a new foothold. I hung for a second my full weight on my fingers until my toe snagged on a protrusion. I pushed up and folded an elbow over the branch, gasping. The ground looked very far below and I closed my eyes, psyching myself for the next push upward. I swung myself up onto the branch and collapsed against the trunk.

I looked down; Jasmine and Alisha were staring up at me, their eyes wide in the darkness. I waved to Alisha to come up. She stepped up to the trunk immediately. Her smaller feet could squeeze into the cracks in the bark, and she scampered up until she reached the place I had paused. I could see her searching for handholds but there were none. I swung myself around, clamped my legs around the branch and leaned down. She reached up, grabbed my hand and scrambled up over me, onto the branch. Then it was Jasmine's turn. She copied her sister exactly and we all sat on the branch, regaining our breath, and listening intently to the forest surrounding us.

From that point on, it was easier; with branches to hold and step on, we soon reached the perch at the top. I brushed the old dead leaves away from the junction of wide branches that radiated away from the trunk, forming the natural seat. Then I swung my backpack round to the front and sat down, resting my back against the tree trunk. Both of the girls snuggled in either side, the perch holding us all easily. From underneath we would be invisible and I could feel the girls relax slightly against me.

I could hear movement in the woods around us; the noises drew nearer, rustlings of people below, moving, searching. We had reached the perch just in time. I sat motionless, cradling the girls, desperate for a drink of water. Finally, after about twenty minutes, the sounds moved far enough away that I could slowly reach into my bag for my bottle. The water tasted like heaven. It was then that I noticed that the girls didn't have their rucksacks. 'Where are your bags?' I said quietly as I handed Alisha the water bottle.

'Mark and Freya took them at the golf course so we could run faster,' whispered Jasmine. I nodded, that had been good thinking on their part. Had they reached the main road? If they had made it out of the woods, their bikes should have taken them well inside the M25 and safe.

I took out my phone; I had a good signal but I was wary of using it. The soldiers were quiet, but I hadn't heard their bikes start up, so I knew they hadn't left yet. I switched it to silent; if it rang, we would be exposed and trapped. The moon had slipped towards the horizon during our flight and the sky was beginning to lighten at the edges, but looking down, the ground below us was invisible. Occasionally the undergrowth rustled; it was probably just nocturnal creatures scurrying through the bracken, but every movement of the leaves sounded loud and clear in the cold dark night. Where was David?... and what was he doing?

On the edge of my hearing there were voices, volume rising; they were moving closer, the girls pressed against me and I sat so still I almost wasn't breathing at all.

The voices were directly below; David and another man.

'We've combed the woods; they're not here, where exactly do you want us to look?' It was a Scottish accent, the voice deep and gravelly with a hint of impatience.

'We can't let them get away,' said David, 'they're due to go and work on the salmon farms and you know how desperate we are for workers, the Scottish employees keep disappearing into the hills.'

'And whose fault is that... no Scot would accept such awful conditions.'

'Could we get more men?' David pleaded, 'surround the woods and work our way to the fence?'

'No. I'm not keeping my men out here any longer, you need to accept that you've lost these ones and get some new recruits, they're not exactly hard to find; the cities are teeming with kids.'

I heard the sound of footsteps converging to our right. The area below was silent and then I heard the sudden jarring roar of a motorbike. Several others started up in concert and the sound increased in volume before slowly fading into the distance.

The sky was lightening rapidly, and I could see that the ground below me was clear. 'Wait here' I whispered to the girls. I shuffled round in my seat, finding handholds and stepping down onto the branches below me. I got to the point where the branches disappeared and, reaching down for somewhere to rest my foot, slipped. I clutched desperately at my handhold but my arm wrenched free and I fell, crashing into the bracken below.

There was a cry or alarm from above, but I lay stunned for a couple of seconds unable to move or reassure them. Then I gave a convulsive cough, rolled over and came to my knees. I looked up at the perch to see two anxious faces peering at me over the edge. I waved weakly. I would have a couple more bruises and scratches to add to my collection, but it had only been a drop of about eight feet and I was fine. I stood up wincing as my ankle took my weight... maybe not so fine, but I could still walk. I brushed myself off, checking my backpack. Everything seemed ok.

I looked around, which way was home? I walked in one direction a little way and then turned back, uncertain. At that moment, the sun rose properly and the rays streamed between the trees. East! That way was east. I smiled and half-turned, just about to call up to the girls to come down, but standing between me and the tree was David, squinting against the sun's rays.

'Zoe' he said. He seemed remarkably calm.

I stepped back, silent.

'Where are the kids?' he asked, stepping forwards.

I stepped back again, and he followed, it was like some weird sort of formal dance. 'I...I don't know,' I said, the words catching in my throat, willing myself not to look up at the girls. I hurt in too many places to count and was tired and limping and he seemed bigger and more threatening than ever, but there was no way he was getting those kids.

He lunged forward, grabbing my arm, the calm disappeared in an instant, 'you're lying' he screamed, spittle flying. From his pocket, he pulled a flick knife and it sprung open, the morning sun flashing along the blade.

I reacted instinctively, arm flicking in a wrist release, and dodging away. 'David, stop, what are you doing?' I said.

'Taking a leaf out of your book.' He slashed with the knife, and I could see the madness in his eyes. 'Do you know what everyone thinks? Irina told everyone how she found me, tied up in your kitchen, towel over my head. I'm a laughing stock.' He slashed again, fury shaking his hand.

I dodged, I couldn't get away; he was bigger and faster. I was going to have to try to get the knife off him. I watched it mesmerised, but then switched focus, he was telegraphing every move, all I needed to do was step in and block inside his wrist. He would drop the knife if I hit his arm hard enough. I had practised the move for years. I could do it, I took a breath, and dodged again as he slashed, then again, he was getting closer and I still wasn't doing anything.

'Do you like my knife?' he said, 'I've been carrying it around ever since you pulled that stunt.' He slashed and I dodged again. 'It's funny, it makes me feel powerful.' He lunged, and in that instant I stepped forward and sliced out with the edge of my hand, hitting his wrist with all the force I could muster. I let loose a flurry of blows to his body and face and he leaned back, teetering, and then fell. There was a dull crack as he hit the ground and he was still.

I stared down at him, adrenaline still coursing through my system. Had I killed him? Remorse flooded through me and I dropped to my knees, leaning over, desperately searching for signs of life. I lay my fingers into his neck as they did in the films, nothing, I pressed harder searching… there… I moved my fingers back a little… and felt the beat against my fingers… a pulse. He was alive.

I sat back on my knees as my heart banged in my chest, my eyes darting. The gleam of metal caught my eye, the knife…by his head. I reached forward to pick it up and saw the grey rock amongst the leaves. He was still unmoving, eyes closed but as I watched closely, I saw his chest rise and fall. I had to know. I leaned forward and felt under his head but my hand came up clean, there was no blood.

There was a sound beside me and I whipped around, standing up, but it was only Jasmine and Alisha, down somehow from the tree and crying into my arms as I crouched again and hugged them to me. Eventually Jasmine pulled away a little.

'I thought he was going to kill you,' she said.

'Me too,' said Alisha.

'No chance,' I said, a smile in my voice, 'it would take a lot more than David.'

I reached forward again for the knife and stood up. It was beautiful, a curved blade honed to a point, with an ornate mother-of-pearl handle. The girls and I stared at it, and then I shuddered, pushed it closed and tossed it into the bramble thicket. There was a groan behind me and David stirred slightly, eyes still closed. He would be ok, but in no shape to chase us. I turned so the sun was at my back, took the girls hands, and stepped forwards, the rays of light highlighting the trunks of the trees ahead of us.

23

Community

We walked through the trees with the sun at our backs, until the track met the chain link fence. The girls were silent, stumbling with tiredness, gripping my hands tightly. They had been up all night, waiting to escape, and the flight through the woods and fight with David seemed to have rendered them mute. We worked our way along the fence, detouring around thickets, until we found the streambed. The bike tracks were clear in the soil so we pushed our way through the gap and followed them to the edge of the wood. We stepped out into the open, the low sun streaming across our faces and I stood, deliberating, with the girls waiting trustingly beside me. Which way? From my left I heard a faint noise, growing louder. A bicycle shot out between the hedges of the lane, flew past, and then stopped abruptly. The rider turned around. It was Alex.

'Don't you check your phone?' he said brightly.

I reached into my pocket and pulled it out, and there, listed on the screen, were three text messages and a missed phone call.

'We've been looking for you guys,' he said smiling.

The road was wet with morning dew but I didn't care as I sank to the ground with relief, the girls crowding against my back. 'Are you ok?' said Alex, most of his casual insouciance disappearing from his voice.

'Yes' I said, speaking for the three of us, 'just so relieved, did everyone else get back okay?'

'Uh huh,' he said, 'they were tired, and upset that you three hadn't made it back. Mark was all for returning himself but we could see he was worn out. He eventually agreed that Leila, Taz, and I should come out and look for you.'

'Where are they?' I asked.

'Hold on, I'll just call them,' he replied.

He gave the news that we had been found to Taz, and then to Leila, then phoned Liam so he could let the others know.

'Taz is up by the landfill site, Leila down by South Mimms,' he said, 'they're both getting worried about being seen now it's morning.'

'We need to cross the M25 to get back,' I said, 'perhaps we should wait until this evening?'

'Yeah.' he picked up his phone and called Leila explaining the problem. 'Leila says there are empty houses in South Mimms,' he said, 'should we wait there?'

I looked around; it was full light and I could see for miles across the fields. It would be better to get out of sight. The soldiers might do patrols, especially if they were looking for more recruits; we were right on the edge of London and people crossing out would be easy targets. South Mimms was too close to Potters Bar to be totally safe, but it would have to do.

'Okay,' I said, wearily dragging myself up and taking the girls hands again when they reached up, silent still.

Alex phoned Taz to let her know and then we began walking south back down the lane. He chatted away about the journey up from Carpenders Park, and then about getting some plants from Robert. I saw him looking sideways at me and the girls, but I was much too tired to respond, and kept plodding along. He had moved on to something about the community hall when, from behind us, the ring of a bell sounded. We turned; it was Taz on her bike. She slowed to a halt and looked at us, concern showing in her face.

'Are you ok?'

I nodded in reply and the girls let go of my hands and stepped forwards.

'Zoe fought with David,' said Jasmine.

'And won,' said Alisha.

'He had a knife and she knocked it out of his hand, just like that,' added Jasmine, miming the move I had made.

'It was cool,' said Alisha jumping around and chopping at Jasmine, suddenly alive again.

Taz looked at me, 'And David?' she asked as the two girls began to play-fight.

'I don't think he will be following us any time soon,' I said.

'Can you teach us?' said Jasmine, turning to me, serious again.

'Maybe,' I said, 'if you promise not to fight each other.'

'How about fighting Alex?' said Alisha as they turned together towards him.

Taz smiled, 'I'll go meet Leila' she said, as she scooted ahead on her bike.

We arrived in South Mimms a couple of minutes later, and found them waiting. Leila looked at me appalled and then guided us into a house.

I'm hungry,' said Alisha.

'Is there any food?' asked Jasmine walking into the kitchen. Taz followed them, and Leila turned to the stairs.

'There are clothes in the closet,' she said, as she led me upstairs, 'and I've boiled a kettle, so you have hot water to wash with.'

I walked into the bedroom and then stopped as my reflection stared back at me from a full-length mirror. I was covered in blood and dirt. No wonder they all seemed concerned.

'It's really not that bad,' I said, 'just some scratches and I fell out of a tree.'

'You what?' said Leila.

'I'll explain later,' I replied, desperate for the bed that looked so clean and comfortable.

I cleaned up as best I could, and borrowed some jogging bottoms and a fleece from whoever had lived in the house. Then I lay down and seconds later was asleep.

Whilst I slept, they found bikes for us, and when I woke, mid-afternoon, gave me some food and sent me back to bed. I checked in briefly with Alisha and Jasmine but they were both sleeping. It felt good to be looked after for a change, and I accepted their help gratefully. I lay there in the peaceful quiet, thinking about David and the way he had slashed at me with the knife. I replayed those few seconds when I thought I had killed him. Somehow, that was even worse; David had a crazy streak but he was just a symptom of the corrupt system.

I thought back to the escape, the hostel, and the mystery guard, Peter. We hadn't really needed his help but the fact he had given it was encouraging. It was clear that, even inside the army, there were people who didn't fully support the new regime. Maybe that was why David was so fanatical, it sounded like the new government still had teething troubles. I turned over and snuggled into the soft pillow, it wasn't my problem, we had escaped, and soon we would be home.

When I woke the second time, it was dark outside and my clothes were folded up neatly on the chest at the foot of the bed. I changed and made my way downstairs and stood at the kitchen door. Around the kitchen table, playing cards, were Alex, Leila, Taz, Alisha and Jasmine. It looked like Alex had just been caught cheating and the teasing and laughter was something to see, after the silence and joylessness of the settlement camp. I could never have stayed there, knowing the truth about their lives.

I stepped into the room smiling, and they sprang out of their seats in welcome. We ate a quick snack and left. I felt refreshed and was eager to get home.

We rode down the A1, retracing our route, and arriving home uneventfully in little more than an hour, but instead of heading for my bungalow, Alex directed us to the community hall. He pulled up in the car park and the others got off their bikes and leaned them against the wall.

'What's going on?' I asked.

'We just need to make a stop here first,' said Alex mysteriously. Leila opened the door and ushered me in. I walked forward along the hallway and into the main room; there was a cacophony of sound, everyone yelling 'surprise'. Looking round I saw that everyone was there, even Nina, carrying William, and Matty carrying Rachel. Both children looked wide awake and were clapping excitedly. I stopped, staring; the improvement was unbelievable. Then I did a double take, 'Matty,' I said, 'you finally woke up!'

'Just in time for the party it seems,' he said, waving a hand at everyone around us, as they uncovered plates of food and poured drinks 'but what happened to you?' he asked.

'I got trapped up a tree,' I said, and then I had to explain to everyone exactly what had happened.

We sat, ate, chatted, and laughed, celebrating everyone's safe arrival and new homes. Taz had found some more unbroken doors, and with Alex's help, they had prepped a couple more bungalows. Everyone seemed settled and happy. I found myself sitting with Nina, watching the kids.

'They seem to be doing much better,' I said, as we watched William laughing, as he was chased by Leila and Taz. I looked at Rachel, playing quite happily with Liam on the floor.

'I've decided to stay with Leila and Taz,' said Liam, looking up at us, 'I like it there and I can babysit William and Rachel.'

I nodded, Liam was only ten and needed someone to look after him, Leila and Taz would be perfect.

Later I sat beside the piano, watching Matty play. The kids always surprised me. I had no idea that Matty was an accomplished musician, playing almost anything that was requested, even some Taylor Swift for people to bounce around to. He had woken up on Wednesday immensely hungry and very weak, but by the next day, after a good couple of meals, had been almost back to normal.

'I found a bungalow with a piano,' he said, 'and I want to thank you for the peppermint tea, I remember you feeding it to me.'

I nodded as I tapped my feet to the music.

'Could I get a piece of the plant to grow?' he asked, 'I seem to have developed a taste for it.'

I smiled; it sounded like we had another gardener on our hands.

Eventually the kids started to get tired and the party died down. Leaving Mark and a few others to do the final tidy up, with Matty still quietly playing in the corner, the groups separated, taking the empty dishes and glasses back home. I walked back to my bungalow with Nina, carrying the children who had fallen into an exhausted sleep, but at my driveway she paused.

'Whilst you were out, I moved into the house next to the girls,' said Nina, 'now that William and Rachel are so much better it was time to get our own place.' We walked a few houses down and into the very bungalow I had earmarked for them and lay the children gently on the beds inside.

'I can't thank you enough,' said Nina, wiping the corner of her eyes as she looked down at them sleeping peacefully. 'You took us in when I was lost and utterly desperate.'

I looked at her... this was why people had opened their doors to the knockers; I felt I finally understood.

'It was my pleasure,' I said, 'see you in the morning.' I hugged her, and then walked back out onto the street. The night was cool and clear, the good weather holding. As I ambled up my drive, I could see an envelope, pinned to the wooden sign I had hung from the door. I reached out in hope and opened it.

'Z, we came by, but you weren't here, will phone soon,
Vik'

So typical of Vik; the briefest of messages... where were they? I would have to wait for him to call. Or go searching, they couldn't be far.

I unlocked the door, and stepped into my bungalow. The electricity was off, and as I moved through the rooms, switching on the solar lamps that were scattered around the house, I could see that everything was sparkling clean. Matty and Nina had obviously tidied before they left. I walked into the front room and flopped down into my armchair with a contented sigh. Feeling a poke from my back pocket, I reached back and pulled out the card Peter had given me. It was blank except for a single uninformative email address. I flipped it over; in the centre of the card was a small x in a square. There was a mystery there, but I was content for the time being to let it be. I was home.

Characters

Zoe, (alias: Zara Ball)
Vik
Nadia (Mum)

Maria
Jenny

Garden Centre
Ben
Catrina
Daisy
Toby
Lucas

Carpenders Park residents
Frank Tipson
Cathy
Beryl & George
Helen & Brian
Robert & Sheila
Nina, Rachel & William
Raj, Rabia and Adam
Richard, Elizabeth
Heather and Andrew

Croxley Green
Anne
John
Tony, Anita, Judith

Wendover/Chiltern camp residents
David
Dr Peterson
Receptionist
Gordon, James
Jonathan, Malcolm
Stephen
Sophie & Imara
Olivia & Millie

Escape Kids
Ruth Sanders
Mark
Leila
Taz
Jack
Alisha Gill
Jasmine Gill
Kai Perth
Eddie Leathers
Drew Taylor
Liam
Alex
Freya
Mateusz (Matty)

Potters Bar
Tanya
Peter

About the Author

Emma Zeth is a pseudonym I created when I was twelve and bored in school.

I am an ex-science teacher, who likes gardening and who used to live in a bungalow in Carpenders Park.

In 2019 I had a whole summer free, so I wrote the book that had been bouncing around in my head for the last ten years. It came out nothing like I had expected, but I had fun writing it anyway.

If you would like to know whether Zoe finds her mum and Vik, and what the x on the business card symbolises, please let me know in an amazon review, and I'll start writing book 2.

Manufactured by Amazon.ca
Bolton, ON